"I'm Kate Rawlins.
I believe we're partners."

He froze, visibly shaken. The friendly look in his eye faded to grim comprehension.

"Small world," she added into the lengthening silence.

A muscle in his jaw jerked. He looked as though he'd rather reach for a rattlesnake, but he shook her hand, then shoved his thumbs into the back pockets of his jeans.

"We'd sorta given up on hearing from you," he said at last. His casual stance belied the cold hostility in his voice.

And I'll just bet you were praying you wouldn't. Kate forced a smile. "I was…delayed."

He glanced at her two lone suitcases. "And you're not staying long?" he asked. The good-old-boy grin had masked the keen intelligence she now saw in his eyes. He was probably calculating financial advantages if she simply packed up and let him become the sole owner of the Lone Tree ranch by default.

"Sorry to disappoint you, cowboy, but I'm staying till July—as my grandfather's will stipulates."

ABOUT THE AUTHOR

Romance Writers of America 1995 Golden Heart winner Roxanne Rustand lives in the Midwest. She and her husband have three children, four horses, and—thanks to the kids—a menagerie of epic proportions. She says she feels truly blessed, now that she's writing for her favorite series.

Her first book, a 1998 Golden Heart finalist, was published by Superromance last August. *Montana Legacy,* winner of the West Houston Emily award, is her second novel.

Roxanne would love to hear from you. Her address is: P.O. Box 2550, Cedar Rapids, Iowa 52406-2550.

Or, you can visit her via the internet at: http://www.superauthors.com.

Books by Roxanne Rustand

HARLEQUIN SUPERROMANCE

857—HER SISTER'S CHILDREN

MONTANA LEGACY
Roxanne
Rustand

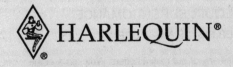

HARLEQUIN®

TORONTO • NEW YORK • LONDON
AMSTERDAM • PARIS • SYDNEY • HAMBURG
STOCKHOLM • ATHENS • TOKYO • MILAN • MADRID
PRAGUE • WARSAW • BUDAPEST • AUCKLAND

ISBN 0-373-70895-5

MONTANA LEGACY

Copyright © 2000 by Roxanne Rustand.

With thanks to Montana ranchers Sharlet and
John Teigen III; Dennis Gardner, DVM; Harry Daugherty,
Chief of Police, Marion Police Department; and
Penny Parrish, Minneapolis Police Department
Public Information Officer.

Any mistakes are mine alone.

Also, with love and many thanks to Larry, Andy, Brian
and Emily, who have learned to equate deadlines with
fast food and major laundry delays, but who have always
been supportive of my dreams. I couldn't have done
this without you all.

PROLOGUE

CRADLING THE TEENAGER'S head in her lap, Kate Rawlins knelt in the weak light at the base of a street-lamp and felt the last of his precious warmth seep away into the cold November mist.

His head was heavier now. Cold and still. The dark red pool beneath him glistened, widened across the asphalt. Sirens screamed in the distance. Patrolmen, investigators and EMTs moved at the periphery of her vision. A crowd milled around in the shadows beyond the crime-scene tape.

News reporters jockeyed for position. Shouted questions. Flashed cameras. The hubbub seemed distant, as if Kate were underwater.

Yet she heard every breath, every sullen murmur of the four belligerent gang members being shoved into two patrol cars at the curb. The last one standing swung his head toward her, his eyes glittering with pure hatred. He started to shout something at her, but his words were lost in a burst of noise and confusion.

With a hand at the back of the kid's head, a patrolman sent him lurching into the back seat of the cruiser.

Kate dropped her gaze to Rico's dark curly hair and the angelic face that had been bright with hope just hours before. An ambulance carrying his young brother had careened around the corner moments ago in a desperate race against time.

With one hand she stroked Rico's cheek. With the other, she fumbled at the catch of her badge with blood-slick fingers. She swore softly, then with a savage jerk ripped the badge free. She'd failed. As a cop, and as a friend. And now this seventeen-year-old boy would never have his chance to go on to college, as she'd promised. He would never leave the inner city of Minneapolis to reach for his dreams.

She'd been set up, with Rico as the unwilling bait, in apparent retribution for the arrest and subsequent testimony she'd given against one of the gang's leaders. Rico's shouted warning as she'd stepped from her cruiser had saved her life.

A split second later, a bullet took his.

Giving the hovering EMTs a curt nod, Kate placed her badge within Rico's curled fingers and gently laid his head down on her folded jacket. She rose stiffly to her feet. Ignoring her patrol car, she stumbled down the cold, barren sidewalk. An icy breeze stiffened the wet fabric of her uniform. Chill mist changed to pellets of sleet, but she felt too numb to care.

From somewhere far away she heard someone shout her name.

She'd been a cop for ten years. Her job had always been everything—her career, her family, her obsession. Nothing mattered more than doing her job right and, in her free time, trying to make a difference for the kids in this neighborhood.

But now, because of her, Rico Sanchez was dead and his younger brother badly wounded. The boys had trusted her. She had should have foreseen the danger lurking in the shadows.

The handcuffed Blood had mouthed the words, "You're next, you—"

It didn't matter. Nothing would wash away the blood on her hands. Nothing would ever erase the guilt from her soul.

Out of the darkness she caught a flash of movement. The glitter of silver. She spun, reaching for her Beretta.

Something hit her with sledgehammer force in an explosion of light and pain. The asphalt rushed to meet her, slammed into her with blinding force.

Then she knew no more.

CHAPTER ONE

Two months later

THE WEEKS HAD PASSED in a blur of frustration and pain and sorrow. Hidden by darkness and the protective cover of littered alleys and helpful cohorts, the shooter had never been identified. For lack of witnesses and incriminating evidence, those arrested at the scene were released within twenty-four hours.

Justice, Kate thought bitterly. Even now, Rico's killer was probably prowling the streets of Chicago or Los Angeles, bragging about his successful escape. Bravado aside, he surely wouldn't have been stupid enough to stay in Minneapolis after shooting a cop.

Lucky for Kate, he hadn't quite hit his mark. A few millimeters over, and she could have been dead. As it was, she'd come through the experience with just a graze wound and stitches in her scalp, a concussion from her fall against a curb, and a two-day stay in the hospital.

Shaking off the memories, she scanned the terrain ahead. The endless sweep of January-brown Montana range stretched to the horizons in every direction, empty and barren as the wasteland inside her chest.

Lone Tree Ranch would be her home for the next

six months, no matter how desolate the scenery or unfriendly the inhabitants. An unexpected sense of loneliness chilled her heart.

A bitter blast of wind slammed against the side of her old Mustang, shrieking through the rusty lace comprising its quarter panels and sending it with a lurch into the opposite lane.

Wrestling the steering wheel into compliance, Kate scanned the empty, rolling grassland on either side of the road. She hadn't seen another car for more than an hour. If she ended up in a ditch, she likely wouldn't be found for months. The co-inheritor of the ranch would probably be thankful if she never showed up.

She checked the odometer, then searched the road ahead for signs of an intersection. According to her late grandfather's estate lawyer, the road leading to the ranch was due within the next quarter mile. The highway seemed to stretch clear to eternity, a faded black ribbon bisecting the rolling land until perspective narrowed it to invisibility.

The sheer desolation made her shiver. She needed a good dose of security right now. The familiar bedlam of rush hour traffic. The smell of exhaust. The crowds and bustle and confusion of a Minneapolis sidewalk.

Reaching for a crushed bag of stale doughnuts on the floor, she almost missed the narrow road leading off to the right. Just one more shade of brown in a monochromatic landscape, it blended with the bleak terrain and dreary sky. Hitting the brakes, she pulled onto the shoulder, bit into the doughnut and wondered if she'd made the biggest mistake of her—

A familiar wash of grief and anger flowed through her. No, she'd made other, bigger mistakes. She'd failed to sense the ambush on that cold November night. Rico had paid for her mistake with his life. And now she would give six months of her own to make sure he wasn't forgotten.

The doughnut crumbled to sawdust in her mouth. After two days of driving on gallons of coffee and a dozen powdered-sugar doughnuts, her appetite still faded at the recent memories. *I'm going to do this, Rico. I promised your mom there'd be a memorial scholarship in your name. And my word is good.*

Collecting the inheritance she'd never wanted to claim would make it possible.

The roar of a truck shook through her as a red dually pickup sped past, its right-turn signal blinking. It stopped, then backed up.

Every sense she possessed went on red alert. An isolated location. A stranger whose broad shoulders seemed to fill the cab of his truck. No cover, other than the rust bucket she was driving. She started to reach for her Beretta, then froze. She was a thousand miles from home, not on patrol. Her holster and gun were packed safely away.

The truck swerved closer, its brakes squealing as it lurched to a halt. If she floored the accelerator—

The stranger leaned across the seat of his truck, tipped back his dusty cowboy hat and grinned at her. Laugh lines fanned out from the corners of his eyes, and vertical grooves bracketed his mouth. With his tanned, rugged face and warm brown eyes, most women probably thought him handsome. He undoubtedly thought he was God's gift to the women of Montana.

She had no interest in men who projected an aura of such confident masculinity. The attitude usually veiled a good dose of conceit and the morals of a stray dog. But unaccountably, those last two doughnuts started doing a tap dance in her stomach, and she felt warmth rise in her cheeks. *Caffeine. It had to be all the caffeine.*

"Car trouble?" He met her gaze squarely. With one wrist cocked over the steering wheel and his other arm draped across the back of the seat, his body language didn't appear threatening. But looks could be deceiving. Out here, totally alone, any man might think her easy prey.

That man would be dead wrong.

"No, but thanks for stopping." She gave him a bland smile. "I'm…expected at Lone Tree Ranch any minute."

"You are?" He gave her a closer look, as if he were assessing *her* for criminal tendencies. "Looking for work, are you?"

"I'm a relative." Ignoring his frown, she gave him a breezy smile and shifted the transmission into drive. "Thanks."

She waved him on, but he held back, so she pulled onto the highway in front of his truck and turned off on the next road. This had to be the right one, but darned if it looked like any traffic ever passed this way. The road was filled with bumps and potholes, and appeared to wind around every bush and scrubby tree in sight. As the Mustang jolted over the rough terrain, its shock absorbers squealed in protest.

Flicking a glance at the rearview mirror, she saw the pickup following her. Was he simply heading for the ranch, or did he see her as an interesting opportunity? She upped her speed another ten miles per hour.

The road forked just ahead. Kate scanned the horizon for clues as to which way to go. Suddenly, her car hit a deep rut and slammed to a halt with bone-jarring force. Despite the shoulder harness, she lurched forward. Pain shot down her neck.

Repeatedly, she put the car into reverse and then in drive, trying to rock it free of the barrier. A cloud of dirt billowed up behind her car as its tires spun...but the front tires were too deeply wedged.

"Hey, take it easy!"

It was that cowboy again, no doubt looking for trouble. And he'd get it if he so much as touched her.

Bracing his forearms on the open window of her car, he leaned down and peered inside. He still wore that affable home-folks grin probably designed to put women at ease.

"I take it you've been to the Lone Tree often, being a relative and all."

"Of course," she shot back.

"You sure picked the hard way to get there. Main road's another half mile up the highway."

Swinging her head around to face him sent an arrow of pain straight down her spine.

The cowboy swung her door open and hunkered down to eye level, sweeping her with a concerned look. His eyes were the warm, deep brown of bittersweet chocolate, shaded by thick lashes. From the strong line of his jaw to the firm set of his mouth, he looked like a man who would stand his ground no matter what the odds.

"Stay here. I'll call for help on my cell phone." He studied her for a long moment, as if debating whether or not she would pass out before he could get to his truck and back.

Mesmerized, she caught herself staring at him and jerked her gaze away. Maybe he wasn't what she'd thought after all. Patrolling inner-city Minneapolis had made her edgy, had honed her sense of caution. Not that it had helped much in the Rico situation. Still, a cop who didn't develop that awareness wouldn't last long, and she'd been on the streets for ten long years. She took a deep, steadying breath and slowly exhaled. "I'm fine."

He'd cocked his hat back far enough that a shock of dark hair swung down over his forehead, but there was nothing boyish about this man. Sinew corded his well-muscled arms; his broad shoulders blocked the view out her door. "There's a doc in Salt Creek—"

"No. I just need to check for damage on my car, and then I'll be on my way." Kate unbuckled her seat belt, steeled herself against the expected pain, then slid out from behind the wheel. The man's large, warm hand cupped her elbow as she stood up. An odd sensation fluttered in her stomach at his touch. Dizziness, no doubt.

He glanced at the front end of the Mustang and shook his head. "You won't be going anywhere in this. Unless you have a spare?"

With a sigh of frustration she shook her head. "This *was* the spare. I had a flat this morning, and the garage didn't have a decent tire the right size. I haven't been through a town big enough for a tire dealer since then."

The front tire had blown on impact. She stared at it, then surveyed the rolling landscape. There wasn't a town, a house or even a cow in sight. Nothing but endless, rolling Montana landscape and one stubborn cowboy.

At least he seemed somewhat civilized. She'd taken down bigger men than this one, though a sixth sense told her she wouldn't want to try. "Can you give me a lift?"

Bracing one arm against the roof of her car, he held out a hand. "You took off before I could introduce myself. I'm Seth Hayward, from the Lone Tree." He paused, sweeping her with a long, slow look. The twinkle in his eye and his easy grin suggested that he liked what he saw. He flicked a glance at the Minnesota State Parks sticker on her windshield. "My foreman's sister lives in Minnesota. Are you Celia?"

Stunned, Kate stared at him, then shook her head. *So this is Seth.* Until this moment, he'd been just a name on a lot of legal papers, and the lawyer hadn't been all that clear on the phone. She'd assumed Seth had been her grandfather's lifelong foreman, and had envisioned him as a wiry, dusty-looking cowboy resembling the hero's aging sidekick in an old western.

This guy wasn't grizzled or aging. Not much over thirty-five, he looked like a smooth-talking charmer who could fool an old man into almost anything. And now he'd inherited the other half of the Lone Tree without any stipulations attached. She'd be doing some serious investigating during her time at the ranch.

"Related to one of the other cowhands?"

"I'm Kate Rawlins." She extended her hand. "I believe we're partners now, Hayward."

He froze, visibly shaken. The friendly look in his eyes faded to grim comprehension.

"Small world," she added into the lengthening silence.

A muscle in his jaw jerked. He looked as though he'd rather reach for a rattlesnake, but he shook her hand, then shoved his thumbs into the back pockets of his jeans.

A chill slithered down Kate's back and lodged in her midsection, extinguishing the tingles of awareness she'd felt at his touch. His initial friendly interest had clearly plummeted to the depths of sheer dislike.

"We'd sorta given up on hearing from you," he said at last. He leaned against the side of her car, arms folded across his chest. His casual stance belied the cold hostility in his voice.

And I'll bet you were praying that you wouldn't.
Kate forced a smile. "I was...delayed."

"For five months?" he bit out.

"My grandfather and I were never in contact. I
didn't even know he'd been ill until his lawyer noti-
fied me about the will." Kate started to say more,
then stopped. She didn't owe this man any explana-
tions.

"Nice, that you found out after he was gone. I
know Bob tried to contact you more than once."

"If he did, he sure didn't try very hard." It had
been twenty-five years since she'd left the ranch as a
toddler, clutched in her mother's arms. Bob Rawlins
had never tried to contact them, hadn't given a
damn—and he'd even ignored the letters she'd sent
as a child.

Nothing less than her wish to fund a scholarship in
Rico's name could have forced her back to her grandfather's ranch. But claiming her inheritance would en-
able her to help a lot of disadvantaged kids...and give
her time to think about her own uncertain future.

"Wilson did tell you that I was coming, right?"

"Wilson?" Seth studied her face, his eyes narrowed.

"The lawyer handling my grandfather's estate."
Kate raised an eyebrow. "I imagine you know him
fairly well by now."

"He's away." Seth stared at her, a muscle flickered
along his jaw.

"I know. He's vacationing in Hawaii," Kate said
evenly. "But there *are* phone connections between

there and Minneapolis. He called me again two weeks ago and promised to tell you that I was coming.''

With a snort of disgust, Seth shoved away from her car and strode to his pickup, slid behind the wheel and jerked a thumb toward the passenger side. "C'mon. I'll get your car later."

"So much for cowboy charm," Kate muttered, hauling her battered luggage out of her car and flinging it into the back of the pickup. Seth gave her a curious look when she climbed into the cab.

"Not staying long?" he asked slowly, glancing back at her two suitcases. The good-old-boy grin had masked the keen intelligence she now saw in his eyes. He was probably calculating the financial advantages if she simply packed up and went back to Minneapolis. If she left, he'd become sole owner of the Lone Tree by default.

"Sorry to disappoint you, cowboy, but I'm staying till July, as required." Kate yanked the shoulder strap across her chest and buckled in. "I pack light."

Seth started the motor, then rested both wrists across the top of the steering wheel and stared out the front window. "Ralph's a damn good lawyer, but he didn't say a word about this."

The temperature outside must have dropped twenty degrees in the last ten minutes. Rubbing her hands together, Kate blew on her chilled fingers and reined in her impatience. She was usually on the other end of interrogations. This end was a lot less pleasant, no matter how subtly done.

"I'm a cop. Until recently, I'd told him I couldn't

leave my job to stay out here for six months. He probably didn't think I'd show up.''

"I'll bet," Seth muttered under his breath, throwing the truck into gear. He backed it in a big arc, then headed out toward the highway. A rooster tail of gravel spewed up behind the vehicle as it lurched forward.

Kate braced one arm against the dashboard. "I've got his phone number, if you want it. He said to tell you he won't be back until he snags a trophy marlin for his office."

"I've got his number." Seth shot a look at her that clearly said, *And yours, too.*

Back at the highway, he headed west. A half mile later he pulled onto a wide unpaved road leading through an open gate with an overhead sign announcing Lone Tree Ranch. The truck shook as it passed over the metal bars of a cattle guard. Dust boiled up behind them as Seth drove down the road.

A strip of pink satin on the floor of the cab caught Kate's eye. She shot a surprised glance at Seth's profile, then reached down to pick up a child's hair ribbon. Cartoon characters danced down its length. "Yours?"

Seth slid her a glance. "My daughter's." The warning note in his voice came across loud and clear.

Apparently the good-looking cowboy was a family man, one who didn't flaunt his flirtations at home. Oddly enough, she felt a twinge of disappointment at the news.

Wise up, Rawlins. He was married, yet he'd sized

her up like a stallion checking out a new mare. Her estimation of him fell another hundred points. But what did she expect? She'd been on far too many domestic calls where the husband had turned into Mr. Congeniality by the time the squad cars arrived. And more than one married cop had tried to pick her up. She had no misconceptions left when it came to men.

After another ten minutes of awkward silence, Seth cleared his throat. "It took Bob a long time to die. It would have meant a lot to him to see his only granddaughter."

"I—"

Seth held up a hand. "That's not my business," he growled. "I may have reservations about Bob's will, but I won't contest it." He took a deep, steadying breath, as if fighting to rein in his emotions. "Now that you're here, we need to establish a good business relationship, or running this ranch is going to be damn hard."

"Right." This cowboy had hit the jackpot with a legacy of half a Montana ranch, yet dared sound honorable about not contesting the will? Of course he wouldn't contest. He'd lose every nickel in the process. A doddering old man, confused and vulnerable, a greedy shark—any judge would see through the situation. She'd certainly done nothing to deserve any part of the ranch, but at least she hadn't been dishonest.

Seth settled his hat lower over his forehead. That same muscle ticked along the side of his jaw. "This place is isolated. We all have to work together. What-

ever family problems you and your mother had with
Bob are old business.''

Kate stared at him in disbelief. ''I'm not exactly
coming out here with my six-shooters drawn, Hayward. I have no memories of my grandfather, and he
certainly never cared about me. I haven't a clue why
he named me in his will.''

Another mile or so of gravel, dust and winter-
brown landscape passed before Seth spoke. ''The
ranch means nothing to you?''

''I didn't say that.'' The vents in the cab provided
lukewarm heat, at best. Kate zipped up her down ski
jacket and eyed the heater controls, but resisted the
temptation to reach out and crank them up full blast.
Seth appeared oblivious to the cold in his battered
denim jacket, so she would manage.

Until she knew him better, her plans were better
left unsaid. Maybe he'd try to find a way to buy her
out, or would welcome the opportunity to sell out
completely so he could start a new life somewhere
else. Maybe his wife had been badgering him for
years about moving to a more populated area. But
starting out on the wrong foot could spell disaster.
And Kate wouldn't take possession and have the option of selling her share for the next six months, at
any rate.

She gave Seth a friendly smile. ''So, what do you
do out here this time of year?''

''Work.'' Seth pulled to a stop at the crest of a
small rise. Below them, the road swung down into a
broad valley. ''There it is,'' he said, his voice low

and proud. "Your grandfather kept this place together through drought, blizzards and economic disasters. Thirty thousand acres, a thousand head of prime Angus, and Angus-cross cattle. He always said this land was his very soul."

This is what he'd loved, instead of his family? Kate suppressed the thought and forced herself to concentrate on the vista below.

Distance gave the scene a surreal look. A sprawling ranch-style house, collection of barns and numerous corrals lay off in the horizon, small as a child's toy farm. Like fly specks, black cattle dotted the shoulders of the hills rising far beyond the buildings.

Even in the raw wind and weak January sunlight, the scene had a wild sort of beauty Kate hadn't expected. Compared to Minnesota's neat patchwork of lush, cultivated farm fields, this terrain looked as untouched as it would have been a century before.

"I half expect to see cavalry riding across the valley floor and the campfire smoke of an Indian village," she murmured, unfastening her seat belt. "It's beautiful."

So this was her grandfather's land. The land of her great-grandfather, and the generation before that. Something deep and unexpected tugged at Kate's heart.

Without intending to, she found herself slipping out of the truck to absorb the impact of that history. *Her* history. She would have grown up here, if Bob Rawlins had shown any compassion toward his daughter and her illegitimate child.

Because he'd lacked a heart, Kate spent her childhood with a mother who never stayed anywhere long, who bounced from one low-paying job to the next, town to town, and never seemed to find peace until the day she died.

All old business, as Seth put it. None of it mattered anymore. Kate drew a deep breath and watched a hawk drift on the air currents high above. The wind rustled the dried grass around her, grass that seemed to flow on forever like an ocean of brown.

"A person could definitely feel a little lonely out here," she said.

Seth stood just a few feet away. "In the city, a person could go crazy from the crowds and noise."

She could feel him watching her, intent and somber. Gauging her reaction, she supposed. "I'm still curious about what sort of work you do this time of year."

"Depends on the weather."

That was certainly informative. She faced six long months out here, shoulder to shoulder with a man who doled out words as if they were too expensive to waste. Without the stress and tension and adrenaline rush of covering her beat, the next hundred and eighty-two days would seem like eternity. "I need to be useful."

"We've got a housekeeper."

A flare of anger shot through her. *Easy, now.* "That's good, because you wouldn't want me in the kitchen. I'd like to help outside, with the cows—"

"Cattle."

"Whatever." She shook off his patronizing tone. "I don't mind getting dirty and I'm not afraid of hard work."

Seth pivoted and headed back to the truck. "I was on my way to water cattle. You might as well come along."

The truck lurched and bucked as Seth sped across an endless pasture. At the bottom of a hill, he pulled to an abrupt stop next to an immense round water tank. Above it rose an old-fashioned windmill.

Kate climbed out of the truck and leaned back against the cold hood to watch the blades spin in the wind. "That thing works?"

"Mostly." Seth pulled a pair of battered leather gloves from his pocket, snugged them on, then rummaged around in the back of the pickup. He lifted out an ax and a couple of pitchforks. "Yesterday there wasn't a breeze, so the water didn't flow. Some of the tanks froze." He handed her a pitchfork.

A pitchfork? Kate fished a pair of gloves from her own jacket pocket and turned up her collar against the raw wind. In contrast, Seth shrugged out of his jacket and tossed it on the hood of the truck. Then he hefted the ax, tested the weight of it in his hands and raised it high over the frozen surface of the tank.

He wore a dark-green flannel shirt and a black turtleneck tucked into well-worn jeans. With each blow of the ax, the sound echoed like a cannon shot through the silence, ice chips flying like glittering diamonds in all directions. With each measured swing, his shirt strained over his back and shoulders. Great shoulders—powerful, well muscled, tapering into a long, lean back and narrow hips.

Kate looked away, uneasy with her unwanted awareness. For better or worse, her ten years in law enforcement had kept her in constant contact with men, and she'd long since learned that a good physique was no measure of the man himself. This one was married, and if she guessed right, he was a con artist to boot. He was also the type who gave orders and expected to see them carried out, no questions asked. Just like her grandfather, if her mother's stories were true. And just like Kent, her ex-fiancé.

If anything made her hackles rise, it was a man who expected docile compliance.

A sudden buffet of wind whipped a strand of hair across her eyes. Lifting a hand to tuck it behind her ear, she glanced at her watch. Just three-thirty, yet the sky was already turning leaden gray. Thankful for her heavily insulated boots, she stamped her feet and shivered, as much from the memories of her ill-fated engagement as from the chill wind.

Kent had been one of the worst mistakes of her life. Handsome enough to draw stares and flirtatious smiles from women age nine to ninety, he'd swept her off her feet with promises of *forever,* and she'd been sure that even eternity wouldn't be long enough.

Then just before the wedding he started pressuring her to leave law enforcement. She'd refused, he'd insisted. Each assumed the other would bend.

On their wedding day, he left her standing alone at the altar, in utter humiliation before a congregation of her fellow police officers and his friends and relatives. Waves of embarrassed sympathy had battered her from all sides as everyone expressed awkward platitudes and then escaped the church.

"Forever" hadn't even made it to the wedding vows—and commitment to a relationship wasn't something she planned to risk again.

Seth swung his ax until he'd broken up all the ice, then he walked back to the truck and exchanged the ax for the extra pitchfork. He flicked a glance toward the horizon. "They're thirsty."

Kate turned around. Behind her, maybe a half mile away, a mass of black cattle spilled over the top of a hill and flowed—slow as cold molasses—over the side. She could hear them bawling. As they hit the bottom of the hill the leaders picked up a shambling trot, then a disjointed lope, heading straight for the tank. Kate edged closer to the truck.

"Come on over here and help," Seth called out. He paused. "Unless you'd feel safer in the pickup."

Safer? Kate gritted her teeth and stalked to the water tank, then studied Seth's movements. He scooped up an iceberg with his pitchfork, steadied the load, then flung it away from the tank, leaving an area of open water. Easy.

She snagged a chunk of ice with her pitchfork and lifted. The weight of the ice caught her off balance. Her feet slipped. She grabbed for the side of the stock tank. The pitchfork clattered against the metal rim, wobbled and disappeared beneath the ice floes on the surface.

Seth continued scooping and pitching ice from the tank with powerful, rhythmic strokes. "Leave it," he said mildly, without looking up.

Kate stared at the black, ice-cold water, angry at herself for failing her first small task. Turning on her heel, she went after the ax leaning against the pickup, then returned to the edge of the stock tank.

Both hands on the ax handle, she started fishing through the water. *Here...no, there.* The blade of the ax hit something solid. If she could snag the tines of the pitchfork, she could lift it out. She reached farther. Her feet slipped a few inches. Again—

At the weight of a hand on her shoulder, she jumped. Intent on her quest, she hadn't heard Seth come up behind her. A frisson of awareness shot down her spine. He jerked his hand back as if he'd touched something hot.

"I'll get it, or it can stay till spring. It doesn't matter."

But it did. She leaned forward to sweep across the bottom of the tank once more. The slushy ice floating on the top and dark water prevented a clear view, but she could get the darn thing with one more try.

"No," he snapped. "It isn't worth falling in."

He reached for her ax. She held it tighter. Frowning, he looked at her then, *stared* at her, as if seeing her for the first time. "You are one stubborn woman," he said finally.

"I'm capable of doing things myself."

"And I don't take risks." A corner of his mouth

twitched as he gently pried her fingers from the ax. "Let's go, so the old girls can have a drink."

Kate whipped her head around. Not thirty feet away, an incredible number of black cattle had formed a semicircle around the tank, the sound of their approaching footsteps masked by the keening wind. Here on the open range, they had a warm, rather pleasant smell. Not at all like those in a stockyard.

Like nearsighted old ladies trying to focus without their glasses, they bobbed their heads up and down, eyeing Seth and Kate with suspicion. One took a step forward. Several others followed suit. Clouds of steam rose from their nostrils as they blew noisily, as if issuing some sort of bovine challenge.

Kate shrank back a step. Again, she felt the warm, comforting weight of Seth's hand on her shoulder. Longer, this time.

"They aren't going to run us over, but we're done here. Let's go." He guided her forward, keeping himself between her and the herd of impatient cattle. "You've just met the lifeblood of this operation. Or part of it. We should have more than nine hundred calves this spring, if all goes well."

"What can go wrong?" Kate gingerly stepped around a steaming plop of something the diameter of an extra-large pizza.

"They were all checked in the fall, and the open cows were shipped—"

"Open?"

"The ones that weren't pregnant."

Kate felt a twinge of sympathy for the cows. "Sort of extreme, isn't it?"

"It's business. Ranchers can't afford to feed cattle that don't produce. We also have to deal with storms, drought, disease and coyotes. Even checking the cattle twenty-four hours a day during calving season, we can lose a lot of calves." The resignation in his voice hardened to steel as he turned to face her. "There's no financial security here. But this is a way of life and a legacy for the future. I won't let anything jeopardize this ranch."

Quite a speech for this laconic guy—and he clearly meant every last word. Kate met his gaze squarely. "I understand."

She understood, all right. Her new partner was a fierce protector of his world, a throwback to an earlier time. He wanted the ranch to stay intact forever...but couldn't afford to buy her out, according to her grandfather's lawyer. On the other hand, she *had* to sell her share, to make good on a vow she could not break.

They were both strong, determined people, and she could already feel a shimmer of undeniable attraction rising between them. There would be no easy victories, no simple solutions. One of them would win, one of them would lose.

And now she knew that Seth would never accept defeat.

CHAPTER TWO

THE PHONE RANG as they climbed back into the truck. Mentally ticking off all of the things that could have gone wrong back at home, Seth jammed the receiver between his head and shoulder, then turned the key in the ignition switch and shifted the truck into reverse. Kate settled into the far corner of the seat.

"Sheriff called." Della's foghorn bellow could have dropped a man at fifty yards. He'd never been able to convince her that she could speak in a normal tone when talking to him on his cell phone. "Somebody going down the highway said we got a cow caught in a fence line. Near the Salt Creek turnoff."

"Anybody out there?" Seth spoke into the phone, then held it away from his ear.

"Cal said he was a good forty-five minutes away. The caller just kept agoin'." Della snorted with disgust. "Stupid tourist. The other boys are still moving heifers, so you're closest. Need help?"

Once Della would have been his choice before any of the hands. Strong, with the determination of a bull and the steady nerves of a gunfighter, the rawboned woman could handle horses and cattle better than any man around. Now she moved slowly on cold mornings and paid the price when she did too much.

"We'll manage," he said, glancing at Kate. *As long as Ms. City Slicker stays out of the way.*

"We?" Della asked.

He was suddenly glad to be ten miles away, knowing what the elderly woman's reaction would be. "Yeah. Kate Rawlins just showed up. If you get a chance, can you clear out the spare bedroom?" The silence on the phone spoke louder than words. "Della?"

She'd hung up. Just as well—given the decibel level of her voice and the close proximity of Bob's long-lost granddaughter. Kate would sense the hostility soon enough.

The entire community knew of Bob's will. Not one person would welcome the arrival of a granddaughter who showed up like a vulture to claim her inheritance yet hadn't bothered to come back while he was dying. Even now, she showed no sign of regret over Bob's death. The chasm in Seth's own heart had yet to heal.

Seth dropped the phone on the seat and maneuvered the truck up the steep slope, turned cross-country to the north, then floored the accelerator. The truck rocked and shook as it flew over the hard-frozen earth. "Can't take you to the house just yet," he said, raising his voice to be heard over the rush of wind and the roar of the motor. "Warm enough?"

"Yeah." Glancing down at her hands, she quit rubbing them together and dropped them to her lap.

Seth reached out and flipped the truck's heater to a higher setting.

"I hope your wife won't go to any trouble," she added. "I don't need much to get along."

Even after eight years, the word *wife* shot shards of ice through his veins. *"What?"*

"Just let her know I can take care of myself."

From the corner of his eye, he caught Kate's swift look of condemnation. What the hell had he said? He'd been polite to a lady in distress on the highway and had offered her a ride to the ranch—even after discovering her identity. "You mean Della? She's our housekeeper."

"Okay, so let them *both* know that I don't want to be in the way." She glanced at the hair ribbon she'd laid on the seat between them. "I know having an extra person around will be an imposition."

Seth felt the telltale jerk of muscle along his jaw-line. Just the thought of his ex-wife triggered regrets and anger he should have been able to deal with long ago. But how could any woman walk away from her baby and never look back? Even after all these years, rehashing the most spectacular failure of his life was still more painful than taking a dead-on kick in the gut by a shod horse. "Mandy, Della and I are the only ones at the house," he said evenly. "Mandy is my daughter."

"Oh," she said faintly. Her gaze flew to his face, then skittered away as a faint blush rose in her city-pale cheeks.

A blush? He would have bet his best boots that Kate Rawlins didn't even know the meaning of the word. Seth pointedly remained silent, though taking pasture moguls at fifty in a truck with bad suspension and a glass pack muffler precluded the possibility of much conversation, anyway.

At the north end of the pasture they rattled over a cattle guard, then Seth turned onto the highway. The comparative quiet of asphalt under the tires stretched into a long and awkward silence. His wariness giving way to curiosity, he shot another glance at her. What the hell was she thinking about right now?

Most women filled conversational lulls with chatter. He found himself wishing that this one would. The ranch was already in serious financial trouble. Did she plan to stay forever? Just the six months and then split? Was she planning to interfere with the operations? He didn't have a clue. Not since his ex-wife had he met a woman with so much power to destroy his life, and the uncomfortable sense of losing control made him want to demand answers here and now.

She was leaning back against the seat. With her dark sunglasses, navy down jacket and stocking cap, he could see just her straight nose and strong jawline. She could have been any anonymous stranger passing through, yet something about her put all his senses on high alert. Under any other circumstances, he might have interpreted his reaction to her as attraction, but that was impossible. He liked women soft and sweet. Nurturing types. Women who might be good prospects for a warm-cookies-and-cocoa sort of mother for Mandy.

Women who were nothing like his ex-wife, and definitely not like this hard-edged lady cop.

But whatever his personal feelings, he needed to get a handle on the situation. "Know anything about ranching?"

She stirred, then twisted in her seat, tipped her sunglasses down with one slim hand and looked at him over the rims. A quick glance told him that she had gray eyes, no makeup. Definitely not the soft-and-fluffy type. So why did she make his stomach tighten?

"I'll learn." Her voice was level, calm, as if she wasn't fazed by the fact that they were total strangers thrown into an impossible situation. Everything Bob had worked for, every one of Seth's dreams now hung in the balance. Didn't she feel it?

Seth turned off the highway onto a rutted lane. Fifty yards ahead, a white-faced black cow lay tangled up in wire, her head tipped up and back at an awkward angle. "Damn."

Kate leaned forward, a hand propped against the dash. "Is she dead?"

"Not yet." Seth slammed on the brakes and pulled to a sideways stop on the shoulder of the lane. Grabbing fence pliers from under the seat, he launched out of the truck. Kate followed close on his heels.

"Stay back," he ordered, bending down and running a hand over the cow's thick ebony hair. Smears of dark blood on the ground told of her desperate fight for freedom. Though her eyes were closed, she stirred, then took a deep breath and weakly struggled against the heavy barbed wire. Steam rose from her sweat-damp hide.

Kate leaned over his shoulder. "Tell me what to do."

"Stay out of my way. She's wrapped up like a Christmas present. She'll struggle, and this wire is dangerous."

If he started in the wrong place, she would struggle all the more and risk further lacerations. Seth scanned the situation, then leaned over and cut the first few strands. The cow bawled.

"Whoa, mama," he soothed, going down on one knee against the frozen earth and reaching for another handful of wire. "Easy, old girl."

Several strands looped around one of her back legs like a gypsy's bangles. Seth two-handed the fence pliers, stifling a soft curse as he laboriously cut each loop away. The twisted double-strand wire was meant to last, not to break. A trickle of sweat trailed down his back.

The cow lurched forward, trying to scramble to its feet. A sharp barb raked across his inner arm, ripping his shirt. Seth threw his weight against her. "Quick, hold her down. She's still caught in the wire."

Kate threw herself across the cow's neck. Seth attacked the last few confining strands and folded the sharp edges back as he severed each one. "Step back," he warned.

With a groan, the cow staggered to its feet and stood spraddle-legged, breathing hard. Blood from a jagged laceration dripped down one of her back legs. No arteries or major veins, thank God.

"Now, that's a first." Kate stared at the cow lumbering away. "I've tackled some good-size suspects, but never anything that big." She looked over at Seth. "I think—"

Her voice caught. She stared at his hands. "Is that her blood or yours?"

Seth glanced down. His battered leather gloves were damp with the cow's blood and pungent sweat, but above them a crimson stain blossomed wet and heavy through his shirt. There was little pain, but then that wire had been scalpel-sharp. "Guess it's mine."

Kate pocketed her sunglasses and reached for his arm. Carefully avoiding the blood, she unbuttoned the cuff of his shirt and gently peeled back the sleeve. She whistled under her breath. "Guess it is. Have a first aid kit in your truck?"

"Nope. It's in the horse trailer back home."

A slash on the inner surface of his forearm extended upward a good four inches from his wrist. Blood ran off his arm in a steady stream. Seth reached into his back pocket for a bandanna. *Empty.* He fought the urge to clamp down on the wound with his free—but dirty—hand. Cow sweat, dirt and rusted wire were a potent combination for trouble.

Kate gave him an assessing look, then whirled and strode back to the pickup. She reached for one of her suitcases and snapped open the latches.

"This will do," she called over her shoulder, withdrawing a voluminous length of white material.

With a sharp jerk she tore the material lengthwise until she had a wide strip a good yard long. In moments she'd neatly bandaged his arm with something worn soft from long use, bedraggled lace trim at one edge. *Her nightgown?* Seth frowned at his arm, then blinked as scarlet seeped up through the layers of fabric. Something within in him stirred at the odd intimacy of her lingerie. His blood. *Hell.*

"Hey, there, are you okay?" Kate asked sharply, searching his face. "It's good enough for now. You'll need stitches, but this will get us into town."

"Uh…thanks." Virginal white cotton on the city cop. With white lace. Who would've thought? Khaki would have been his first bet. In camouflage-green print. He shook his head, trying to clear his thoughts. "It'll be fine…like it is."

Frowning, she grabbed his good arm and steered him toward the truck. "Come on, cowboy. I'll drive."

Her voice brooked no nonsense, her gray-eyed gaze didn't waver. Seth envisioned her on the streets, handling emergencies on a daily basis. Risking her life as a cop. She certainly took things in stride. There couldn't have been any cattle on the streets of Minneapolis, but she'd handled this situation as if she'd done it all her life. And she hadn't blinked at the sight of blood. Seth's curiosity about her rose.

She might be the callous granddaughter who broke Bob's heart, but she could handle herself well. Maybe—just maybe—she would fit in at the ranch on a temporary basis. It *would* be only temporary. Seth knew that from experience. He would help her pack the minute she decided to leave.

Any rancher with sense knew that city women didn't last.

SETH WOULD HAVE GONE back to the ranch. But sure enough, Kate turned the wrong direction when they hit the highway, ignored his protest and drove the twenty miles west to Salt Creek in stubborn silence. For someone who couldn't weigh more than a hundred-fifteen, she was one implacable woman. Still, if it hadn't been for all the blood he'd lost, he would have made her turn around.

At Doc Anderson's cramped office—just a rural satellite clinic for the larger office in Folsum—she stood in the corner of the single exam room, her arms stiffly folded, watching Doc work. As if she were assessing his expertise and making sure the job was done right.

She'd taken off her hat. Dark blond hair hung loosely at her shoulders, and without the sunglasses her face looked pale and drawn. Those gray eyes were steady, but a lot more emotion lurked beneath the surface than she betrayed. Every motion, every flick of a glance telegraphed tension and a significant amount of exhaustion.

She was too thin to even be called slender, so again he had to wonder why his heart had skipped a beat when he'd first seen her out on the highway. He liked buxom brunettes. Curvy redheads. Quiet, easy camaraderie. This woman was the antithesis of everything he appreciated in women. Worse, she would be underfoot for months to come. He glanced heavenward. *Thanks, Bob.*

"Got a sidekick, I take it? Just what you need!"

Doc winked at Seth, then waggled a snowy brow in Kate's direction. "'Bout time."

"It's not what you think." Debating for a moment, Seth watched Doc tie off a stitch. Gossip was inevitable, but maybe this would be a good time to start it off right. "She's Bob's granddaughter."

Doc's head jerked up. His wire rims slid down his nose as he turned to give Kate a narrowed glance. "This'll be interesting," he muttered, reaching for a roll of cling bandaging. "Did she just get in?"

"Yes, I did," Kate interjected. "I'm Kate Rawlins."

"Humph." Doc surveyed his handiwork. "Just a tetanus booster, and then you're done." He gave Seth a friendly cuff on his good arm, then turned to Kate as he peeled off his latex gloves. "Bob was a good man. There's not a person around here who doesn't miss him."

"I didn't know him."

Doc stepped on the pedal of a stainless steel trash can and threw the gloves away. "Real sad thing, dying without any blood kin at your side."

"That's true," Kate said quietly. "But I never heard from him. Ever. And until his lawyer's letter arrived, I didn't know about his death."

Doc sent Seth a surprised glance that quickly faded to patent disbelief. Looking down, he scrawled some notes on Seth's medical chart. "Lucky he had Seth here."

"Now, Doc—"

"Hold your horses, Seth, I'm just stating facts."

Doc cleared his throat. "Bob and I were friends. Life-long friends."

Kate tipped her head in acknowledgement. "I'm sorry about your loss."

Doc nodded to himself as if confirming an opinion, then turned back to Seth. "Make sure you take it easy for a while. I want to see you back here in ten days."

Another trip to town, during what would be the start of calving? There wouldn't be time. "I can just take these stitches out myself. I do the same on cattle."

Kate frowned at Seth, then gave the Doc a determined smile. "I'll make sure he gets back here."

Doc regarded her for a long moment. A suspicious twinkle gleamed in his eyes when his gaze shifted back to Seth. "Like I said—this'll be interesting."

BY THE TIME they pulled up at the ranch, Kate couldn't have forced a smile if her life depended on it. Her grandfather's lawyer had assured her that everything was set, that there would be no problems. She'd been too caught up in her grief over Rico and her own physical recuperation to see the situation in Montana clearly.

Grabbing one of her suitcases in his good hand, Seth motioned her toward the double front doors of the rambling two-story house. She snagged the other suitcase and led the way up the long flagstone walk. Once inside, she felt his somber gaze on her as she turned slowly around to study the spacious great room.

The dark pine paneling and heavy stone fireplace, complemented by colorful throw rugs and rugged furniture, might have been part of a high-country hunting cabin instead of a year-round home. Southwestern prints of horses and wild country hung on the walls. An antique shotgun hung over the fireplace, topped by a mounted elk's head. The subtle earth tones of the room felt cozy, welcoming.

But none of it felt familiar. Not the room, not the atmosphere. Disappointment washed through her. Somehow, she'd imagined she would feel a sense of belonging. *Yeah, right. Like you'd know what that is.*

"Remember anything?" Seth asked.

She finished surveying the room and shook her head. "Nothing, really. I was a toddler when my mom left with me."

From the back of the house pots and pans clanged. Heavy footsteps came down a long hallway, and then a ramrod-straight woman appeared at the arched entryway across the room, both hands jammed in the deep pockets of her denim apron. Her steel-gray hair, scraped into a ponytail, matched the steely look in her eyes. There wasn't one hint of softness among the deep lines and furrows of her sun-cured flesh.

"Kate, I'd like you to meet Della Grover. She's been a part of the family here since before I can remember."

Kate moved forward and extended her hand. Her face impassive and eyes downcast, the older woman gave Kate's hand a single shake. A dim memory surfaced, too vague to recall, at that contact. Just in time,

Kate kept herself from glancing at the arthritis-gnarled hand within her own.

"Were you here when I was born?" Kate's curiosity grew. Perhaps Della could provide answers about the past, answers Kate's own mother had refused to give.

Della shrugged. "Don't recall."

But from the woman's brief, intense glance, Kate would have laid odds that Della could remember what she wore and what she had for breakfast three years ago last Tuesday. Her demeanor was anything but that of a forgetful elderly woman.

The housekeeper looked over Kate's head at Seth. "The room's ready. Supper's in ten minutes."

Kate fixed a pleasant smile on her face and looked Della in the eye. "I look forward to visiting with you."

The older woman grunted an unintelligible response and disappeared back down the hall.

Seth watched her leave, then shifted his gaze back to Kate. He smelled of leather and pine and the sharp scent of antiseptic on his bandaged arm, scents that seemed to curl around her like a beckoning hand. She could almost feel his physical warmth. But his manner was as cold as the winter wind outside.

"It will take us all a while to get used to this…arrangement," he said, the tone in his voice suggesting the others at the ranch would do so or live to regret it. "Want to see your room?"

Kate nodded, then followed as he led the way up an open staircase. "Is your daughter here?"

Seth's grip tightened on the handle of the suitcase. *Ever the protector,* Kate thought with amusement. *As if I'm any threat.*

"She'll be back tomorrow noon," he said. "School's out for teacher's inservices, so she's at a friend's house overnight."

Four bedrooms flanked the open balcony on the second floor. Seth ushered her through the door at the far end. The room was softly lit by a bedside lamp; its pine-log walls glowed like warm honey. A colorful Navajo rug lay on the floor, while a matching quilt of crimson, gold and navy covered the brass double bed. The dresser was bare except for a black telephone circa 1950.

Seth dropped her suitcase inside the door. "Will this be okay?"

Kate took a deep breath, nearly overwhelmed. "Perfect, thanks." *Would this have been my room all these years?*

Seth started to leave, then paused with one hand braced high on the door frame. The motion emphasized the breadth of his shoulders, the powerful line of his back. "We've got to talk. If you aren't too tired, perhaps we could start after supper?"

"Of course."

He shut the door behind him. His footsteps retreated along the balcony, and then back down the stairs.

Exhaustion poured through Kate like molten lead. Almost paralyzed by the weight, she turned and collapsed backward onto the bed. The quilt enveloped her, warm and comforting as a cocoon. So soft...

A distant tapping sound grew louder, more insistent. Kate sat up, confusion swirling through her thoughts as she stared at her surroundings. She'd been drifting and dreaming about her barren, generic white apartment, the buzz of her alarm clock, the pressing need to report for duty on time. Innocuous dreams, for the first time in months. Usually her nightmares ravaged what little sleep she could manage, leaving her cold and exhausted by dawn.

She shoved a hand through her hair—long past needing a good shampoo—and fought an urge to sink back into the warm quilt. The glow of the brass bedside lamp threw dark shadows against the walls. The windows revealed night had fallen.

"Are you all right?" A deep male voice vibrated through the bedroom door.

Seth. "Be out in a few minutes."

A steaming hot shower and a change of clothes made Kate feel almost human again. After towel-drying her hair, she finger-combed it back and headed downstairs in her stocking feet. The grandfather clock bonged eleven times as she crossed the darkened living room toward the glow of light coming from the kitchen.

Seth was leaning back in one of the kitchen chairs, his long legs stretched out in front of him, one hand curved around a steaming mug of coffee on the table. He nodded toward a second cup sitting across from him.

A flash of awareness shot through her. Followed by the humiliating memory of her unconscious reaction when he'd told her that he didn't have a wife. *As if that matters, Rawlins. After Kent, the last thing you need is another guy.*

She could only hope Seth hadn't noticed the heat rise in her cheeks. She never, ever blushed. And she was not interested in a cowboy who'd somehow finagled his way into half ownership of the Lone Tree. She would be investigating Seth Hayward, not wasting her time on foolish attraction.

But she couldn't deny that he was one good-looking man. For the first time, his head was bare. Thick, nearly black hair, long past the need for a cut, swept back and brushed the back of his collar, though one stubborn lock curved over his high forehead. His high, chiseled cheekbones suggested the possibility of Native American blood. Stunningly attractive, in a rough-hewn way.

He tipped his head toward the carafe in the center of the table. "Decaf. Black?"

Kate slid into a chair across from him and poured herself a cup. The aroma sent contentment curling through her tired muscles. She took a slow sip, then gratefully cradled the cup in both hands. "Thanks."

"Supper leftovers are still on the stove, if you're hungry."

Shaking her head, Kate ignored the answering rumble in her stomach and scanned the room. Lit only by a light above the sink, the room felt warm and welcoming. White eyelet curtains hung at the windows, the walls were buttercup yellow. Indian pottery and wildlife prints added the finishing touches. An open archway led into a small mudroom, where a pile of crumpled cowboy boots was banked up at the back door and a locked gun cabinet stood in the corner.

None of it was familiar, yet it was all as she'd imagined the ranch might be. Solid. With a strong feeling of family, of continuity.

Life out here had obviously gone on very well without her. The old pain nibbled at her heart, though she'd made peace with her grandfather's disinterest long ago. Kate felt Seth watching her and jerked her thoughts back to the present.

She took a slow swallow of coffee, then propped her elbows on the table to savor the rich, dark roast aroma and study him over the rim of her cup. With the angles and hollows of his face shadowed in the dim light, he looked as solid as Mount Rushmore.

"So tell me. How long have you lived here?" she asked.

"Almost as long as I can remember." He crossed one long, lean leg over the opposite knee and studied the frayed hem of his jeans as if it held the answers to the universe. After a long pause his gaze shifted and met hers. "Your grandfather took me in when I was thirteen, and I've been here ever since."

"Your parents?"

A shadow flickered across Seth's face. "Gone."

"I'm sorry."

"It's been a long time."

He might as well have been a Marlborough poster

model on a billboard for all he had to say. But then, straightening in his chair, he suddenly pushed his mug aside. "The terms of the will require you to stay six months and take an active part in the operation. This isn't a dude ranch. I'm not sure what your expectations are, but calving starts within two weeks, and none of us have time to entertain a guest."

"I hardly expect to be entertained." Kate managed a smile. "You tell me what needs to be done, and I'll pitch in."

He gave her an assessing glance. "The boys brought in a herd of heavies today from the north pasture—a hundred heifers we bought last fall when prices bottomed out. They'll be calving soon, and that's a round-the-clock deal. If the weather goes bad, one of us is out there every hour. You up to that?"

The expression on his face suggested he didn't think she was. The note of condescension in his voice made her wish she could take him out on a graveyard shift back in Minneapolis. Just once.

"Show me what to do," she said, keeping her voice level.

"I won't ask you to do anything I wouldn't do myself."

"Fine."

He stared pensively at her. "After your time is up in July, you could opt to stay here or head back to Minneapolis and become a silent partner. What are your long-range plans?"

Kate shrugged, dropping her gaze to the coffee cup in her hands. "I suppose anything could happen."

"I want one thing clear." Seth's voice turned cold. "Stay away from my daughter."

"You want me to ignore her?"

"She misses having a mom here. I don't want her thinking you're a part of her family and being hurt when you leave."

Kate had seen the same intense look of warning in the eyes of a rottweiler protecting its master. "I wouldn't do anything to hurt a child."

Seth studied her for another moment, then settled back into his chair, apparently satisfied. "Do you ride?"

Two summer camps...a few trips to a rental stable north of St. Paul...she had a good dozen hours under her belt. Easy. "Of course."

A corner of Seth's mouth lifted. "We use four-wheelers at times, but mostly we use horses to work cattle. Do you need a broke horse, or can you handle something green?"

A sparkle lit the deep warmth of his brown eyes, and Kate suddenly wondered what it would be like if he were to turn on his charm. "Whatever."

"Then I've got the horse for you." A vertical slash deepened in his cheek as his mouth curved into a half smile. "Rowdy needs some long hours on his odometer."

Rowdy? Kate feigned a casual shrug. "No problem."

Right. She was going to die under the hooves of some wild-eyed horse named Rowdy who probably ate greenhorns for breakfast. She'd never been able to easily back away from a personal challenge, especially when she was being patronized. Making her way alone in a man's world had only hardened her competitive streak. And now she was going to pay.

Studying the look in Seth's eyes, she knew she'd been cornered into facing spectacular failure. He hoped she would crash, burn and head back to the city, leaving his daughter and his precious ranch safe from her evil clutches. He was dead wrong if he thought she would ever give up.

She just hoped she wouldn't end up dead proving it.

CHAPTER THREE

THE HORSE BLEW NOISILY through his nostrils, his ears swiveling like crazed radar detectors. Kate bit her lip and gathered the reins in one hand at his withers, then tentatively put her left foot in the stirrup. Rolling his eyes, Rowdy sidled sideways. Kate hopped along on one foot beside him to keep up.

"Whoa!" she muttered, well aware of the spectacle she was providing for the host of grizzled cowboys lined up along the fence.

Rowdy swung his rear end away from her, pivoting on his front feet, and bobbed his head.

"Gotta move a little faster, ma'am," a scratchy voice called from the fence. "That horse don't have all day."

Kate took a deep breath, caught part of the gray gelding's mane with her rein hand and launched herself up into the saddle. Rowdy froze. His muscles bunched and tensed like a coiled spring beneath her. Unbidden, the words of some long-ago sermon danced into her mind. *Pride goeth before a fall.*

"All set?" Seth asked.

"Sure," she called back. A dozen yards away he lounged in his saddle, one forearm resting across the saddle horn, the other arm crossed above it, the reins held loosely in one hand. With his dark sunglasses and the brim of his black hat tipped low, his expression was unreadable. He looked impossibly masculine on that horse: tall, lean, supremely capable. Maybe it was his innate confidence that struck a chord within her. Maybe it was the easy drawl and dry wit. Either way, she would need to keep her distance. Although for now, the point was moot.

His horse stood with its head down and a back hoof cocked peacefully. *Her* mount felt like an atom bomb between her legs. Kate debated the wisdom of nudging Rowdy into forward gear. Lighting his fuse could mean a fast trip into the dirt for her, face first. Standing still much longer would decimate whatever pride she had left.

From the rail came a wheezy laugh. She turned and tracked its source to a gray-haired guy with a battered black hat and an even more disreputable old denim jacket. ''Give him a big ole whomp and he'll get agoin' *real* good,'' he offered.

A younger cowboy with red hair—aptly nicknamed Freckles, from the raucous banter she'd overhead earlier—gave the old geezer a dirty look, then turned his earnest face back to Kate. ''Rowdy's all bluff, ma'am. He was in a camp string once and figured out how to stay in the barn. He'll be okay, honest.'' The others turned away in disgust at Freckle's revelation. Not one of them had even smiled at her, much less said hello. They were waiting to see her fail.

''Thanks.'' Collecting her courage, Kate forced herself to relax in the saddle. She nudged Rowdy's ribs with her heels. Then again, a little harder. "Come on, fleabag," she muttered under her breath.

She'd been set up. Nothing she hadn't experienced before, as a rookie on the police department.

Rowdy shambled into a slow walk, apparently disappointed that his ruse had been detected. If a horse could pout, this one was doing so right now with its head hung low and ears bobbing in time to each step. Kate let out a long, slow breath and sank deeper into the saddle. The release of tension turned her backbone to jelly.

Seth gave her a curt nod and reined his sorrel out toward the pasture. Lifting an arm, he gestured to the distant north, where the cattle looked like tiny black polka dots against the rolling pasture land. "We're going out to check them, then today or tomorrow we've got to bring in the herd that's up on the Jefferson place."

Seth's horse eased into a slow lope. Rowdy followed suit with minimal riderly input and matched his speed to Seth's horse, so Kate gave him his head and concentrated on the flow of his three-beat motion. His fluid stride gathered and surged beneath her, powerful yet smooth as a rocking chair.

Exhilaration sped through her veins at the crisp air. The endless expanse of sky overhead. The sensation of flying across the grasslands. The vast, undulating landscape seemed to go on forever, blending into the faint blue silhouette of the Bull Mountains at the horizon. Those mountains were more than sixty miles away, Seth had said, though that seemed impossible.

Kate breathed in deeply, absorbing the day and a sense of freedom she hadn't felt in a long, long time.

They cut across hills too rugged for a jeep to cross. Seth might as well have been relaxing in a favorite chair, but Kate felt every twist and turn of Rowdy's body as he negotiated the steeper slopes. She kept Rowdy a few lengths behind Seth's horse so he wouldn't see her greenhorn efforts, and prayed that somewhere, among the boxes stashed in the trunk of her car, she had a bottle of good liniment.

Seth eased his gelding into a slow jog and held out an arm, signaling Kate to slow down as they approached the herd. Rowdy took the hint without so much as a touch on the reins.

No doubt the old coots back at the barn were still laughing at her, the dumb city girl who'd been fooled by Rowdy's wild-horse routine. Kate reached forward and stroked his neck, where powerful muscles played beneath his furry winter coat. "Does Rowdy try to scare everyone, or was it just me?"

Seth pulled to a stop and gave Rowdy a thoughtful look, then shifted his dark, somber gaze to Kate. "The ones he doesn't fool he generally dumps."

Either the man had the driest sense of humor this side of dirt, or she'd been one lucky woman. Rowdy halted next to Seth's horse as if preprogrammed, and only then did she catch the twinkle in Seth's eyes. He did have *some* degree of charm. How else could he have wormed his way into her grandfather's heart and inherited half the ranch?

She needed to start investigating.

A herd of maybe a hundred black cows grazed on

the winter-dried grass ahead of them. A few raised their heads to inspect the visitors, then dropped back to the business at hand.

"Can they graze like this all winter?"

Seth scanned the herd. "They'll paw through snow to graze, but once a heavy snow lasts three or four days we start 'em on hay. We've been lucky so far this winter."

With a barely perceptible touch of a rein to his gelding's neck, he headed slowly into the herd, studying each cow he passed. "Once we start, they have to stay on hay until spring. Busiest time of the year, haying cattle and calving."

Tossing hay bales at cattle and watching calves being born didn't sound challenging. In fact, the calving part sounded like fun, but judging from the ominous tone in Seth's voice he didn't take much pleasure in helping the little critters arrive. "I look forward to learning all about it."

Seth snorted. "In a month or so I'll remind you of what you just said."

"What exactly are you looking for?" Kate shivered, wishing she'd had the foresight to pack more long underwear. Her toes were numb inside her Western boots, and her fingers were stiff with cold. The wind had picked up again, ruffling through Rowdy's mane and whipping her hair across her eyes. Between frostbite and aching muscles, she'd be ready to sell her soul for a hot tub by nightfall.

Seth rode ahead. "These heifers are due for their first calves starting the next week or so, according to the ultrasound reports they came with last fall." He leaned forward to peer under one of the cows, then shifted back into his saddle. "Some of these might go a little sooner. We'll trail this bunch back to the ranch in case they need any help."

Two riders. A hundred cows perfectly content to stay exactly where they were. The odds for success didn't look good, especially if one of those riders was a city cop who'd been lucky to simply stay on top of her horse. "I sure hope you know what you're doing," Kate whispered, giving Rowdy a pat on the neck. "Get me through this and I owe you an apple."

Motioning Kate to head in the opposite direction, Seth circled to the outside of the herd, bringing in stragglers at the perimeter.

"Move on. Move along!" he shouted, rhythmically slapping a gloved hand against his thigh.

Biting her lip, Kate gave her horse a tentative nudge with her heels. Fortunately he seemed to know his business. A cow darted to one side in an escape attempt. Rowdy lowered his head, pinned his ears and launched after the cow like a missile, then slid into a neat pivot and turned the cow back into the herd. Kate grabbed at the saddle horn just in time. Her leg muscles screamed in protest. Pain shot down her neck. But—miracles did exist—she managed to stay aboard.

From the corner of her eye she saw Seth watching her, a concerned frown etched on his face. *So I'm not John Wayne, hotshot.*

The cattle moved across the valley floor toward the ranch buildings. Seth flanked the opposite side of the herd. Twice, the animals started to veer off to the south, but each time Kate managed to head them back. "*Two* apples," she whispered, leaning forward to rub Rowdy's neck beneath the heavy fall of his mane. "You're making me look like a pro."

Seth gave her a nod of approval, then urged his horse forward to tighten up another set of stragglers. He looked as if he'd been in the saddle since the day he'd been born. She watched him closely for a while, unable to detect the cues he gave his horse. Maybe he and that gelding shared ESP.

From a distance he fit the visual image of a dark-and-dangerous cowboy drifter, one who could steal cattle or a lady's virtue and never look back. A shiver of awareness skittered down Kate's back. Without a car or highway or power line in sight, they might have been trailing a herd in the 1800s. Once again, she felt an uncanny sense of heritage seep through her. Had her grandfather ridden these same hills? Great-grandfather? Maybe this stay wouldn't be so bad after all. During her leave of absence from the force she could deal with the doubt and disillusionment that had been escalating since Rico's death. After six months she could return to her beat, and to the career that had become her job, her family, her reason for living. She could prove to her precinct sergeant that she had settled her inner demons.

Two hours later, they drove the last cow into a pasture just north of the barns. Seth dismounted and latched the gate. The cattle continued on and spread out over the gently rolling hills.

"They've got just fifty acres to roam on here," he said, swinging back up into the saddle. "We'll get their vaccinations done this afternoon and start checking them every day.''

He'd been polite from the moment they'd met, but the cool look in Seth's eyes ranked her well below the sort of company he preferred to keep. As they rode toward the barns, they passed a ranch hand nailing up a plank on a corral, and two who were saddling a skittish colt in a round pen. The glances those men gave her bordered on sheer dislike.

She'd faced gang situations where tempers were explosive and rival factions shared only an intense hatred of the law as exemplified by her. There were subtle undercurrents of that same sort of antipathy here.

''Guess I'd better not campaign for Miss Popularity,'' she muttered to herself, watching Seth dismount at the door of the horse barn and tie his mount to the rail.

Flipping a stirrup up over the saddle horn, he deftly uncinched his saddle and settled it on the rail, then draped the sweaty blanket to dry out. Steam rose from his sorrel's damp back.

Kate waited until he turned away, then slid out of her own saddle, suppressing a heartfelt wince. Her leg muscles were on fire; her knees turned soft as spaghetti when her feet hit the ground. She upped her medical needs to liniment *and* a double dose of ibuprofen.

Rowdy turned his head to look at her and bumped her hip with his nose, as if fishing for a reward. Kate chuckled. ''I owe you, fella.''

''Daddy!'' From around the corner of the barn sped

a blond-haired dynamo who tackled Seth at the hips. Rowdy jerked backward, nearly pulling the reins out of Kate's hand.

"Mandy!" Seth warned, firmly extricating himself from the child's grasp. "What have I told you?"

The child stepped back and dug one toe in the dirt. "Not to run."

"Where?"

"At the horses."

Seth ruffled her hair. The warmth in his eyes and the genuine smile on his face made him one handsome guy. "Because?"

Mandy kicked up some dust. "'Cause someone could get hurt." She looked up, a broad smile displaying several missing teeth. "It was cool having two days off this week. I wish teachers had lots more meetings! Nicki and I had a really fun overnight." Her brow furrowed. "But I'm glad to be home, Dad. I missed you!"

Mandy grabbed him around the waist with both arms and he hugged her back. "Good to see you, honey."

The warmth of his expression faded as he looked over Mandy's head at Kate. "This is Kate. She'll be staying with us for a while."

Without releasing her Dad, Mandy looked over her shoulder. "Staying?" Her voice wavered with uncertainty.

"Until July. I sure hope we can be friends." Kate tied her horse to the hitching rail, ignoring Seth's darkening expression. "Maybe you can show me around sometime?"

Mandy hesitated, then nodded.

Kate smiled and studied the little girl from head to toe. "Hmm...I'll bet you're at least in fifth grade."

Mandy stood a little taller and stuck out her chest. "Third."

Kate managed a suitably impressed expression. "No!"

Seth dropped a protective hand on his daughter's shoulder. "Honey, you need to let Della know you're back. I'll see you in a few minutes at dinner, okay?"

As soon as Mandy disappeared, Seth pinned Kate with a searing look. "Remember what I said. This situation is strictly business."

Kate's mouth fell open. "You don't want me to be friendly?"

"Mandy is...vulnerable. She wishes she had a mother who..." Seth shifted his gaze to the cattle grazing on the hill. When he looked back at her, his expression hardened. "Just keep your distance. I don't want her to think you're the answer to her prayers."

Inexplicably hurt, Kate turned away and busied herself by hooking the stirrup over Rowdy's saddle horn, then releasing the cinch just as she'd seen Seth do.

Of course, she wasn't planning to stay past July, but never in a thousand years would she intentionally hurt a child's feelings. Yet after knowing each other less than twenty-four hours, Seth already assumed the worst of her. No wonder he hadn't remarried. The man had the sensitivity of a rock.

Behind her, she sensed Seth's hesitation, then heard

him swear under his breath. "When you're done, put Rowdy in with Drifter, then head up to the house for dinner. It's almost noon."

Kate's hackles rose at his orders, but the thought of a hot meal and a soft chair stifled her automatic retort. Once he'd led his horse away, she took a deep breath, prayed her muscles would hold up and wrestled the saddle off Rowdy's back. The saddle blankets fell into the dirt. The heavy leather cinch slid over his back, whacking her on the cheek.

Her knees wobbling and cheekbone stinging, she lugged the saddle forward a few steps and hoisted it onto the rail, then shook out the blankets. Rowdy bumped her shoulder with his soft nose.

"You're my one friend here, buddy. And even you didn't like me at first," Kate murmured as she rubbed him behind the ear.

He stretched his nose out and closed his eyes in apparent enjoyment. She chuckled, then untied him and led him into the corral, where the Seth's horse was rolling in the dirt.

As soon as she unsnapped the lead rope, Rowdy nosed the ground, turned in a tight circle and collapsed in a billow of dust. Legs flailing in the air, he rolled back and forth, wiggling his spine against the hard earth. The rapture expressed in his closed eyes and bared teeth made her laugh aloud.

"Old-timers would call him a three-hundred-dollar horse."

Startled, Kate spun around. Just a few paces away, the old ranch hand she'd seen this morning stood with an immense syringe in one hand and a coiled lariat in the other. Standing straight he might have topped five foot ten, but he was curved and bent with age and untold injuries. A mottled gray Australian shepherd sat at his feet.

"What?"

"A hundred dollars a full roll, fifty for half way." He leaned to one side and spat tobacco juice. "Barometer of the horse's condition, they used to say."

"And not just how itchy the saddle blanket was?" Smiling, she stepped forward and offered a hand. "Kate Rawlins."

"Cal." He ignored her gesture.

Kate let her own hand drop to her side. Judging from the scowl on his face, the old guy probably didn't make many new friends. She glanced at his hand and tried another tack. "Something—or someone—isn't going to be happy to see that needle coming."

"Been done. Had to treat the cow that got hung up in the fence." Eyes narrowed, he spun the syringe in his hand. "I 'spect you'll be staying till summer."

One more person who would like to see the taillights on her car. There were going to a be a lot of disappointed people on the Lone Tree when she made it to that sixth month, but July was beginning to seem like a lifetime away. "That's right."

With a snort, he turned away and snapped his fingers. "Belle." The dog rose to follow him across the barnyard.

Kate did a double-take at the dog's oddly rolling gait. Belle was missing a hind leg, yet she managed to lope along at a steady pace. Her owner was a gruff old coot, but Kate had to give him credit—he'd been kind enough to give the animal a second chance. Given his surly tone, Kate doubted he'd even give her one.

What did these people expect? Bob Rawlins's will had been explicit. She wasn't here scheming to take something he hadn't offered. If it hadn't been for Bob's cruelty toward her mother, Kate might have experienced a normal, carefree childhood on this ranch. Nothing in the past had been her fault.

Maybe from somewhere above, or far below, Bob was enjoying his last laugh. He'd lured her back, knowing she wouldn't fit in, expecting that she would leave long before her time was up. Perhaps he'd considered this his final, humiliating insult.

Except he didn't know his only grandchild. She'd been an outsider her entire life; the opinions of a few ranch hands and one stubborn cowboy wouldn't affect her at all.

"Dinner's on!" Mandy flew across the sweeping lawn at the back of the house and hung over the fence. She cupped her hands around her mouth. "Dinner!"

Kate waved an acknowledgment and started for the house. Mandy scrambled over the fence and raced up to meet her. "It's fried chicken! My favorite. Della made it just for me because I was gone."

Kate hid a grin. "I'll bet she'll be happy just seeing that smile on your face."

"I went to my friend's house." Mandy fell in step with Kate. "She has puppies. Do you like puppies?"

"All kinds."

Seth had sauntered toward a distant barn, and now

several hands strolled out the door, all wearing dusty, trail-worn Western hats and long, faded jeans that crumpled loosely over their boots. Seth spoke with them for a few minutes, then the other men vigorously shook their heads and strode toward a beat-up truck. Squinting against the bright winter sun, Seth came toward Kate and his daughter. The purpose in his stride made his intention crystal-clear.

"Sweetie, your dad is coming. I'll bet he wants you to scoot inside and get your hands washed."

Seth was faster than she'd thought. In seconds he'd caught up and sent Mandy on ahead. "You have a sweet little girl, there," Kate murmured. "You must be so proud of her."

"Yes." He fell in step with Kate, his eyes focused on the house ahead.

"In case you didn't notice, your daughter approached *me*. It would hurt her more to be rudely ignored." She glanced down at his sleeve. "How's your arm?"

His silent, careless shrug relegated twelve stitches to the category of splinters and bug bites.

At the back porch Kate reached for the door, but Seth's longer arm caught it first. He started to usher her in, then stopped. He was so close she could feel the warmth of his body behind hers and feel his breath at the back of her neck.

Her skin tingled. And elevated awareness of him slid through her, making her want to step aside to escape. He'd made it all too clear that he thought her an interloper, an undeserving heir.

He touched her shoulder. Cleared his throat.

"Uh...Della is like family around here," he murmured. "Do your best."

Surprised, Kate spun around. "Excuse me?"

But instead of cold criticism, she met an expression of concern. His gaze was centered on the kitchen behind her. "Afternoon, Della," he said, sidestepping around Kate. He disappeared down the hall.

Della stood at the kitchen counter with a stack of plates held in the crook of one arm and a fistful of silverware in her misshapen right hand. The denim apron she wore added a measure of domesticity to her threadbare jeans and faded Pro-Rodeo sweatshirt, but her strong, nearly masculine build spoke of far different endeavors during her earlier years.

"Dinner in five minutes," she snapped. "Your mail is on the settee."

Kate chose to ignore the woman's rude tone of voice. *"Mail?"*

"I go after it every day at noon."

Kate nodded her thanks and headed for the living room. Who on earth would have written? She hadn't bothered to tell anyone her address for the next six months, and never used credit cards except for her computer on-line service.

The paneled walls of the hallway leading to the living room were covered with framed photographs. Show cattle and their handler—maybe Bob, as a young man?—posed behind massive trophies. Cutting horses. People Kate had never seen. Were they relatives? Kate looked closer. None were of her mother, nor were there any baby pictures of Kate. Then her breath caught in her throat. There were many of a much younger Seth in various sports uniforms, holding baseball bats and footballs. And some of him on horseback with trophies and ribbons. All lovingly framed and displayed.

No wonder her grandfather hadn't cared about her, she realized, looking at the long row of lovely gilt frames. He'd found a replacement and had done just fine. She'd known that he had never pined for the daughter and grandchild he hadn't seen in more than twenty years, but seeing proof of his affection toward another child reawakened some of the old pain in her heart. Childish hurt that belonged in the past. Resolutely, she turned away and walked on down the hall.

In the living room she found her mail—from Ralph Wilson, the absentee lawyer, postmarked Hawaii. The guy who hadn't bothered to let anyone at the ranch know of her impending arrival. The day she met him in person would be a day he remembered well.

Ripping open the letter, she scanned the contents as she went upstairs to her room. He hoped she'd arrived safely. Promised to contact her when he got back into town. Said he'd work on the details if she decided to sell out her share. *Yeah, right. As if I need an incompetent lawyer.*

After splashing some water on her face and changing into a warmer sweater, she tossed the letter into the drawer holding her lingerie and beneath that, her laptop. When her fingers brushed against an old, ribbon-tied box next to the computer, her hand stilled.

Kate closed her eyes as memories rushed through her. Her mother, pressing the small box into Kate's hands a few years ago and making her promise to safeguard the heirloom brooch within. Her mother, wearily trudging off to yet another minimum-wage job, warning Kate to "stay inside, no matter what." And the long, hot afternoons that followed, spent in a cramped apartment, when Kate had felt sweat trickle down her back as she'd watched other children playing out on the street, and wished with all her heart she could join them.

She opened her eyes and took in the simple beauty of burnished log walls surrounding her, the double-wide windows looking out over the ranch. Her mother had been so very young, so alone when she'd fled this house. If Bob were still living, Kate would have more than a few things to say to him about the importance of forgiveness and love.

The phone rang as Kate strolled into the kitchen. A platter of chicken and a large bowl of mashed potatoes in her hands, Della took a step back toward the phone. The pile of chicken shifted. She shot a frustrated look at Kate. "Get that, would you?"

Kate nodded and picked up the phone. "Lone Tree."

The caller breathed in sharply, then chuckled…a low, sultry sound filled with surprise. "Well, well."

"Can I help you?" Kate asked automatically.

After a long pause, the woman sighed. "Is Seth there?"

"Just a minute, I'll go find h-" Kate heard a crackle of static and a burst of noise at the other end of the line. "Hello? Still there?"

"Er…I need to go. Just tell Seth I'll call later on, around five or so. This is Alison."

The delicate click at the other end of the line sounded as feminine as the caller's voice. An unexpected—and totally inappropriate—flash of something akin to jealousy flooded Kate's thoughts. The woman's lush, sensual voice would entice any guy with a heartbeat, Kate guessed. She envisioned Alison as a seductress in black lace and red satin, her crimson nails toying with the telephone cord. Toying with Seth. Kate gritted her teeth. A man who looked like he did surely had a variety of girlfriends. What he did was his own business. But she'd bet her Beretta that none of them would be happy about another woman living in Seth's house.

Kate replaced the receiver on its hook. "Someone named Alison says she'll call Seth again this evening around five."

A scowl darkened her features as Della set a massive bowl of creamed peas and a basket of dinner rolls on the table. "Damn fool. She knows he's never in this early."

Seth entered the kitchen and headed for the table, Mandy close at his heels. "Who?"

"Alison plans to call back at five," Della grumbled.

"Or so," Kate added, feeling the inexplicable urge to defend the poor woman against Della's obvious dislike.

"We've got a hundred heifers to vaccinate, and I've got an appointment at the bank this afternoon. If I miss her, tell her I'll probably just stop and see her while I'm in town."

Della harrumphed her displeasure as she motioned

for everyone to sit down and say grace. The table could seat ten, but for just the four of them Della had set places at one end. Mandy slid into the seat next to Kate. Her eyes lit with pleasure as Seth held the platter of crispy fried chicken in front of her.

"Why didn't Cal and the other hands come in?" Mandy asked, selecting two chubby drumsticks.

"Errands." He met and held Kate's gaze as he passed the platter on to her. "I'm sure they wish they could have been here."

Mystified, Kate accepted servings of the food being passed. It didn't take long to understand. After the first bite, her gaze flew to Della, who sat across from her. If there'd been any sort of seasoning in the kitchen, it hadn't come within fifty yards of the food on the table. If there'd been any sort of natural flavor to the food prior to preparation, it had been neatly dispatched. No wonder the hands had fled before dinner.

Kate cast surreptitious glances toward Mandy, who was busily consuming her dinner with obvious pleasure, and toward Seth…who was neatly sectioning pieces of chicken from the portion on his plate into ever-smaller fragments. Fascinated, she found herself watching his large, strong hands making surgically precise cuts. Finally, with a sigh, he gave Della an approving nod and began to eat.

Della methodically polished off two plump thighs, then attacked the potatoes on her plate. Then the peas. One item at a time. For one crazy moment Kate imagined the woman was a robot of some sort, capable of stowing away food to keep up appearances.

Seth gamely proceeded. Mandy seemed to love every morsel. And it was a long, long way back to town for anything edible. Kate silently apologized to her stomach and began picking at her meal. Again, she stole a look at Seth…whose stoic expression spoke volumes.

He'd been cold, he'd been rude. He'd weasled his way into the Lone Tree and ended up with half of it. Yet what sort of man would put up with a house-keeper who couldn't cook and face this sort of food every day? A masochistic man with no surviving taste buds, or a warmhearted guy who couldn't bring himself to fire an incompetent employee? After a moment's thought, Kate voted for masochistic.

Kate reached for the platter of chicken and passed it to Seth. "More?"

His eyes glazed. "Plenty, thanks. But please, go ahead." He glanced at Mandy. "How about you, honey?"

Mandy's blond braids bounced as she nodded her head, and she actually beamed as her father slid an-other chicken leg onto her plate. Poor child.

"So," Kate began, twisting in her chair to face Seth, "what are we doing this afternoon?"

He gave her a cool look. "The boys and I are vac-cinating heifers."

"Great! I'd like to help."

"No."

No. A word that triggered memories of all the times she'd been told that she couldn't, she shouldn't, she wouldn't be allowed to do something because she was a woman. Kate crumpled the napkin in her lap into a tight ball.

"Show me what to do. I should be learning all of this."

"You know how to rope? Had much experience at injecting cattle with vaccine?"

"No, but—"

"Real good on a horse, are you?"

Oh, yeah...and after this morning's ride her traumatized leg muscles just might be healed within a month. Or two. "Uh..."

"As I said, the boys and I are vaccinating this afternoon." He tossed his napkin on the table and rose. "You can...do whatever else you want."

Kate bit back a sharp reply. "Then I'll go to town. I need to set up my bank accounts here and buy some warmer clothes."

"The boys brought in your car last night, but we don't have any tires that would fit. You can use the black pickup parked out back." He gave her a doubtful look. "That one has a stick shift. Can you handle it?"

He might as well have asked if she was capable of tying her shoes. The man was a master at making her blood pressure rise. "I think I can manage."

"While you're in town, find a new nightgown and I'll reimburse you. Yours is probably beyond repair."

Della gasped, her shocked gaze darting from Seth to Kate.

"Not what you think, Della." Kate gave her a wry grin, then shifted her attention back to Seth. "I do plan to stay, Hayward. I plan to become a part of this ranch, and I will be an equal partner once I satisfy the terms of the will.''

Della sucked in a breath. Mandy's gaze flew from her father, to Kate, and then back again as Seth silently jerked on his boots and grabbed his jacket from a hook at the back door. In a flash he was gone.

"You have no idea what you've done, coming here." Della's voice shook with anger. "You don't belong. There's people around here who aren't gonna take this real well."

Kate rose and gave her a level look, thinking of her mother's suffering in this house at the hands of her father. Young, scared and only eighteen, Lorna Rawlins hadn't been strong enough to stand up to him.

For the first time, Kate saw beyond her intention to sell off her part of the ranch to fund Rico's memorial. She owed this to her late mother, too. In her mother's name, Kate would reclaim the home and security that had been so cruelly taken away from her. Kate would reclaim it, and then she would sell out, proving to all the ghosts of the past just how little she cared for Bob Rawlins's beloved legacy.

Kate rested both hands on the table and looked Della straight in the eye. "I'm sorry you and the others aren't happy about my arrival," she said gently, "but you can pass this along to anyone concerned. I'll be glad to cooperate. I would rather be friendly. But I don't back away from trouble, and I don't give up."

Della froze. Kate looked over at Mandy, whose widened eyes revealed a glimmer of admiration. "I'm sorry, sweetie. We shouldn't talk like this in front of you.''

Mandy nodded gravely, but a twinkle in her eye gave her away. ''No one gets away with talking back to my dad. Are you going to be in trouble?''

''Nope, but we'll all be more polite in the future, okay?'' Kate reached over to ruffle the child's fluffy bangs. ''I'm going to town for a while, but I'll be back in a few hours.''

Mandy smiled eagerly as she stood up. ''Can I come?''

''No!'' Della fixed the child with a stern look. ''Your—''

''Your father wouldn't want you going anywhere without permission,'' Kate interrupted smoothly. ''But we'll check next time, okay? Now, let's help clear these dishes.''

Mandy gave a melodramatic sigh as she gathered plates and headed for the kitchen. A platter and bowl in hand, Kate turned to leave as well, but a prickling sensation at her nape made her stop. She looked over her shoulder.

Della still sat in her chair, her eyes closed and her deeply wrinkled face twisted into something akin to grief. ''You shouldn't have come back here,'' the old woman muttered to herself. She clenched her hands together on her lap.

From their first meeting, Kate had noticed that Della's hands were gnarled with arthritis, the right one more misshapen than the left. Apparently self-conscious about the deformity, Della kept it mostly out of sight. But Kate had felt a dim sense of familiarity surface when she'd shaken Della's hand, and now that vague memory slid into sharp focus. That claw-curved hand wasn't just gnarled with arthritis. It was scarred, and the little finger was missing; something even a very young child might remember well. Yet Della had denied living at the ranch when Kate and her mother were still here. A chill shot down Kate's spine. Why would Della try to hide the truth?

ALISON WRIGHT FACED her husband from across the expanse of the polished cherry dining room table, her hands clutching the back of a chair. Between them sat a massive bouquet of fresh flowers, artfully arranged and delivered weekly by a florist. Eric insisted on fresh flowers here and in the expansive marble foyer, whether they were entertaining that weekend or not. She might have enjoyed the delicate scent of flowers, but the heavy red roses he ordered each week were meant to focus the eye on the fine wood and the grandeur of the room itself. Not to please her. *Appearance means everything,* he always said.

Too bad that the house he'd created was little more than a front for a shallow, self-centered man and his embittered wife. Still, Alison managed a bright smile. "I'm so happy you got home early today," she said, infusing her voice with as much warmth as she could muster. "I hope you had a good day."

He'd been staring at the bloodred roses with a smirk of satisfaction, but his eyes narrowed as he lifted his head to look at her. "What the hell are you wearing that for?" he growled, gesturing toward her mauve sweats. "You look like a goddamn bag lady."

"I—I was going jogging."

"You aren't going outside looking like that."

Alison felt her smile slip. "There's no one out on our lane. If I go up and back a few times I can get in two miles. It's so boring down on the treadmill."

"Change your clothes."

"But—"

"Alison—" He seemed to loom over the table, Nordic-pale and tall and quietly menacing. She'd once challenged him, and had regretted it for nearly a week. He'd had the foresight to hit her only where it wouldn't show. She backed away from the table and nodded, then turned to go.

"Oh, and Alison," he added, his voice silky. "I would be extremely unhappy if I ever caught you with that ex-husband of yours."

"I have no interest in Seth." God, how she hated her voice. Meek, soft. Where was her spine? "But Mandy…"

"You can bring your daughter here, but I don't want you going to the Lone Tree anymore. That's clear enough, isn't it?"

It was clear all right. Alison turned and slipped out of the room, then fled up the open, curving flight of stairs to the second floor. She'd tried leaving twice, but he'd come after her both times and had made her very sorry she'd tried. His compulsive need for absolute control meant he would never let her go. Marrying Eric had been a foolish mistake, and now she was going to pay for the rest of her life.

CHAPTER FOUR

LOST IN THOUGHT, Kate headed for the parking area beyond the side of the house, stopping for a pair of sunglasses from her car before heading for Seth's pickup. Della was testy enough to end conversations without regard for social niceties, but that didn't explain her reaction in the kitchen. Muttering to herself, with her hands clenched in her lap, the woman had looked exceedingly upset. Why?

Kate had the passenger door of her car open and was reaching for the glove compartment when she realized that nothing was where she'd left it the day before.

Someone had searched her car.

Della's warning, *You shouldn't have come here,* thrummed in Kate's ears as she scanned the interior of the old Mustang. There hadn't been anything of value to steal, but papers from the glove box were strewn on the dashboard, and the inconsequential litter of the past few years had been excavated from beneath the front seat. Nothing much: just an outdated map of Wisconsin, a flashlight, a long-forgotten novel. Her canvas gym bag, containing old running shoes and gray sweats, had been emptied onto the floor along with the crumpled bag of doughnuts she'd nursed all the way from Minneapolis.

If the perpetrator had hoped to find anything of value, he'd hit the wrong vehicle. Kate Rawlins traveled light. With the exception of the laptop computer, her Beretta and her mother's heirloom brooch, which were already stowed in her bedroom, she didn't own anything that could generate a fast profit on the street.

She stepped back and slowly turned around. Not a bush stirred. Not a sound rose above the rustle of breeze-tossed grasses at her feet. Yet the hair at the back of her neck prickled with awareness. She'd have bet a week's pay that someone was watching her from within the deep shadows of the outbuildings.

She moved slowly around the car, searching the brittle grass and winter-hard earth for clues, then swung open the front door and did an inch-by-inch visual search of the interior.

Back in the Twin Cities she would have dusted for prints—or superglue fumed them—and sent them to the lab. Out here, she had no equipment and no lab, but the logical suspects included a limited population of ranch hands, a cranky elderly woman and their surly boss. A boss who, incidentally, would profit in a major way if she left before her time was up. She would be giving Seth's office a visit in the near future.

When he wasn't around to give her a tour.

Force of habit made her double-check the ignition for extraneous wiring. She chuckled under her breath at her own suspicions. Surely no one out here would dare go that far. It wasn't likely that any of them even knew how.

Returning to the trunk, she lifted out the shredded tire, then pitched it into the back of the old black pickup parked nearby.

After scraping a heavy coating of frost from the front windshield, she climbed in and started the truck. It turned over on the first try—surprising, given its battered appearance. She flipped the defroster knob to high and blew on her cold-stiffened fingers.

The air felt heavy today. Heavy and damp and full of promise for snow. After letting the truck warm up for a few minutes, she checked the rearview mirror, backed around and headed out to the highway.

Her new partner may have denied her the opportunity to work cattle, but he'd given her a better one: the opportunity to start checking out the locals, to learn more about him from the people who knew him best.

And just maybe, she'd learn something about her grandfather. He'd never bothered to answer the letters she'd written him as a teenager, never tried to find her. It might be interesting to hear another side to the story of what had happened all those years ago.

Though maybe it would be better if she never found out.

AFTER KATE DISAPPEARED down the road, Mandy released the curtain clutched in her hand and watched it fall back into place, then flopped backward onto her bed against her collection of stuffed animals. Fishing a familiar shape out from beneath her, she stared into Bear's remaining eye, and then hugged him close. A warm tear trickled down her cheek.

Coming home from the McArthurs' house always made her sad, even though Nicki was her best friend. Spending time with a mom who gave hugs and kisses and baked wonderful cookies made Mandy feel lonelier than ever.

What would it be like to have a mother like Joanna? Guilt speared through Mandy at the disloyal thought. Her own mom would be like that, when she finally left her crummy second husband and moved back to the Lone Tree. No one could want to live with a creep like Eric Wright.

And when her mom came back, everyone would be happy. Mandy would have her mom every day, instead of just sometimes, and all of those pushy ladies would stop chasing her dad. They thought he might decide to marry one of them, but of course that would never happen. He'd been married to the most beautiful woman in all of Montana, and no one else could take her place.

She'd overheard Della talking on the phone about Alison being too shallow to catch rainwater, but it wasn't her mom's fault that she couldn't have Mandy visit more often. Eric made her travel with him, and she was really busy. Once she left him, she could come back to the ranch for good. Loneliness and anger gnawed at Mandy's stomach.

Maybe Kate was lonely at the Lone Tree, too. Della sure didn't seem to like her, and Dad acted like he was mad at her or something. But Kate was nice, and she wasn't afraid of Dad or Della. A flutter of happier thoughts wriggled through Mandy's chest. Maybe Kate would like to be friends.

Wiping away a last tear, Mandy reached for the drawer of her nightstand and withdrew the small photograph hidden beneath a jumble of books and papers. Dressed in a shiny red dress, with a tumble of blond curls falling over one shoulder and a bright smile, Alison Hayward Wright looked exactly like a movie star clear down to her long fingernails and sparkly rings. Too beautiful to stay out in the middle of a ranch with only a plain little girl and a cowboy to keep her there.

Mandy levered up on one elbow and studied herself in the mirror over the dresser, then fell back against the bed in disgust. Except for the blond hair, she didn't look like her mother at all. Della had muttered "Thank God for that" every time Mandy asked why she couldn't have looked more like her mom. Della didn't understand. Dad didn't, either.

What if he sent Kate away? Mandy would be alone once again, with only silent Della for company. Launching herself off her bed, Mandy grabbed her jacket from the doorknob and raced down the stairs. She nearly barged into Della as she skidded through the kitchen and snagged her boots from the pile at the back door.

Della frowned at her. "Where you going?"

"Gotta help Dad." Mandy hopped on one foot and then the other as she pulled on her boots. "I promised."

"But—"

Mandy darted out the door before Della could ask any more questions. "I'll be back in an hour," she called over her shoulder.

Mandy raced across the frozen ground toward the sound of bawling cattle and thundering hooves in the north corrals. Dad always warned her to stay away if anything dangerous was going on, but she could stay on top of the fence and watch.

And if he took a break and came over to give her a hug, she could try hard to convince him that Kate had to stay. From the look on his face over lunch, he was likely to tell Kate to pack her bags before supper, if he had the chance.

Mandy couldn't let that happen.

THE URGE TO TURN AROUND, pack her bags and head back to Minnesota hit the moment Kate drove into Salt Creek. Barely four blocks long and dominated by a church at one end, a grain elevator at the other, and at least five bars in between, it hardly seemed like a bustling community. But the people in those buildings must have bustled to the windows as soon as she hit the first block.

Unlike in the resort areas of Montana, a stranger in this town was apparently a major curiosity. No doubt the state on a license plate, type of vehicle and appearance of the driver would become an instant topic of conversation over coffee and pie at the local café. And though she was driving a battered Ford pickup with Lone Tree emblazoned on the side, they still noticed the stranger behind the wheel. All along the street, heads turned and people stood at store windows peering out.

Kate pulled into an empty parking spot in front of

Jim's Diner and decided she would meet that wave of curiosity head-on.

From the second she walked into the diner, she knew her assessment had been right. The occupants of the stools at the long Formica counter swiveled in unison, just far enough to cast surreptitious glances at the front door. Newspapers rustled and lowered to half-mast, and a dozen pairs of eyes peered at her from the booths along the wall.

"Hello," she said to no one in particular, making her way across the floor to the counter. "Beautiful day."

If she'd known about the Jim's Diner dress code, she would have grabbed a denim jacket and battered Western hat from the ample collection in the mudroom at the Lone Tree.

"Can I help you?" The lanky teenager behind the counter gave her a cocky grin, though from the blush on his cheeks she could tell that he was well aware of all the attention she had attracted.

"Just coffee." She grinned back at him. "I'll bet this is the best place in town for lunch, though."

He ducked his head in silent acknowledgement, and brought her coffee in record time. "Cream? Sugar?"

Kate shook her head. "Nice town. Have you lived here all of your life?"

Before he could answer, the elderly man sitting next to her swiveled toward her and raised a snowy eyebrow. "You're new around here, right?"

"Right. Just got in yesterday."

He took a long swallow of his coffee, watching her expectantly over the rim of his cup.

A perfect opportunity. Kate gave him a bright smile. "I'm staying out at the Lone Tree," she said. "Until midsummer."

He pursed his lips, narrowed his eyes. "Related to one of the ranch hands?"

After seeing Doc Anderson's reaction to her, this would be interesting. Kate took a deep breath. "Bob Rawlins's granddaughter."

The man stared at her, the muscles of his jaw working. The friendly look in his eye faded. "Been a lot of years, ain't it." He swiveled back toward the counter and set his cup down with a thump. "Guess I'd better get back to work."

He rose, dug through a pocket of his denim jacket and tossed a crumpled dollar bill onto the counter. "Thanks for the coffee, Jess." Without another word, he strode out of the café.

Jess watched his departure with fascination, then gave Kate a wary look. "Uh…can I get you anything else?"

"Nope. Who was that guy?"

"Sam Hilton. He runs the feed store in town."

With a faint scent of delicate perfume and the rustle of her nylon jogging outfit, a petite woman slid into the empty seat. Early-thirties, with short, wind-blown brown hair and lean features, she had the type of classic good looks that would last into old age.

Kate offered her hand. "Afternoon."

Her eyes twinkling, the woman extended her own. "Looks like you ran Sam out of here pretty fast. Not that it's much loss. The man's the most inaccurate gossip in town. I'm Joanna McArthur. And you are?"

"Almost afraid to say." Kate gave her a rueful grin. "I'm Kate Rawlins."

Joanna gave her a head-to-toe glance. "We've all sure heard about you."

"Since—"

Joanna's laughter pealed through the café. "Forever. But a lot more often since you came to town."

"Since *yesterday?*"

"This is a small town. We hear about it when someone sneezes. I suppose talk died down for a few decades after your mama ran off, but Lorna Rawlins was once big news." Leaning an elbow on the counter, Joanna crossed her legs, as if settling back for a long chat. "Mandy and my daughter Nicki are good friends, so you and I will be seeing each other quite a bit."

She wore no wedding rings. Charming, pretty, surely this woman was the type a man like Seth would fall for. Kate felt a sliver of—no, she wasn't even attracted to Seth. She certainly felt nothing akin to jealousy over his romantic involvements. He could parade a dozen beauties through his house and she wouldn't bat an eyelash. "I'll be here at least until July." After a heartbeat of hesitation, she just had to ask, "How do you and your husband like Salt Creek?"

"I'm single." Giving Kate a look of open curiosity, Joanna drummed her fingernails on the counter. A slow smile crinkled the corners of her eyes. "So…what do you think of Seth?"

If this woman was a girlfriend, either she didn't view Kate as a significant threat, or was far better at hiding her emotions than most of the cops Kate had worked with over the years. "I won't…interfere, if you and Seth…"

Joanna laughed aloud. "Half the women in the county are going to be worried, but not me. Seth and I are casual friends, nothing more." She leaned a little closer and wiggled an eyebrow. "Actually, I think Paul is a fairly interesting guy."

"Paul?"

"The sheriff, Paul Cameron. Not that he seems to be noticing how charming *I* am." She flicked a glance up at Jess. "The usual," she drawled. "If you've got a minute."

Caught eavesdropping, the teenager reddened and spun away, then quickly returned with coffee and a handful of creamers.

Joanna added enough creamers to turn the coffee nearly white. Cradling the cup in both hands, she shifted her gaze back to Kate. "So," she said, her smile wry, "made any lasting friends since you got here?"

"Hardly. This isn't the most friendly community I've seen."

"People here take care of their own. They would give the shirts off their backs if need be."

"That's a bit hard to envision."

"But true." Joanna took a sip of her coffee, then added another dose of creamer. "I'm relatively new here myself, and not too popular, either. I'm the administrator of Meadowbrook, a youth facility. Some of the locals resent the 'dangerous' element we bring into the area."

"Dangerous?"

"By the time these kids get to us, most of them are on the verge of serious trouble, and all of them will soon be too old for juvenile court. We offer a last chance to turn these kids around."

"Working with teens was the best part of my job back home," Kate said wistfully. *At least until Rico died.*

"I heard that you're a cop. We may call on you this summer for a little volunteer time. Are you planning to stay after your six months are up?"

Feeling a little dazed, Kate stared back. In Minneapolis she'd been anonymous, except when wearing her uniform and badge, and even then she had been a law enforcement officer, not Kate Rawlins.

Joanna laughed. "Sorry. How long you stay isn't my business."

Kate found herself grinning back. "I don't mind. It's just a touch of culture shock."

"I know. It hit me, too." Joanna's tone was light and laughter genuine. "You'll be an even greater target of curiosity, with your mom running off and all."

Kate had never discussed the past with anyone, had never revealed the years of hurt and loneliness she'd felt. But suddenly it seemed right to do so, to have at least one person understand.

"My grandfather was—" lowering her voice, Kate shot a look at Jess that sent him bustling to the far end of the counter "—a violent man. My mother fled when I was just a toddler."

Joanna's mouth dropped open. "Bob? Violent? He

was strong and determined, but he wouldn't have killed a mosquito.''

Memories of years of her mother's fear and anger, the endless moves from one town to the next, years of a nearly homeless existence rushed through her. *We've got to go, sweetie. I'm sorry…you'll like your new school a lot better, I promise.…*

''My mother was afraid he would track her down, declare her unfit and try to take custody of me.'' Kate's emotions threatened to swamp her, to make her reveal things to this stranger that no one should ever know. She slid a dollar onto the counter. ''Excuse me, I really should be going.''

Startled, Joanna reached over and touched Kate's arm. ''Please, I'm sorry. I didn't mean to tread where I shouldn't.''

Kate had to turn away from the compassion brimming in the other woman's eyes. She didn't want sympathy or understanding. ''Really, I do have some errands. It was nice meeting you.''

Joanna followed her out to the sidewalk. ''Have a—''

Her voice faltered to a stop as a silver Ford Bronco cruised by.

Curious, Kate shifted her gaze to the driver. *Pale blond hair, well-cut. Medium frame, mid-forties…*

''Have you met him?'' Joanna asked.

Kate shook her head. ''Doesn't sound as though you like him very much.''

''That's Eric Wright. He's Alison's second husband, and Mandy's stepfather. I wouldn't trust him any farther than I could spit.''

"Why?"

"The guy gives me the creeps. He's some sort of real estate investor. He seems to go after people who are desperate, like widows and people who are in financial trouble. I've overheard the man talking, and anyone who brags about his 'steals' is pretty low in my book." Joanna glanced at her watch. "Oops, gotta run." With a wave of her hand, she darted across the street toward the drugstore.

So the woman who'd called the ranch was Seth's ex-wife. Kate looked down the street and memorized Eric's license plate, then smiled ruefully to herself. In a town this size there couldn't be another silver Bronco.

A quick stop at the grocery store, farm supply and the drugstore yielded some personal essentials and a new tire, but little else. After being met with either wary curiosity or frank suspicion at every stop, she found the blessed silence of the drive home a great relief. She would have to wait awhile before trying to get any information about Seth and the Lone Tree.

The brief conversation with Joanna replayed through her mind as she crossed the desolate land of the ranch. Joanna was wrong. All of those years of fear, of running, of one dingy apartment after another hadn't been for nothing. Her mother had done the right thing. She had fled from a violent, unpredictable man, to keep her little daughter safe. Her mother had been right.

Hadn't she?

THAT NIGHT THE DREAM came again. The alley, dark and dank. Rats squealing and rustling around a pile of refuse. The dim light of a single streetlamp glowing through the swirling mist.

This time there were a hundred forms lurking in the shadows, darting past the windows of the abandoned building looming above the alley. The glitter of a gun barrel, the glow of a cigarette and the flash of silver neck chains symbolic of the local gang darted at the edges of her peripheral vision.

At the end of the alley crouched a young boy, pale as death, his eyes huge and frightened in his thin face. All she had to do was run the gauntlet, but even as she started down the alley it lengthened. Darkened. With every stride she took he seemed farther away. She ran harder, faster, her breath tearing through her lungs.

The soulless creatures lurking in the windows shrieked with laughter. When she'd nearly reached the end of the alley they took flight, then rocketed to earth. Toward the terrified child. *Rico.*

His screams tore through Kate's consciousness. He grabbed for her arm. Bolting upright, she fought the familiar confusion and fear careering through her mind. Felt the cold sweat of fear.

And felt a child's warm hand on her arm.

"Kate?" Mandy's pale, frightened face looked ghostly in the sliver of moonlight streaming through the curtains. "Are you okay?"

Kate stared at her for a minute, willing her heartbeat to slow down and her voice to steady. Clad in a flannel nightie and clutching a disreputable teddy bear in one hand, the little girl looked much younger than she had in the daylight. Yet she'd left the security of her own bed to make sure Kate was okay. Touched, Kate swung her feet onto the floor and reached out to give Mandy a hug.

"Thank you, sweetie. Guess I just had a bad dream."

Mandy scooted onto the bed and hugged her back. "I have bad dreams sometimes, too. My Dad stays till I go back to sleep. Should I stay with you?"

Looking down into Mandy's earnest face, Kate felt her heart expand with unfamiliar warmth. "I'll be fine. And I'll bet you'll sleep a whole lot better in your own bed."

"Maybe. Do you want me to tell you a story, first?"

Even though the old Baby Ben clock on the night-stand read 2:00 a.m., Kate wanted to savor Mandy's presence a few minutes more. "Is it a short one?"

Nodding, Mandy cleared her throat. "My mom is a beautiful princess. As pretty as anyone you ever saw in a movie, with long golden hair and silk dresses. Long ago she fell in love with a handsome cowboy— that's my dad—and came to Montana, but after she had a baby—that's me—she got sort of mixed up and went away." Mandy stifled a yawn. "My dad has been really lonely ever since. No one will ever be as beautiful and perfect as her, and someday she's going to come back."

Heavy footsteps came down the hall, stopped in the vicinity of Mandy's bedroom, then came closer. "Mandy?" Seth whispered from the doorway. "Are you in there?"

Deep in her own thoughts, Mandy continued. "Maybe we can be friends. You're not like all those pretty ladies who think my dad should marry them. But that won't ever happen, because my mom is coming back someday soon. And then we'll all be to-geth—"

"Mandy!" Seth pushed the door open a few inches and peered in. "Why aren't you in your own room?"

Startled, Mandy looked up.

The door swung open. Seth filled the doorway, clad in a hastily tied robe. In the dim moonlight he looked almost menacing, with a dark five o'clock shadow and an even darker expression in his eyes. Disconcerted, Kate gathered the frayed edges of her nightgown at her throat.

"What the heck are you doing in here?" His late-night voice was even deeper than usual. Some men might look disheveled and unassuming, even cuddly, in a robe. But with his long, muscular calves bare and broad chest partially exposed, Seth Hayward was one very imposing man. One who looked exceedingly annoyed.

Yet...Kate felt her skin grow warmer. Heard her heartbeat pick up a faster rhythm. And wished that robe would slip just a little. Her fingers curled as she wondered what it might be like to run them across the hard curves and planes of his chest. His skin would be hot, smooth....

Damn. Blinking, she shifted her gaze back to safer territory—the top of Mandy's head. "Your daughter thought she heard something."

"I did! Kate had a nightmare. Didn't you hear her

scream?'' Mandy snuggled closer to Kate's side. ''I came to help. Just like when you come to help me.''

Seth's gaze shifted to his daughter's earnest face. ''Back to bed, young lady.''

''But, Dad!''

He pointed to the hallway. ''Scoot!''

''You always stay with me if I have bad dreams,'' Mandy wheedled.

Seth held out a hand. ''I mean it, punkin. Morning comes way too early around here.''

''Sorry.'' Mandy slithered off the bed and whispered, ''Do you want my bear?''

Kate fought a smile. ''You'd better keep him. He would miss you, I'm sure.''

Ruffling his daughter's hair, he laid a hand on her shoulder and ushered her out the door, but then looked back. ''Are you okay?''

An unfamiliar sense of comfort flowed through Kate. How long had it been since someone had said that to her? ''I sometimes have…vivid dreams, but it's nothing.''

He frowned back at her with an expression of concern, then looked over his shoulder. ''Get back in bed, Mandy. I'll be there in a minute to tuck you in again.''

''But—''

''Now, Mandy.''

Mandy sighed. ''G'night, Kate.'' Her footsteps faded down the hall.

Seth stayed at Kate's door, watching his daughter's departure, and then leaned one shoulder against the door frame as he turned back toward Kate. *"Night-mares?"*

Kate shrugged. His raised eyebrow conveyed willingness to talk, but there was no point in sharing her terrifying dreams. He would feel obligated to express sympathy and support, just like the counselor back at the precinct, but the nightmares would keep coming, and talking about them only made her appear weak and foolish. "It's nothing."

He searched her face, his eyes dark and compassionate. "I expect you've had a lot of experiences as a cop that you'd rather not remember."

Though he didn't move away from the door, the deep resonance of his voice made her feel as though he'd enveloped her in a gentle embrace.

The old memory crystallized, anyway, still sharp as a stiletto twisting in her heart. *Rico.* Once again she could feel the boy's warm blood on her hands, hear the deafening silence after his last breath. The EMTs had arrived ten minutes later. After seeing the number of bullet holes in the boy's chest and the ocean of blood on the street, they'd radioed the ER and hadn't attempted heroic measures.

She willed her voice to steady. "Goes with the job, I guess."

She caught her breath at the unexpected emotion that flashed through his eyes. It must have been just a trick of the moonlight, the late hour. She could not have seen a depth of pain and loss as deep as her own.

Seth straightened, hesitated. For just a moment he looked as though he might stride into the room and gather her close. But just as quickly, he faltered and spun away.

"Dawn will be coming soon," he said, his voice rough. "Get some sleep."

Kate listened to his footsteps moving down the hall and the closing of a bedroom door, then settled back against the headboard and stared at the ceiling. *Six, seven, eight...* she counted the pine planks across the ceiling, then started counting the knotholes on those planks, one by one.

She'd be exhausted by morning if she didn't sleep, but falling asleep meant risking the nightmares. She should have known it would happen.

Her own private hell had followed her to Montana, and would never let her go.

CHAPTER FIVE

PAIN SLAMMED THROUGH HER with each heartbeat, like a chisel hammering through the side of her head. Inch by agonizing inch, Kate managed to lever herself up into a sitting position, where the blinding force might ease. The severe headaches were less frequent, but might recur for several more months, according to the doctors back in Minnesota. The graze wound and force with which she'd hit the cement had left her with a tangible reminder of the night Rico was killed.

She hadn't been able to sleep after Mandy and Seth left, so she'd started up her laptop, hooked up to the phone line in her bedroom and had initiated a public records database search on Seth and Della. After coming up dry, she'd e-mailed a P.I. back in Minneapolis who had access to more extensive search methods. When she felt better, she would ferret out the legal names of the ranch hands—who all seemed to answer to nicknames—and start on them. Someone had searched her car…and with the exception of Mandy, no one wanted her here. It wouldn't hurt to know just whom she might be dealing with during her stay.

But for now, the intensifying pain in her head shattered her ability to think, to move.

Exhausted, she gingerly sagged to one side and leaned against the headboard of her bed. Across the room, in the dresser, lay the bottle of prescription pain medication that might help dull the agony to a bearable level.

It might as well have been on the moon.

A soft tap against the door rocketed the pain level higher yet. "No…" She willed the sound to go away, but again, there was a soft tap. "Please…"

"Rise and shine!" Seth's voice slashed through the silence. "You wanted to be a part of the operation, and we're hauling cattle today. Be ready in ten minutes."

Kate forced open one eye and stared at the door. *Go away. Please…*

After a pause, Seth rapped at the door. "Are you in there? I'm opening the door, so I hope you're decent."

The door swung open with a shriek that must have awakened the dead in four counties. Flinching, Kate fought the urge to close her eyes and die.

Standing in the doorway, Seth studied her, his eyes narrowing and mouth curling in apparent disgust. "I won't even ask what you took, or how much you drank, but take this as your one-and-only warning. I won't tolerate anything like that here, no matter what Bob's will said. Is that clear?"

He thought she'd taken *drugs?* A faint glimmer of humor surfaced through the throbbing sensation in her brain. His opinion of her certainly couldn't have been more clear.

A wave of nausea hit. With a soft moan she closed

her eyes and moved a hand slowly to her midsection, praying for a reprieve. The bathroom was roughly a hundred miles away, and even rising to her feet would take more courage than she could summon. Whatever happened, would happen right here—there was no other conceivable option. *Go away, Hayward, you arrogant jerk....*

She heard him move across the room, felt his proximity as a warm, tangible force when he stopped at the side of her bed. He gently touched her forehead. "What's going on here?"

"Go. Away." Kate breathed. "No...wait. Top drawer. Please."

She heard the rasp of a wooden drawer opening, the slither of lingerie, then the blessed rattle of tablets in a plastic bottle. After a moment of silence—while he considered the script on the bottle, no doubt—he left the room, then returned to the side of her bed.

"Here, it says to take two." He shook a couple of tablets into her hand. "And here's some water."

He waited until she'd finished, then set the glass and bottle on the bedside table. "I know you don't feel like conversation, but...I'm sorry. I shouldn't have jumped to conclusions."

Kate managed a smile of thanks, then sank back against the headboard and closed her eyes. "These headaches don't hit very often anymore, thank goodness."

Again he touched her, this time laying a cool cloth across her forehead. *Heaven.*

His voice was soft and low. "I'm hauling a load of cattle to a sale and won't be back till supper. I'll tell Mandy to be quiet, and I'll have Della check on you later.''

He left so quietly that Kate might have thought him still in the room, until she heard him descend the stairs. Damn. The cowboy was good to look at, but that had been his one redeeming quality. Now she'd felt his gentle touch, experienced the impact of his protective side.

The wife who'd let this one get away had made a major mistake.

BY LATE AFTERNOON Kate was on her feet and, if a little worse for the wear, at least functioning well enough to hunt for something to eat in the kitchen. Della wasn't anywhere to be seen.

On the first floor she changed her mind, turned away from the kitchen door and headed for Seth's study. This could be the only time she would have the place to herself.

Bookshelves lined every wall. Classics, business law, several sets of encyclopedias...and further in, behind the desk, an eclectic grouping of agronomy and animal husbandry texts interspersed with the latest mystery and suspense bestsellers.

Kate paused. Listened. Then moved to the desk. Neat stacks of receipts and bills were positioned by a desktop computer. A banner of tape from the adding machine to the right cascaded over the edge of the desk and hung to the floor.

After a quick glance out the window, she thumbed through files in the cabinet next to the desk. *Bingo.* Each employee had a file containing insurance and payroll records, and all the personal data she needed to facilitate background checks.

Kate copied down names and numbers, then stuffed the piece of paper into her jeans pocket. A dog barked. A car door slammed. Quickly she replaced the files, then slipped into the kitchen.

Through the windows she could see Della talking to Cal over a corral fence. Mandy had stopped to play with Belle, the three-legged dog. *Close, Rawlins,* she muttered to herself.

Foraging through the refrigerator, she found some cheese and ham, then she sliced a thick slab from the loaf of whole-wheat bread left to cool on the counter.

Settling at the kitchen table with a glass of milk, she gazed out the window toward the ranch buildings, where the hands were sauntering around, doing whatever ranch hands did. The skies were leaden, and every now and then one would cast a glance upward, as if he expected precipitation.

Maybe she should go out and offer to help. She smiled to herself, imagining their responses. With the exception of Freckles, none appeared eager to give her the time of day, much less pointers on how to be useful.

The back door squealed and Mandy burst in, her cheeks rosy above the upturned collar of her pink jacket. She dropped her school backpack and shucked off her boots in a flurry of impatience.

"Hi! Isn't it great that it's Friday? It was a pretty good week, though, since we had two days off—" She covered her mouth with one hand, a look of horror in her eyes. "Oh, I'm sorry," she whispered. "I forgot about your headache!"

Kate smiled at her. "It's okay, I feel a lot better now."

Her eyes still wide, Mandy drew closer. "Did my dad say you had to leave?"

As if he could. "No…" Kate casually took a bite of her sandwich. "Was he planning to?"

Mandy rattled the lid of a cow-shaped cookie jar on the counter, grabbed a handful of chocolate chip cookies and settled into a chair next to Kate's. "He's never been so grumpy to anyone in our house before. I figured you might be gone by the time I got home from school." Mandy sighed heavily. "I'm glad you're still here!"

"Grumpy?" Seth had been so gentle this morning, more than solicitous over her splitting headache. "Oh, you mean yesterday, at dinner? When he said I couldn't help him with the cattle?"

Mandy nodded.

"He was just making himself clear." Kate tipped her head toward the backpack at the back door. "So how was school?"

Slumping in her chair, Mandy frowned at the cookie in her hand. "Okay."

This was familiar ground. Kate had put in a lot of volunteer hours at the youth center back home. Not one of the kids ever said more than "fine" when she asked them about school.

She tried a different tack. "What was the best thing that happened today?"

Mandy shrugged, her gaze still fastened on the cookie.

"The worst thing?"

Mandy started picking crumbs off the edge of the cookie. "Nothing."

Kate hid a smile. "You got sent to the principal's office?"

"No!"

"Your best friend called you names?"

"No…"

"Failed the biggest test of the year?"

Mandy looked up. "'Course not!"

"Hmm…you fell down the stairs, knocked over three teachers and sent the janitor flying out the window?"

Mandy fought a smile. "No." Her smile wavered, then her eyes began to fill. "I have to be in a play next week."

"So? Won't that be fun?"

A tear slipped down her cheek. "It's supposed to be about pioneers, and everyone will have long dresses and bonnets. Nicki's mom always makes her something really cool." In a smaller voice, she added, "The other moms will all come to the play, too."

Kate's heart went out to the little girl. She looked so sad, and Kate could sympathize. Her mom had always been too busy or too tired to come to any of Kate's school events.

"So…do you have any ideas for a costume?"

Mandy shook her head.

Kate had brought a meager collection of clothes from Minneapolis. Jeans, sweaters, sweatshirts, nothing that could be altered into a style from the pioneer era. She didn't even own a dress, come to think of it. "What about the attic? Or the closets?"

"There wouldn't be anything." Mandy's voice broke. "If there was, I would just look stupid. Dad always says to ask Della or Nicki's mom, but just once I wish I could have something really special."

Kate nodded to Della as the older woman came in the back door, then turned back to Mandy. "Maybe we could do some alterations, if we found something that would work. Have any ideas?"

"Try the storeroom out in the barn. I already told her to look there," Della grumbled as she shucked off her coat.

"The *barn?*"

Della turned but didn't meet Kate's gaze. "All the old things are out there."

Mandy shot a nervous look out the window. "It's getting dark. And there's mice."

"The lights work, missy." The older woman smoothed her iron-gray hair back with both hands, slapped them against her faded jeans and hobbled into the kitchen. The cold, damp weather had to be playing havoc with her arthritis.

"But it's…*creepy* in there!"

Della hitched one shoulder as she peered into the refrigerator. "Then you should go while there's still daylight." Withdrawing a package of thawed beef, she turned toward a cupboard and pulled out a deep roasting pan.

"Would you come with me?" Mandy gave Kate a hopeful look. "It won't take long, I promise."

After Della's warmth and compassion, Kate couldn't have said no to walking a mile on broken glass. "No problem." She picked up her empty plate and glass, loaded them into the dishwasher, then chose a lined denim jacket from the hooks by the back door. "We'll figure out something that your friends will envy, okay?"

Hurrying through the cold rain with Kate close on her heels, Mandy led the way to the largest barn.

In the dim shadows at the back, Kate could make out the hulking shapes of two immense tractors and several other farm implements. Ancient harnesses hung from pegs along the alleyway, and above, the soaring roofline arched over a vast number of hay bales. Scents of hay, dust and motor oil tickled her nose.

Two fat calico cats immediately appeared and wound around Kate's ankles, their loud purrs sounding like the steady hum of machinery. "What are their names?" Kate asked, reaching down to rub the smaller one behind its ears.

Mandy scooped up the other one. "That's Fluff, and this is Spots. They're going to have kittens."

Any minute, if appearances meant anything. "Won't that be fun?"

Straightening, Kate turned toward the heavy storeroom door. Apparently it hadn't been opened in some time. Thick rust and debris crusted the hinges, while swaths of dust-laden cobwebs swooped low in front of the door frame. A shiver crawled down her spine. Spiders capable of such an engineering feat had to be the size of city rats. Rabid dogs, pet pythons on the loose and feral alley cats she could handle. But never had she overcome her aversion to spiders.

Mandy gave Kate a curious look, then reached for a rusted scoop shovel hanging from a nail. "Use this," she said, offering the unwieldy tool.

Kate swatted at the webs, then gingerly swept away a handful of the sticky strands and opened the door. "Isn't this sort of a problem, storing things out here?"

Mandy shuddered. "This is just the really old stuff. Della says we should burn it all."

With one hand on the door frame, Kate peered inside. Dim light filtered through a haze of dust from the small window at the far side. A jumble of trunks, boxes and furniture leant a mysterious air. A tug on the string dangling in front of her nose bathed the huge storeroom in light.

"Wow. They didn't ever throw anything away around here, did they!" She turned in a circle. "Has anyone ever come in here looking for something and actually found it?"

Mandy stayed close by Kate's side. "I don't know."

Moving into the center of the room, Kate looked around slowly. "I'll bet they even stored the covered wagon and oxen in here. Think we'll find them?"

"I hope so!" Mandy giggled and ventured a few steps in a different direction. "Once I was out here with my dad and we found some cool stuff. I'm pretty sure there were some trunks that had lady's clothes inside, really old."

Kate's initial hesitance to go through someone

else's possessions eased as she realized, with a sense of wonder, that almost everything must have belonged to her grandfather, and to the generations before him. In an odd sense, she was touching her past, a history no one had ever shared with her. Who might have worn this ancient, moth-holed jacket? Or the pretentious hat with plumes swooping off to one side? The shadows and cobwebs held secrets Kate longed to uncover, but Mandy's cries of frustration precluded a more leisurely search.

Twenty minutes later Mandy plopped down on an old horsehair sofa. "Guess I'll be the only one without a good costume," she mumbled, kicking at a box by her feet.

"Giving up will guarantee it." Kate brushed a cobweb out of her eyes and pressed her hands at the small of her back, then sat down next to Mandy and gently lifted her chin with a forefinger. "Let's look a little more, okay?"

Ten minutes later, Kate was ready to quit when she spied a trunk pushed against a far wall, almost hidden by a tangle of Christmas tree lights draped over its arched spine. Kate leaned over and blew at the dust obscuring the shipping label pasted at one end. *Lorna Rawlins.*

Stunned, Kate sank to her knees and ran a hand over the surface, her heart racing. How could it still be here, after all these years?

"Did you find something good?" Mandy leaned over her shoulder, brimming with impatience. "Quick, open it!"

Emotion clogged Kate's throat and turned her stomach to lead as she lifted the lid.

"Is there a dress?" Mandy leaned over so far that Kate felt the child's warm breath tickle her ear.

Something brown and dry had been laid carefully atop a mass of tissue paper. A corsage, with a fragile bow of pink ribbon edged in tarnished gold. The color long since gone, it still bore a faint, musty scent of roses. From a high school prom?

Her mother had rarely talked about her life at the ranch, had refused to answer any questions. But this corsage spoke of youthful joy and anticipation...of a girl who had found happiness in some parts of her life, even if she'd refused to acknowledge them as an adult. Had Lorna's prom date been the boy who had gotten her in trouble, and then abandoned her?

This might have been from my father.

Mandy leaned over and peered into Kate's face. "You look kinda sad."

Kate managed a smile. "No...it's just nice to be able to touch the past. See, this trunk has my mother's name on it." She slowly lifted the brittle corsage and set it on the protective lip of the upturned lid of the trunk, then ran a hand across the tissue paper laying inside. With careful, probing fingers she moved it aside and tested the size and weight of the next object. "This might be what you're hoping for, kid."

It was heavier than she'd expected as she lifted the item out and began to unwrap several more layers of brittle tissue. Kate caught her breath.

Mandy squealed. "It's beautiful!"

It was. Simple, probably of moderate cost for its

day, the bodice of heavy pink satin glowed in the dim light. Kate stood and shook out the full-length skirt and heavy netting beneath. With a scalloped hem and high, puffed sleeves narrowing into fitted cuffs, there were few decorative touches, but the lines would have flattered her mother's slender figure.

Her mother's high school prom dress—a dress in which she must have felt like a princess. What had Lorna Rawlins been like before bitterness and fear ruled her life?

Mandy reverently stroked the smooth fabric. "It's too pretty for me to use. Is there anything else in there?"

After wrapping the dress within its protective cocoon, Kate set it aside and reached deeper into the chest. Costume jewelry. Baby clothes.

Mine? Kate thought with wonderment, tracing delicate bunny embroidery on a white bib. And then there were packets of baby pictures...yellowed Polaroids and curling color photos. After a lifetime of feeling no connection to any place on earth, here was a treasure trove of her own history. The discovery nearly took her breath away.

"Can I see what's underneath?" Mandy jiggled from one foot to the other in anticipation. "Maybe we'll find huge diamonds or a million dollars!"

Laughing, Kate reached around and gave her a hug. "I've already found some pretty special things, sweetie, but let's take a look." She withdrew a length of royal blue calico.

"That's it! It's perfect!" squealed Mandy, spinning around with glee. "That's my pioneer dress." Her face fell. "Unless maybe it's special and I can't use it."

"I think this was called a 'granny dress' back in the sixties," Kate mused, holding up the floor-length dress for inspection. The bodice was of cranberry calico, the sleeves long and full. "It would be just right for your costume."

Mandy enveloped Kate in a bear hug. "You're the best."

Kate held the garment up. "Maybe we can shorten it and figure out a bonnet from what we take off."

Her eyes sparkling, Mandy twirled around the small space. "Now I can't wait to be in the play." She flopped backward onto the sofa, sending up a billow of dust, then sat forward. "That's your *mom's* trunk? Really?"

Nodding, Kate lifted out an empty purse, some old books…odds and ends of a life on the ranch that had ended with a midnight departure and a bus ticket to nowhere.

"What's that? It looks important."

In the shadowed corner of the bottom lay a shoebox tied with red ribbon. Kate reached in to get it.

"That's the hidden treasure!" Mandy breathed, her eyes wide.

Kate tapped her lightly on the nose with a forefinger. "Not likely, squirt. It's probably just Christmas ornaments or old underwear. Be my guest."

Mandy pulled a free end of the ribbon and watched, entranced, as it fell away. With a flourish, Kate lifted the lid.

It was filled with old letters.

Mandy's face fell. "Rats. We could have been rich!"

She thought for a moment. "Maybe they're mushy love letters!"

"If they are, we won't read them." Kate started to close the box, then stared at the return address on the first envelope. Stunned, she lifted out the letters and fanned through them.

Time stood still.

These weren't teenage love letters to her mother. These were from the past couple of decades, and they'd all been returned unopened. Every return address read "Bob Rawlins, Salt Creek, Montana."

He had written. Kate's heart pounded in her throat.

Gathering up the calico dress in her arms, Mandy gave Kate an expectant look. "Can we go back to the house?"

Kate blinked, trying to clear her thoughts. "Yeah…sure."

She hesitated as she packed away her mother's things. The letters were private correspondence, but her mother and grandfather were both gone. Maybe now she could find the answers she'd wanted all her life. Kate picked up the letters and followed Mandy back to the house.

AFTER ANOTHER TRULY forgettable supper, Mandy buried her nose in her homework at the kitchen table while Kate shortened the granny dress. After trying to envision the design of a pioneer-style bonnet using the extra fabric, Kate finally gave up. Hemming pretty much encompassed the extent of her sewing capabilities, and Della apparently possessed even less. The older woman had looked over her shoulder, grunted, then disappeared into her bedroom just off the kitchen.

At nine Mandy went to bed. Outside, the wind keened through the trees and icy pellets rattled at the windows. Twice, Cal rapped at the back door and then stomped in, glared at Kate as if the weather and late hour were all her fault, and asked if there had been any word from Seth.

At eleven, Della came back into the kitchen, paced the floor on the pretext of straightening the already-pristine countertops, and darted glances at the clock on the wall every few minutes.

"Shoulda been back before dark," she muttered, scrubbing at the stove with furious strokes. "He shoulda made it back for supper."

Kate looked up. "Want some coffee? It's decaf."

Della shook her head. "Icy roads, that empty semi, I just don't like it."

"Maybe he stayed in Folsum."

"Woulda called." Della started swiping at nonexistent dust on the cupboard fronts. "He always calls and he don't take chances."

Crusty as she was, the elderly woman obviously cared. She sounded just like an irritated mother hen. "I'll listen for the phone, if you want to turn in," Kate offered.

After another ten minutes of cleaning, Della's limp grew even more noticeable. With a sigh, she leaned against the counter and gave Kate a stern look. "You'll wait up?"

"Promise." Kate crossed herself and held up two fingers. "I'll take a quick shower, and then I'll stay up until I hear from him."

After some consideration, Della put down her dish-cloth and nodded. "Thanks."

A major first step—Della expressing thanks. Kate smiled at her, but she'd already turned away.

KATE CURLED UP in the fuzzy warmth of her worn chenille robe and held the box of old letters in her lap. The kitchen was dark, save the muted light from a single light fixture over the sink, and silent, except for the soft tick of the wall clock above the stove and the occasional buffet of wind against the window-panes.

It was a cozy place, but even her long, hot shower hadn't made her sleepy. Her thoughts spun from Seth, who still hadn't called, to the letters she now held, and then back to the nasty weather outside. Where was he? Della had said he should have returned hours ago.

Seth Hayward was no fool. He wouldn't be out taking chances with an expensive rig. Maybe he was in Folsum, having a good time with friends in some bar. Maybe he was in Salt Creek with some woman…holding her in his arms….

An unfamiliar flutter of jealousy worked its way through Kate's midsection. *She can have him. The last thing I need is some stubborn, irritating cowboy who thinks I'm a lower life-form than mold.* Kate shifted her attention to the box in her lap.

Feeling like a voyeur, she lifted the lid and

thumbed through the envelopes. They had been stored in order of postmark date, filed with care. Why had they all been returned? And why in heaven's name had Bob kept writing, despite the fact that many—perhaps all—of his letters had been sent back?

He'd either hired an investigator to find out her address each time she moved, or had spent a lot of time at the task himself. He'd definitely followed his daughter's trail.

Some of the envelopes had been rubber-stamped as Address Unknown. Most had been "refused," and the refusals had been written in her mother's hand.

How could Kate have missed such an important detail? She flipped through the stack, then went through them again, slower.

And then stopped.

Some envelopes were addressed to Kate. And her mother had written Refused on those, as well.

Kate leaned back in her chair, her mind spinning. Anger rose within her as she remembered the years she'd spent wondering about her grandfather. From the few things her mother had said, she'd imagined him to be a heartless and uncaring monster. His failure to answer the letters she'd written as a teenager had only confirmed her childhood beliefs.

Now she looked down on the unopened letters, and her mother's betrayal twisted like a knife in her heart.

In all fairness, perhaps Bob had been as violent as her mother had once said—perhaps even more so. But Lorna Rawlins had denied Kate the right to make her own decisions, and in doing so had robbed her beyond measure. And with Bob and Lorna gone, there would never be an opportunity to find out the truth.

Wind blasted against the side of the house. The back door blew open, slamming against the wall and sending a rush of cold air swirling through the kitchen. Startled, Kate shot to her feet and spun around.

Seth stood there, tall and lean, filling the doorway. His windblown dark hair and five o'clock shadow gave him the look of an Old West gunfighter, but his stance was that of a cowhand who had been on the trail for months. He definitely hadn't been out having a good time, judging from the glaze of ice on his jacket and haggard look in his eyes.

He looked exhausted and disheveled, and Kate's first impulse was to go to him and take him in her arms as she would an old friend. She caught herself just in time.

CHAPTER SIX

"LONG DAY," SETH GROWLED, peeling off his ice-encrusted gloves.

Kate gathered her robe at her neck with one hand and drew closer. "What on earth happened? Everyone has been worried about you."

He hung up his jacket, then tried shucking off his boots, but his efforts were slow and awkward. "Cell phone went dead. Couldn't…call."

Kate took his arm and led him to a chair, ignoring his bemused expression as she pulled off his boots. "You look awful. Does the other guy look worse?"

Seth closed his eyes and stretched back in his chair. "I wish there'd been one around. I could have used some help."

She tossed the boots toward the pile at the back door, then turned and went to the sink. "Did you make it to the sale, or did you spend your time in a ditch somewhere?" she asked, rinsing out the coffee-pot. "From the looks of you, you weren't out partying."

"Made it to Folsum okay, got the cattle sold."

At the grim tone in his voice, Kate stopped measuring the coffee grounds and looked over her shoulder. Getting information from him was like trying to get a confession out of an ex-con. "That's good, right?"

He lifted one shoulder in a noncommittal shrug.

"It's not?"

He didn't respond.

After starting a pot of coffee, she returned to stand in front of his chair. She'd thought he was simply in his usual taciturn mood, but when he finally opened his eyes, she caught her breath at the raw emotion she saw there.

"Can you elaborate just a tad?" she asked gently. "You went to the sale. You sold the cattle. That wasn't success?"

"Not when you watch thirty years of careful breeding go through the ring for a fraction of what it's worth." He shoved a hand through his hair. "Those heifers should have been part of the future here. Now they're gone."

Kate frowned. "Can't you no-sale livestock if the bidding is lousy?"

"And do what? Tell the bank that we'll get around to paying them in a few months, when it's convenient? This will cover what has to be paid right now. But next month…"

"What about other cattle here? Could they have been sold?"

"The younger beef stock wasn't at market weight. The rest of the cows are good breeders, in a proven herd we've culled every year." He let out a long breath. "I did what had to be done. I'm just sorry it was necessary."

Kate pulled up a chair next to him and sat down,

looking up into his face. Without thought, she laid a comforting hand on his thigh. The muscles bunched and tensed beneath her fingers.

He covered her hand with his own, as if to move hers away, then exhaled slowly and curled his fingers around hers. "Had any more headaches?"

Warmth spread through her at his touch, and at the lazy gleam in his eye as he looked down at her.

"Uh...no." That seductive warmth reached her brain, melted her thoughts. Clearing her throat, she started to pull away, but he rubbed his thumb over the back of her hand, and then turned her hand over and caressed her wrist.

Maybe it was the late hour and the stress of the day that had lowered barriers and lifted caution, leaving them both open and vulnerable. Maybe it was mutual loneliness, or long-untouched emotions that lurked beneath the surface of their relationship. But the effects of his touch escalated, spiraled through her. Her gaze drifted to his sensual mouth. The dark, masculine shadow on his lower jaw. His even, white teeth...

He was smiling at her.

The man who had looked so exhausted moments before didn't look very exhausted now. Heat sparked in the depths of his eyes. His gaze felt like a caress, an unspoken invitation. And heaven help her, she wanted more.

It had been so long since she had been close to anyone. Not even Kent had made her pulse race at a mere touch, and he'd been her fiancé. Thoughts of Kent brought back reality. In six months she would be back in Minneapolis. The idea grew less appealing with every passing day.

The coffeepot gurgled and spat, and with equal sensations of regret and relief, she stood. In a few minutes she had a plate of sandwiches, chips and a cup of steaming coffee in front of him. She took a chair at the opposite side of the table.

"Thanks." He looked at her over the rim of his cup. "A few hours ago food and a warm house seemed mighty far away."

She watched him polish off everything on his plate, then made him more sandwiches and saw those disappear as well. When he finally sat back, his coffee cup in hand, she stood.

"Guess I'll go on up," she said. "I hope you sleep well."

"Don't"

"What?"

"Don't go. Let's take the coffee into the living room and sit for a few minutes. I still feel like I'm driving that damn truck, and I sure as heck won't be falling asleep any time soon."

In the living room, Kate slipped past him and settled into one of the two oversize recliners on either side of the fireplace, then curled her feet beneath her. The massive logs started earlier in the evening had burned down, leaving gently flickering embers. Seth took the matching chair facing hers.

Surely she would be able to think more clearly with enough space between them. "I know the ranch means a great deal to you," she said, dragging an afghan over her lap. "And I know you're a good manager. So tell me about the Lone Tree's financial picture.''

He looked at her for a long moment. ''We've got good stock. And yes, I manage this place well. But Bob's medical care costs were...catastrophic.''

Which translates to untold suffering, Kate thought. If she'd known, she would have come to Montana much earlier. ''Didn't he have insurance?''

''He'd always been proud of being healthy as a horse and never would buy any. And then the last two years...'' Seth lifted his gaze to the dark windows flanking the fireplace. ''We had minimal snow, followed by one of the driest years I can remember. No rain, no hay crop. Drought means hay is impossible to find and worth gold when you can.''

''Aren't the cattle out on pasture for most of the year?''

''No rain, no grass,'' Seth said in measured tones. ''So we either buy hay or sell cattle.''

''Oh.''

''Without cattle, we've got nothing,'' he added, driving the point home. ''Just mounting debts and semiarid land that isn't anyone's idea of a golf course or housing development.''

She might have thought his words were intended to discourage her, but the pain lurking in the depths of his eyes told her that the situation was all too real. ''You know this business too well to go under without a fight.''

''There's no chance in hell that I'll let the ranch go under,'' he bit out. ''But we're facing some lean years. If you thought your inheritance meant substantial profits, you were wrong.''

"You haven't thought about selling out?'' she ventured. "Maybe doing something else?''

Seth launched to his feet and stalked to the window, then turned around. "And fail? Know that I couldn't keep this ranch together?''

"There are other careers.''

He gave her an incredulous look. "This isn't about *careers*. This is about heritage, stability. Maintaining an entire life-style that can't be reclaimed if it's lost.'' He swore under his breath. "I don't expect you to understand.''

Kate bristled. "I didn't grow up here, but I think I can grasp the concept.''

"It goes deeper than that.'' The grandfather clock in the corner ticked away a full minute of silence, then he gave a resigned sigh. "My mother was Lakota Sioux. Both sides of the family were furious when she and my father married. Her family disowned her. My dad's side of the family didn't even come to her funeral.''

There weren't any relatives at my mom's funeral, either, Kate thought, feeling growing empathy for him. "Family relationships can be tough.''

Seth tipped his head in acknowledgment. "Dad never got over mom's death and times were hard. Drought, then a brucellosis outbreak…he borrowed heavily trying to expand the ranch operation, but extended himself too far. One night he lost control of his pickup during a storm and went into a ravine. People said he killed himself. I was thirteen.''

Kate's heart twisted at the thought of the young boy losing his parents and facing the whispers of the community. *Only thirteen.* "I'm so sorry," she whispered.

"Our ranch was auctioned. Everything. The legacy my father wanted for his children and grandchildren was gone. I stayed and watched until the last shovel and dinner plate were sold."

Now at last she understood why he was driven to keep the ranch intact and safe. In her mind's eye, she could see him as a child, standing at that sale, shell-shocked and alone, watching as everything in his life was carted away.

She wished she could wrap her arms around him and give him the solace he'd needed then.

"I've got a second chance to build a legacy for my own children, thanks to Bob," he added heavily. "You and I will share the Lone Tree, but there is nothing on earth that I wouldn't do to save it."

"My life changed when my mother walked out of this house, but I'd imagined that you had the kind of childhood I only dreamed of, because you had…my grandfather." The words sounded so petty, she wished she could call them back.

Seth fell silent. "He did love you and your mother," he said finally. "He never stopped."

Yesterday she would have argued the point. But that was before she found the unopened letters. Letters Bob had continued to write for *years.* Maybe it was time to start thinking as an adult, instead of the hurting child she'd been. "What was he like?"

"You've met Doc, the boys here at the ranch,

maybe some people in town,'' Seth countered. ''Tell me, Officer, what you know about him so far.''

Kate gave him a rueful smile. ''People seem to miss him a great deal.''

''Why do you think that is?''

She shrugged one shoulder, still struggling with her new image of her grandfather. ''I guess he must have mellowed into a likable sort of guy.''

Seth raised one brow. *''Likable?''*

''Yeah.'' Kate gave him a challenging look. ''My mother didn't rate him much higher than serial killers and IRS agents.''

''She sure never gave him a second chance, and that broke his heart.'' He scowled at Kate. ''I've kept you up long enough. Why don't you go upstairs. I've got some work to do.''

Although Kate recognized that the truce between them was over, an unexpected feeling of compassion stole through her as she followed him into his office. He must have loved her grandfather very much. ''Let's start again,'' she murmured, taking a leather wing chair by the window and offering him a smile. ''Hey, Seth, we've been worried about you. How did the sale go?''

He picked up a red pen and tapped it against the polished oak desktop. After a moment, she saw the tense muscles across his shoulders relax. Where there had been pain, there was now just resignation in his dark eyes. ''I guess it was a success. Of sorts. On the way back an oncoming pickup swung wide on a curve and I took the ditch.''

A dozen scenes from her past sped through her

thoughts. Highway accidents with semis twisted in a ditch, bodies strewn across the road. Cars crumpled like tin foil. The smells of spilled gasoline, burning rubber, blood.

Kate leaned forward. "He didn't stop?"

"It was dark. Probably didn't realize where I'd gone."

She scanned Seth's broad, muscular shoulders, his face, the flat plane of his belly, resisting the urge to run her hands over him to be sure he was okay. "Any damage?"

At his cocked eyebrow, she added, "To the truck."

"Just a long wait for someone to stop. Most people are pretty shy about pulling over for a stranger after dark, but a neighbor finally came by. Ty Kirkwood."

From the warmer tone in his voice, Seth apparently considered the man a good friend. "Rancher?"

Seth nodded, then studied the pen in his hand. "He told me the Peterson's J-Bar is going on the block March 1st."

Kate thought of her plan to sell her share of the ranch, and suddenly wished it didn't have to happen. "Sometimes it's for the best," she added mildly. "New beginnings and all that."

"They've got just a month left. Do you think Mary Peterson will like leaving the ranch where she raised her three kids? Will Hal like hunting for a job in town, with a lifetime of experience out here?" The pen in Seth's hand snapped in two, sending a spray of red ink across the desk.

Kate swiftly reached for a tissue from the box on the desk, but Seth shook his head. "Just...go and get some sleep.'' He spun his chair around and jerked a bottle of Jim Beam from the bookshelf that ran the length of the room.

Disappointment speared through her. She hesitated. ''That isn't going to help, you know.''

He twisted the cap open and raised the bottle in mock salute, then poured some onto the desk and cleaned away the spill himself. After replacing the cap, he put the bottle back on the shelf. ''That was your grandfather's alcohol, not mine. Once he knew his prognosis, he…grew despondent.''

That fit the image she'd held of Bob Rawlins; a man given to moodiness, depression and the bottle.

Giving her a knowing look, Seth tipped back and hooked one foot over the opposite knee. ''You think he was a surly drunk. You imagine him smashing bottles against the fireplace, beating innocent women and children.''

''My mother must have had some reasons for leaving.''

Seth shook his head. ''I moved to the Lone Tree when I was thirteen. I never saw your grandfather drunk, and I never saw him lose his temper. What happened earlier in his life, I don't know, but it's damn hard to imagine Bob losing control.''

Kate glanced at the bottle of whiskey on the shelf, then shifted her gaze back to meet Seth's. ''Maybe he changed *after* my mom left.''

''I'll never believe he could have harmed anyone.''

She fought back the urge to rise out of her chair and pursue the argument toe to toe. ''So…what happened at the J-Bar? Poor management? Beef prices?''

"The same thing we're facing here. Drought. Cost of feed. The current market." His expression grew pensive. "I'm heading over to the Petersons' tomorrow to see if there's anything I can do. You should come to that sale."

"To help?"

"To see what ranching means to those people."

"Despite what you think, I do understand." Kate rose and turned to leave.

"You don't understand a blessed thing."

His voice was low and soft, but a tone of indictment ran like steel through every word. "Out here, we help one another out. We work together. We're like *family*. It's a loss to all of us when someone goes under."

"I'm sorry" was all Kate could say. As she left the room regret washed through her. What would happen to his dreams when she had to put her half of the Lone Tree up for sale?

SETH STAYED at his desk long afterward, lost in thought.

What was it about this woman that sent his guard up, made him want to confront her at every turn? She had a right—by blood—to be here. But she didn't care about the land, the heritage she held in her hands. Something had given her a hard edge, an attitude that stood one hundred and eighty degrees opposite of everything he cared about.

Yet she was Bob's granddaughter, and Seth would have to deal with her forever. The one bright note was that she would surely leave as soon as her six months were up, and then they could communicate by business letters and e-mail.

With a flare of surprise, he realized he would miss sparring with her. Had she really only been here three days? It had been so long since he'd had an adult to talk to over coffee in the evening or at the breakfast table. Della was nearly as silent as old Cal. And Mandy was so full of childish chatter and exuberance that she left him winded.

Maybe someday he would start thinking about remarriage. The next time around, he would be practical and find a woman born and bred in Montana, who understood the hard work, long hours and loneliness of life on an isolated Montana ranch. He'd married for love once, and that marriage had been a disaster from the first moment. He mentally ticked through the most obvious possibilities.

Georgia.

Cindy.

Kathy.

Hannah.

Intelligent, attractive women—any one of them would be a good influence on Mandy and would help her through those upcoming teenage years that everyone had been warning him about. Though now those women all seemed even less fascinating to him than they had before.

Kate.

The name conjured up her fresh lemon scent, the husky tone of her voice. The way her no-nonsense manner and surprising sense of humor continually caught him off guard. Seth swore softly under his breath as he flicked off the lights and headed up to his room.

No, definitely not Kate. The last thing he needed was a lady cop, a woman more at home dealing with criminals than the local PTA.

THE SWEET AROMA of frosting filled the air when Seth and Kate came into the house the next afternoon. He'd gone to the Peterson ranch first thing in the morning, and then he had taken Kate along to ride fence in the east pasture.

She gave him an elbow in the ribs and nodded toward the hallway leading to the front entrance. The top of a bright red Blazer was just visible through the front window. "Looks like you've got company. Is it your birthday, cowboy?"

She'd slipped into a good-ole-boy attitude toward him that rankled, though he couldn't think why. Better that than continuing as adversaries. "Not mine." Seth glanced down the hallway, then shucked off his boots. "Joanna must be bringing Nicki out to play with Mandy."

Mandy, kneeling on a chair at the kitchen table, looked up at them both and grinned, her face aglow in a blaze of candlelight topping a monstrous birthday cake despite the late-afternoon sun streaming through the kitchen windows. She wore purple-and-pink frosting smudges on one cheek, and held a frosting-smeared knife in one hand.

"They're out looking at kittens. Della said I could invite them for supper," she chirped. "And since this was Grandpa Bob's birthday, Della said we could make a cake.''

"She had to light the candles, just to see how it looked," Della snorted.

Seth felt his heart twist. He could still hear Bob's shout of surprise and delight over Mandy's annual efforts, each more garish than the last, and still see him envelop her in a bear hug that lifted her off her feet. Last year, Bob had been too weak to do more than give her a gentle squeeze, and his voice had lost much of its robust volume. And now he was gone.

From behind him, he heard Kate's sharp intake of breath, and sensed the tension in her stance. He looked over his shoulder at her. "Quite a decorator, isn't she—"

The confusion in Kate's eyes stopped him. "You didn't know when his birthday was, did you?" Seth asked quietly.

She shook her head, then dropped her gaze to her boots and began yanking them off.

Seth waited until she was standing upright again. "He was like a grandfather to Mandy. He read her stories when she was a baby, helped me raise her after her mother…left. He was a good man."

Kate nodded, but kept her gaze averted as she sidestepped around him. "Quite a job there, kid."

Mandy blew at the candles, and grinned from ear to ear. "My mom is coming out, too. She said so, when I asked her."

Across the room, Della frowned and shook her head. Seth stared back at her. A cold feeling washed through him. *Not again. Not another chance for Ali-*

son to hurt their daughter. The pain in Mandy's eyes tore at his heart every time Alison neglected to show up, every time she failed to remember a special event.

Seth dropped his gaze to his daughter's eager face. "She might get awfully busy, honey," he said carefully. "But I'm sure she wants to be here." Moving forward, he gave Mandy a hug, frosting and all. "I'll bet it took a long time to decorate that cake."

Della, stirring something in a pot at the stove, didn't turn around, but she snorted again. "As long as it takes to mix two pounds of powdered sugar into six colors of frosting and get it all onto a single cake."

"Mmm." Kate moved to Mandy's side and studied the neon-bright assortment of colors. "When you grow up, I really want to see your wedding cake. It will be the prettiest ever."

Mandy looked up at her and smiled, then her smile faded. "I really miss Grandpa Bob."

The oven door creaked as Della opened it to peer inside. Opening it wider, she removed a loaf of bread and set the pan on a trivet. The smell of fresh bread wafted through the kitchen. "Remember how Bob took you sledding out on the ridge?"

Mandy's face brightened. "And how he always took my class for hayrack rides at Halloween?" She lifted her arms and held them wide as she could. "He always found the biggest pumpkins ever and carved any face I wanted. And if dad was too busy, he took me to town for trick or treating. He was always Wild Bill Hickok."

"He started teaching you trick riding, until your

dad caught on.'' Della's voice was surprisingly gentle.

''Sounds like a lot of fun.'' Kate sounded subdued, her smile looked forced. ''You must have loved him a lot.''

Apparently unaware of her impact on their visitor, Mandy babbled on. ''And at Christmas, he was always Santa. He thought none of us knew, but I did. Ever since I was four. He would be all dressed up, and he would have a big sack with presents. And he would knock at the door instead of coming down the chimney—'' her eyes danced ''—because he'd had too many cookies at the last ranch.''

Kate ruffled Mandy's bangs and smiled down at her. ''I think I need to go upstairs and wash up for supper.'' Her voice caught on the last word.

Mandy put down the frosting knife and watched her leave, then turned back to Seth. ''Did I say something wrong?''

''No, honey. Nothing at all.''

Della harrumphed as she started running hot water into the sink. ''Maybe she's realizing that she doesn't belong here.''

''Della,'' Seth warned, sliding a glance toward his daughter.

''I like her, Dad. I want her to stay.''

Della poured a good dollop of detergent into the sink and started clattering through a pile of dirty dishes. ''She could have come back long ago. Now she's probably thinking you are mighty available. She'd have it all if—''

The back door swung open with a crash, and Nicki

McArthur barreled in with a rush of frigid air, her mother close on her heels.

"You little dickens! I'll outrun you yet!" Joanna shut the door behind them, then swept off her bright red stocking cap and stamped her feet. "Hi, Seth, Della."

Nicki shed her coat and boots and bolted over to the kitchen table, her eyes wide. "Wow! When do we eat?"

"Nicki!" Laughing, Joanna caught her daughter around the waist and spun her around. "It looks like Della has supper almost ready. Why don't you and Mandy go wash your hands? You can tell her which of those kittens are your favorites."

With a squeal, Mandy shouted, "I'll race you!" Both girls tore out of the kitchen.

Seth found himself grinning. "They're quite a pair, aren't they?"

Joanna nodded, her smile fading. She lowered her voice. "Mandy says her mom is coming out tonight."

"Yeah, well...and cows fly. Nine out of ten times the woman never bothers to show."

"Have you talked to her?"

"There's not a damn thing I can do about it. She's got as much maternal instinct as a rock, and not a lick of responsibility. I've got full custody, thank God, but I can hardly deny Mandy the right to see her mother."

Joanna stepped closer and laid a comforting hand on his arm. "Mandy's lucky to have a father like you."

At the sound of approaching footsteps, they both

looked up. Seth cleared his throat. "Joanna, have you met Kate Rawlins?"

With an uncertain look on her face Kate hesitated at the door, as if thinking she'd interrupted something personal. Then she moved forward with a smile. "Nice to see you again, Joanna."

Joanna eyed her thoughtfully, then gave Seth a knowing look. "So, how is everything going out here? You two getting everything settled?" She waggled one eyebrow. "You know, Seth, that half the women in the county will want a report when I get back to town."

"Jo," Seth warned.

"Joanna!" Kate gave her a startled look.

"You know it's true," she said blithely as she collected a stack of plates from the cupboard, then handed them to Kate. "Come on, we can visit while we set the table. You're coming with Seth to Mandy's school play Saturday night, right? We can all meet for supper in town afterward. You and I are going to be *real* good friends."

Seth stared after them as they left the room, Joanna chattering a mile a minute. The meaning behind Joanna's question—and her knowing look—disturbed him. She was wrong. *Nothing would be settled the way she implied. Not between him and that city cop.*

Life had gone on after Alison left. Yet earlier today, riding fence with Kate tagging along on Rowdy, he'd been thinking again about how it seemed so right to have a woman by his side once again. He'd found himself thinking about loneliness and growing old, thoughts that hadn't surfaced until Bob's stubborn, complex granddaughter showed up with her two little suitcases and an independent attitude bigger than the Montana sky.

She would be leaving midsummer. Allowing himself to feel anything for her would only lead to trouble, yet he often found himself watching her from across a room, and had even started feeling a little empty if she wasn't with him.

After Alison left tonight—if she bothered to show up at all—he was going to find his old address book. Distraction was exactly what he needed to get through the next few months.

By 2:00 A.M. KATE FIGURED that sleep was a wishful thought and pursuing it would only add to her frustration.

Mandy's growing hurt, as the evening wore on and Alison failed to show, had been painful to watch. The child's stoic acceptance of her mother's lame excuse, when the woman finally bothered to telephone, had cut straight to Kate's heart. How could anyone squander such a precious gift as a child's love?

The urge to track Alison Wright down and to shake some sense into her had grown exponentially since that call. With an ex-wife like her, no wonder Seth hadn't remarried.

Kate wandered to the window and peered out into the dark, wishing the moon were full and that she could at least see the rolling terrain. From some faraway hill came the lonesome, eerie howl of coyotes. A horse whinnied. A cow bawled. At first she'd thought the silence overwhelming. Now she realized that the ranch was alive with smells and sounds and a rhythm of activity that pulsed like a heartbeat day and night.

Resisting the urge to pull on sweats and slip out into the night to run until she was exhausted enough to sleep, she sat at the foot of the bed. The box of letters on the top shelf of her closet caught her eye. She retrieved them and sat cross-legged on the bed with the box in front of her. Surely it didn't matter if someone read them now.

After flicking through the pile, she withdrew the one with the oldest postmark. Yellow with age and still sealed like all the rest, it was addressed in a slashing, bold hand. She slid a finger under the flap and pulled out the letter. The scrawl inside was even stronger, and had torn through the paper in two places.

Dear Lorna,
I figure you'll be back soon, because you'll realize what a mistake it was for you to take off like that. What kind of life is it for a kid? Katy and you will have a better life here.

I swear, if you come back, things will be different. I never meant anything I said, you know that....

Kate lowered the letter to her lap and closed her eyes, feeling her grandfather's anger and frustration rising like waves of heat from the paper. Visions of angry outbursts crowded through her thoughts. Old memories, or just a composite of all the domestic disturbance calls she'd answered over the years?

With trembling fingers, Kate reached for another letter. And another. Remorse. Entreaties. And in a letter dated a year later, the words Bob hadn't been able to write before.

> Lorna, the guys and I all miss you so much. Please come home. I love you, and want you and Katy here at the ranch.
>
> > Love, Dad.

As she stared at the letters in her hand, guilt washed through her for all the stories she had believed without question, for all the years she might have sought the truth. Her mother's failure to forgive had cost Kate the stable family life she'd longed for as a child.

Images of Seth as a powerful, loving protector drifted through her thoughts. His gentleness with Mandy touched her heart, making her regret what she had missed all the more.

Placing the handful of letters back into the box, Kate closed her eyes, remembering how close she'd once been to having a husband and a family of her own. Then, at the last minute, that future had been swept away. She'd learned how fleeting happiness could be. She'd vowed then to never again take any chances with her heart.

But maybe that would be the greatest mistake of all.

She stood to put the box back on a high closet

shelf. At that moment she sensed something was… different.

Frowning, she scanned the closet shelves, then fingered over the dozen or so hangers of clothing, which weren't quite how she had hung them. An uneasy prickle skittered across the back of her neck as she pivoted slowly and surveyed the room. A lower bureau drawer hung slightly ajar. Had someone been here?

Her leather shoulder bag, hanging from a hook in the corner of the closet, still contained her Visa and the forty-two dollars that had been in it yesterday. She knelt at the dresser and pulled open each drawer, breathing a sigh of relief as she found her laptop computer beneath her lingerie, and the fragile old box with her family heirloom still tucked inside a faded sweatshirt.

She withdrew the box and opened it. The old emerald-and-diamond brooch sparkled in the soft light, ageless and breathtaking as ever. Heaven only knew its current value. A decade ago she'd had it appraised and insured for more than she'd believed possible.

She was going to find out who was searching her belongings, and at the first opportunity she would take the brooch into Folsum for appraisal, adjust the insurance policy, then rent a safety-deposit box. Her mother had chosen to live in near-poverty rather than sell it.

Kate would keep it safe.

CHAPTER SEVEN

"YOU'LL COME WITH US tonight, won't you?" Mandy shifted from one foot to the other, her eyes filled with hope. "Please?"

Kate looked over her head toward Seth, who met her glance and then turned away to shoulder on his jacket.

"It would mean a lot to Mandy," he said.

"Please?" Mandy reached for Kate's hand. "The play is great, and you made my costume the best of all."

All week long she'd gently declined any intrusion on this father-daughter outing, but Mandy's pleas were all too poignant, especially considering the likelihood of the child's mother not bothering to show up.

With a sigh, Kate smiled down at her. "Okay. Let me change clothes, and I'll be back down in a minute."

Jingling a set of keys in his pocket, Seth curved an arm around Mandy's shoulders and herded her out the door. "Let's go start the truck."

Upstairs, Kate pulled out several sweatshirts, tossed them aside, then considered a soft lilac sweater that would go with her one pair of good slacks. Or maybe a good pair of jeans. Not that it mattered what she wore. This was a school play, not a date.

Seeing Joanna again last weekend had been delightful...but had also made the past week more difficult. Her teasing innuendos about a possible relationship between Seth and Kate had been playing through Kate's mind ever since. Impossible thoughts, which surfaced relentlessly day and night. And if Seth had been remote before, he was now even less approachable.

Of course, he wouldn't be harboring any wayward thoughts about her. Despite Jo's denial, Kate had seen firsthand the warm relationship Joanna and Seth shared. Seth's quiet strength and her outrageous sense of humor were a perfect contrast. And Jo was the kind of woman Mandy needed. Kate would stay out of the way and let nature take its course.

Light snow sparkled in front of the truck's headlights as they drove into town. By the time they walked into the school gymnasium, snow was blanketing the trees and swirling past the streetlights. It was a beautiful, pristine night, a Christmas-card sort of night. Kate reached for Mandy's hand, feeling a rush of peace and fulfillment.

"I need to go backstage and get ready," Mandy announced.

In a flash she disappeared into the small crowd milling around in the entryway. Suddenly adrift, Kate searched for a familiar face, but no one looked her way.

Ahead, Seth spoke to a cluster of fellow ranchers as he shrugged out of his jacket, then turned toward a stunning brunette in mile-long jeans. Grasping his arm with both hands, the woman leaned close to say something, then tossed back her head with laughter, and soon the whole group was chuckling.

The brunette's gaze skidded over to Kate. After a brief once-over, she turned back to the group. The ranchers grew somber. One gave Kate a narrowed look and shrugged, then turned toward a dour woman who might have been his wife and walked away.

Around her, eddies of people swirled into sociable groups, then moved into the rows of chairs set up on the gym floor or up into the bleachers set at either side of the large room. She felt many curious glances, saw whispered comments spread through the crowd. If she'd been standing in front of them naked, she couldn't have felt more conspicuous—or more of an outsider.

At one end of the room was a stage, its black curtains billowing with the activity taking place behind. Now and then a wide-eyed youngster peered out, then pulled back in a dramatic flourish of velvet.

Feeling alone despite the sea of people around her, Kate started for the bleachers. A warm, steady hand at her waist startled her.

"Let's get closer," Seth said, his hand still touching her back. "Mandy will want to see us." He scanned the entryway, and then studied the bleachers as they walked forward.

"Damn," he muttered under his breath. "She isn't here."

Kate had no doubt about the absent party. Alison, a woman who didn't deserve such a wonderful little girl and who seemed bent on breaking Mandy's heart at every turn. "Maybe the weather…"

Seth's expression darkened. "She lives outside of Folsum, but it's straight highway from here to there. This night meant a lot to Mandy."

He cupped Kate's elbow and pointed to an open section of the bleachers. As he followed her up, he spoke to almost every person they passed.

"Is there anyone here you don't know?" Kate asked wryly, "You should run for mayor."

Settling down next to her, he lifted one shoulder. "Small community, and I've been in these parts all my life."

Kate sensed the disapproval of that community in every glance that came her way. Apparently gossip had flown thick and fast about poor old Bob's heartless granddaughter who had returned only to collect her inheritance. Anyone who hadn't known the score before was getting the low-down tonight.

The lights dimmed, and a spotlight shone on a balding, elderly man at the podium set to one side of the stage. After a lengthy welcome and even longer litany of thank-yous to the community volunteers who had helped with the play, he stepped aside. The national anthem—a little rocky, but recognizable—swelled from the school band and the crowd stood.

Unaccountably, Kate felt her heart hitch a beat looking down at the earnest young faces of the band members and the expression of pride on the parents in the audience. Family. Community. Permanence. What would it be like to live where everyone knew you, where people rallied to help instead of standing silently by when tragedies occurred?

Kate felt a tap on her shoulder as they sat down. Twisting around, she saw a plump, elderly woman balancing a toddler on her lap.

"You're Bob's granddaughter?" Her voice seemed to echo out over the expectant silence that had fallen in the gymnasium.

From the corner of her eye, Kate saw a small figure step out on the stage. She nodded and started to turn back toward the stage, but the woman nudged her shoulder again.

"I went to school with him. Knew him all my life." Her eyes narrowed. "It broke his heart, you know, when you and your mom never came back. Not even when he was adyin'."

"I didn't know—"

Seth slid closer to Kate and put his arm around her shoulder. "Good to see you, Martha," he said in a low, even voice. "Enjoy the play." He pulled Kate closer, then turned his attention back to the stage.

Kate fought the urge to lean into Seth's embrace, to feel a part of his family and this community. She could feel the strength in his arm, the play of powerful muscles. His masculine warmth radiated through her, while his gesture telegraphed a message of acceptance to all concerned.

Caught between gratitude and an unexpected heat that slid clear down to her toes, she firmly ignored the urge. He was protecting the interests of the Lone Tree, nothing more, by showing a unified front to the people of Salt Creek. Any additional wayward thoughts…sensations…desires…were out of line.

Still, it felt so right, sitting here with him, waiting for the play to begin. "Thank you," she whispered, her eyes trained on the stage. Mandy would be on-stage soon. Perhaps she'd pick them out in the semi-darkness and wave. *Family.*

The audio system crackled, barely carrying the voice of the young boy who was apparently announcing the beginning of the play. With a rustle of activity several rows down, someone stood, turned and clambered up through the people already seated, heading straight for Kate.

Kate closed her eyes, praying that there wouldn't be another scene. *Once the play is over, I'm out of here!*

With a bulky coat over her arm and a floppy knit hat shielding her eyes, the woman wasn't recognizable until she sank down next to Kate and gave her an extra little shove that sent Kate right up against Seth's chest.

"Hi, Kate," Joanna whispered, shooting a dark look over her shoulder at Martha. "It was wonderful of you to come. Mandy must be so glad you did!"

Kate nodded. "How's everything going with the kids at Meadowbrook?"

"Got a couple of new challenges this past week. Lots of potential beneath a lot of bad experiences, I think."

Kate felt a sudden twinge of nostalgia for the youngsters she'd worked with in Minneapolis, followed by a familiar rush of sadness over Rico's death. "If you ever need help, just call."

Joanna chuckled. "You have no idea how busy you'll be on that ranch."

A sharp crackle of static over the sound system brought a hush over the auditorium. The lights dimmed.

Kate shifted her weight to give Seth more space, but his arm stayed curved around her, keeping her snug at his side. He looked down at her, his lashes lowered and a quarter-smile curving the edge of his mouth.

"Stay," he said quietly.

That single word dove like a missile, straight for her aching heart, tripping up her pulse and sending heightened awareness shimmering through her.

It had been so long since anyone had wanted her close.

She'd accepted the weight of Seth's heavily muscled arm for what it was, a casual gesture of friendship, a message of acceptance to everyone present. But now she felt an overwhelming longing to turn into his casual embrace for more.

What would it be like to kiss him deep and hard, to feel his mouth moving over hers? In the darkness it might have been just the two of them. Alone.

But the gymnasium wasn't *that* dark. They definitely weren't alone. And she wasn't that foolish. Taking that step would be far too dangerous to her heart.

The play began. The children's voices were almost inaudible, until they sang in unison. Mandy spied them up in the bleachers and gave a furtive wave, then searched the crowd. For her mother, no doubt.

The play seemed to involve George Washington, given the papier-mâché cherry tree on center stage, but concentrating was tough. Seth's faint, clean scent of aftershave and the masculine strength of his body kept her senses humming…and the sight of Mandy's crestfallen face onstage nearly broke her heart. Time and again, Kate scanned the crowd of latecomers by the entrance, looking for someone who might be Mandy's mother, but to no avail.

A round of raucous applause and whistles erupted when the play ended. The lights came on, blinding now after the darkness.

Kate felt Seth stiffen. She followed his gaze to a woman standing in the doorway. Ripples of silky blond hair cascaded down past her shoulders, caught at one side with a glittery pin of some kind. Even from the distance, Kate had no doubt that the coat was fine leather, the sparkles at her ears and throat were measured in carats.

Seth swore under his breath. He stood abruptly, looked at his watch, then started down the bleachers. Bemused, Kate gave Joanna a wave and followed him down. Mandy broke away from the other children milling around on the stage and ran across the gym floor, where she and her father collided in a big hug.

"Wasn't it great? Was I good?" Mandy looked from Seth to Kate, then turned to search the crowd filing out of the gym. Her smile faded. "Mom didn't come, did she?"

"Of course I did. I was in the back." The elegant,

beautiful blonde who stepped forward might have stepped off a fashion show runway.

No matter what tentative feelings might have begun unfurling in Kate's heart, she now knew she'd never have a chance with a man who had been married to a woman like Alison. He would never look twice at some plain-Jane cop who hadn't owned a good dress in five years.

Your money was better spent, her subconscious whispered. Rico and his friends...

Alison gave Kate a brief glance. "Who's this?" she asked, a hint of amusement in her voice.

At Seth's cursory introduction she gave a delicate shrug, then dropped to one knee and gave Mandy a fierce hug. "I've missed you, punkin. You were wonderful in the play."

Mandy pulled back a few inches and gave her an accusing look. "But you weren't here!"

"I...I was just a tiny bit late, but I saw you up on stage and you were fabulous!"

She's nervous, Kate realized with growing surprise, as she studied the lines of tension bracketing Alison's mouth and the stiff set of her shoulders. But why? The love for her daughter was clear, but the woman was obviously upset.

Joanna and her daughter Nicki came up beside Kate. "Hello, Alison," Joanna said, her voice cool.

Kate nearly missed the flash of uncertainty in Alison's eyes.

"Joanna." Alison gave a brittle laugh. "Eric is waiting for me at home, so I have to run. We're heading for Billings tonight. We'll catch an early-morning flight to Denver, then we're off to Cancún.'' She released Mandy and straightened, and as quickly as that her cool mask was firmly in place—belied by the nervous chatter that left no opening for conversation.

After a quick hug and a kiss for Mandy, she was gone.

"Bye, Mom," Mandy called out. "I love you!" She edged next to her father, the joy fading from her eyes as Alison disappeared through the double doors at the back of the gym.

Seth rested a hand on Mandy's shoulder. "She did come, honey. Wasn't that great?"

Mandy sniffled and looked down at her armload of clothes. "I forgot my boots. Will you come backstage with me, Dad? I think they already turned out the lights back there."

It was none of her business. But in that moment, seeing the hurt in Mandy's eyes, Kate wanted nothing more than to have a few minutes alone with Alison. Did the fool have any idea of how much she was hurting her daughter by barely saying hello?

"Go ahead, and I'll go out to start the truck," Kate offered.

Seth tossed her the keys. She strode through the thinning crowd to the exit, then paused on the snowy steps and looked out. Several dozen pickups and a few cars were still in the parking lot, and at least half of them had their lights on.

Bingo. At the far end, a bright red Corvette hummed to life beneath a security light.

Kate crossed the parking lot at a fast clip. Alison had given her daughter less than five minutes on one

of the most important school events of the year, yet
she must have driven a good hour to get here. It made
no sense.

Not that a cool beauty like Alison probably had
any. When Kate's reached the car's back bumper, she
knew her guess of the vehicle had been correct—she
could see long blond hair and a leather coat. But, at
any moment, the woman could peal out of the lot and
the chance to talk might not come again.

As Kate reached the front door, she realized the
woman behind the wheel wasn't going anywhere in a
hurry.

Alison's forehead rested against hands tightly grip-
ping the top of the steering wheel. She jerked away
from the window, startled at seeing someone standing
by her car, and wiped furiously at her cheeks with a
gloved hand.

Kate saw what the woman's artful makeup had
concealed.

A faint, yellowed bruise showed along her cheekbone. The haunted look in her eyes suggested that it
hadn't been an accident.

Instinct made Kate move closer, to reach for the
door, but Alison was faster. With a look of alarm, she
floored the accelerator, sending snow and gravel flying as her car fishtailed across the parking lot.

Stunned, Kate stared after her. Alison had appeared
glamorous and aloof after the play. But the clues were
there—tension, the avoidance of people who might
notice bruises, a fear of arriving home late. Alison
was in trouble. During her years in law enforcement

Kate had seen far too many abused women not to recognize the symptoms.

The sense of responsibility and concern didn't end when a cop took off her badge. For Mandy's sake, Kate would try her best to help Alison.

As Kate turned back toward the gymnasium, a motion in the shadows caught her eye. Someone was standing behind the bushes at the corner of the building...watching her. A car leaving the parking lot obstructed her view.

Kate waited for the car to pass, but the figure had disappeared.

SETH WATCHED KATE LEAVE the gymnasium, then he turned to follow Mandy backstage. *I could have been an actor,* he thought grimly, nodding at the stragglers coming down the rickety stage steps. The sheriff hadn't been more than ten feet away when Alison had approached them. If Paul had read his thoughts, Seth would have been in jail for planning to commit murder.

She had disappointed their daughter once again. What did that do to Mandy's self-esteem, knowing that her own mother couldn't find the time to follow through on her promises?

Seth and Alison had been married only a few months when Alison had become restless and unhappy on the ranch. Both of them had known almost from the start that their marriage wouldn't last. Different interests, different goals in life...they'd been too young to see their infatuation for what it was.

But he would have repeated every hour of that painful history just to have Mandy.

With the increasing snowfall outside and his own darkening mood, the thought of socializing over supper in town no longer seemed appealing. Seth offered apologies to Nicki and Joanna, gathered up Mandy and her costume and headed out the door.

Kate had driven to the doors of the gymnasium. She climbed out and left the door open for him, then rounded the front of the truck toward the passenger door.

A figure wove down the sidewalk toward them. *Who the hell is that?* Seth hesitated, halfway behind the wheel. The figure stopped close to Kate. A unexpected surge of protectiveness shot through him. In a split second he was out of the truck and at her side.

"So," the drunk slurred, sidestepping to keep his balance. The miasma of unwashed male and hard liquor surrounding him was enough to fell an ox. "Just like your ma, I'll bet. Whoo-eeee, she was a hot one."

Kate gasped and took a step back. "Pardon me?"

"Get on your way, buddy," Seth growled.

"Jus' havin' a li'l conversation. No harm in that."

"Come on, Kate," Seth murmured, curving an arm around her waist. He felt her tense, and had a sudden image of her using some sort of police move that would have the drunk face first on the ground with a broken nose. Which would mean waiting around forever for the sheriff to show up, and having to file some sort of incident reports.

Worse, Kate would make the local paper, and heaven knew what sort of spin the editor would put on it. Assault—Trained Police Officer Attacks Pathetic Old Drunk? "Let's go. He's not worth your time."

"Good ole Lorna was sure worth mine," the guy chortled, and lifted his head to get a better look at Kate. "Gotta few minutes for an ole friend?"

"I don't think so, bozo," she said evenly. Seth could feel her crouch slightly, as if she were ready for any move the guy might make. "I'd be thankful if you didn't talk about my mother that way."

He was vaguely familiar, beneath several weeks' growth of beard and all the grime, but Seth couldn't fit a name to the face.

"Dad?" Mandy tugged at his coat sleeve. "Who *is* that?"

Seth turned and scooped her up into his arms, and put her in the back seat of the crew-cab. "He's no one, punkin. We'll be on our way in a minute."

He turned back to Kate. She'd moved closer to the man and was saying something to him in a low voice. Scowling, his eyes glittering in the dark folds of his face, he grunted something in reply and then shuffled away.

Seth expected to see a confident gleam in her eyes, maybe an expression of triumph. He never expected to see a sheen of tears. "I'm sorry," he said quietly. "I should have moved faster."

She swallowed hard and took a deep breath, clearly gathering herself. "It's okay," she said finally. "He was just some old drunk without many brain cells left."

"About what he said…"

"It's nothing. Let's get back to the ranch, okay?"

Seth stared down at her, then enveloped her in an embrace. Just as an offer of comfort and support.

But the moment he held her in his arms, he found himself holding her more closely than he'd intended. One hand, apparently on its own volition, cupped the back of her head and snuggled it beneath his chin. The other drifted down her back. The soothing motion slid into something far more...sensual.

Tipping his head back, he looked down into her eyes, then dropped a swift, hard kiss on her mouth. Time stood still as powerful emotions raced through him, compelling and seductive and dangerously hot, and it was all he could do to release her and step back.

Under a bright security light, with people still trailing into the parking lot and his daughter's face pressed to the truck's window, he had no business kissing her.

They stared at each other; her eyes wide and stunned. He reached out and brushed a thumb across her cheek, then let his hand trail down the column of her throat. The hammering pulse beneath his thumb told him all he needed to know.

"I shouldn't have done that," he said finally. "This situation is complicated enough."

"There's no sense making it worse," she agreed, her gaze fastened on his mouth. "Big mistake."

"Business partners."

"Right."

"You'll be back in Minneapolis in no time."

"I guess so."

"I've got my daughter living at the ranch."

"And I don't believe in casual relationships. So we're all set, then." She frowned, then murmured, "Actually, you never even kissed me."

Seth laughed. *As if I can forget.* "Right."

From behind them, a truck door squeaked open. "Aren't you guys ready to go?" Mandy called out. "I'm getting hungry."

Seth took one last look at Kate, wanting the moment to last just a little longer, knowing that once they drove back to the ranch there would be no more moments of intimacy to share.

It's for the best, he reminded himself. He and Kate needed to forge a strong partnership for decades to come. Personal issues would only make everything that much harder in the future. And from the tone of her voice, he knew Kate had meant it when she said she didn't go for casual affairs.

The roads were snow-covered as they drove through town, but a few miles out they grew treacherous with loose snow drifting over sheets of ice. The wind across the open land sent finger drifts across the highway—narrow drifts interspersed with bare ice. The truck bucked as it hit each drift.

Mandy was silent in the back of the pickup, her eyes round and face tense whenever Seth flicked a look up at the rearview mirror. Kate lounged easily against the door of the front seat, but she hadn't taken her eyes off the road since they'd left town.

A heavier drift than the rest caught the belly of the truck. It hesitated, then lurched ahead on its own momentum. The tires spun on the bare ice beyond.

"Daddy!" Mandy cried, leaning forward.

Seth turned into the skid. The tires caught at the shoulder, and he was able to ease back onto the highway.

Kate turned, resting her arm across the back of her seat. "It's okay. Your dad's a good driver, and we'll be just fine," she soothed, her voice steady. "You'll be in your jammies drinking hot cocoa in just a few minutes."

Seth let out a slow breath and focused on the road ahead, listening to Kate talk to his daughter. Her voice, low and soft, might have been sultry in another context.

After a few minutes Mandy was quiet again. Seth glanced at the rearview mirror. She was cuddled into the corner of the seat with the spare blanket that was always kept in the truck. Her eyes were closed.

"Thanks for tonight," Kate murmured.

"It meant a lot to Mandy."

"I meant, thanks for coming to my aid. That woman behind us wasn't too happy to meet me." With a sigh, Kate slid lower in her seat and leaned back against the headrest. "I didn't expect to make lifelong friends here, but I honestly never expected to encounter such hostility."

"People here know each other better than they know themselves, and they care. Your grandfather was one of the best. He may be gone, but they're still defending him, I guess."

"I wish I'd known him." She glanced back at Mandy, then lowered her voice. "I need to talk to you about Alison sometime."

The hurt in Mandy's eyes tonight flashed through Seth's thoughts. Just hearing his ex-wife's name made his blood pressure rise. "That would be never," he bit out.

"We need to—"

"No." Seth tugged the brim of his hat lower and jerked one shoulder. "We don't."

"For Mandy's sake. And Alison's, too."

"That's private. Family business."

Kate said nothing. From the corner of his eye, Seth could see a look of concern cross her face. But dammit, he was doing the best he could, trying to cooperate with Alison, trying to hide his feelings about her from Mandy.

The mistakes he'd made in the past couldn't be changed.

CAL MET THE TRUCK as they pulled in, his shoulders hunched against the driving snow. If not for his voice, Kate wouldn't have recognized him beneath the lowered cap, layers of heavy coats and scarf over his lower face. "Troubles," he barked. "Heavies we brought down two days ago. Gotta chilled calf under the warmer and a heifer with problems. I'm guessing twins."

"Damn." Seth launched out of the truck, turned and reached under the seat for his gloves. "Upper meadow?"

Cal stamped the snow from his boots and shook his head. "Freckles kept an eye on her for a couple hours, then he trailed her down to the shed. You got time to change."

Mandy sat up and yawned. "We're home?"

"Just." Kate smiled as she tugged on her own gloves and slipped out of the truck to join Seth. The raw wind tore at the hem of her jacket and whistled down its collar. She hugged herself against the cold. "Twins. Two for the price of one?"

Cal snorted and turned back toward the barns. Seth shook his head as he pivoted and headed toward the house. Kate and Mandy had to jog to keep up with his long strides.

"A heifer is a first-time mom, and they're more likely to have problems, anyway," he called over his shoulder. "For any cow, twins can create sort of a log jam on the way out." At the house, he held the door open for Kate and Mandy, then shook the snow off his shoulders and stepped inside.

"How do twins fare after they're born?"

Shucking off his snow-caked boots, Seth frowned. "Not as well. Even an experienced mother cow does better with a single calf."

The kitchen was dark, save for a dim light glowing over the kitchen sink. Della appeared in the doorway, tying the belt of her robe with the hard, decisive movements of a roper hog-tying a calf in a rodeo. She glanced up at the clock, then clucked her tongue at Mandy.

"Past bedtime," she said. She looked up at Seth and frowned. "Bad roads?"

"Fair." He shrugged, then leaned down to Mandy for a good-night hug and a kiss. "I need to go back outside, honey. Calving started. Be good for Della, okay?"

"Can't I help? Please?"

He straightened and tousled her hair. "There will be lots more calves. You gals can turn in for the night."

You gals? Kate cleared her throat. "I'd like to help."

"Then stay in the house."

Ralph Wilson had returned from Hawaii a few days earlier, and had called to ask her how she was doing. From the tone in his voice, he'd expected to hear that she was packing her bags. Seth still expected her to sit idly at the sidelines. Neither man understood her at all.

She was right on Seth's heels when he went back outside.

CHAPTER EIGHT

THE OTHER BARNS PROVIDED brief respite from the bitter wind as Kate followed Seth across the yard toward the long, low building farthest away.

Large rectangular corrals fanned out from the various barns, but the calving shed opened up into a funnel-shaped corral bordered at the far end by a several-hundred-acre pasture. The "maternity ward," Cal had called it—the pasture where heifers and other cows with potential calving problems were kept for closer observation. A heifer in trouble could be trailed in, headed into the funnel and have no option but to go on into the shed.

Kate could only wonder at how a reluctant, half-wild, thousand-pound patient would react to a helping hand.

Stepping inside the calving shed, out of the harsh wind and darkness and into bright light, the sweet smell of hay and the warmth generated by several space heaters felt like entering a whole new world.

In a small pen near the door, a heat lamp glowed warm over a shivering calf. Farther down, Cal and Freckles both had hooked a booted foot on a gate and were watching the cow inside.

"This poor baby," Kate murmured, touched by the

huge, liquid eyes and downy soft fur of the lone calf. "Doesn't he need a blanket?"

Seth moved next to her and leaned over the rail to brush a hand against the calf's spine. "He's coming around. We'll get him warmed up and send him out to his mama in an hour or so."

Surprised, Kate turned to stare at Seth. "But it's freezing outside!"

"And he isn't a house pet. An hour ago he was probably too cold to even shiver. After a few hours of warmth most chilled calves do fine. Sometimes we'll put one in the heated cab of the pickup for an hour or so, if we're way out in the pastures."

Kate knelt in the straw outside the pen and reached through the bars to stroke the calf's soft black coat. He swung his head around, then suckled vigorously on the cuff of her jacket. Dissatisfied, he butted at her wrist, then latched onto her fingers. Startled at the strength of suction and sandpapery feel of his tongue, she laughed aloud. "He wants his mom."

"And she wants him, too. Can you hear her calling for him? The boys trailed her in and she's just outside."

"Can't she come in and be with him?"

Seth walked down the straw-strewn aisle to join the other men. "Too dangerous, with that heat lamp. But don't worry—she'll recognize his scent when we give him back."

Kate followed and stood beside him to peer at an ebony cow inside. Steam rose from her damp flanks. Even a novice could see the bow in her back and the crink in her tail were signs of discomfort. Oblivious to her audience, she lowered her head and strained, walked a step, then arched her back higher and groaned.

"We'd better check her before she goes down." Seth took off his jacket and tossed it on some hay bales, then stripped off his sweatshirt.

After squeezing a generous stream of antibacterial soap into a bucket of clean water at his feet, he scrubbed the solution high up both arms. His navy T-shirt clung to his torso like a second skin, emphasizing the muscles of his chest and upper back.

He looked sexy—and very cold—as he drove his hands deep into a bucket of water once more. Kate shivered in sympathy. "Is this cow tame enough to handle?"

Cal snorted. "*Heifer.* And nope, she ain't tame. But right now she's got just one thing on her mind."

Both men entered the stall and slowly approached her, Cal at her head and Seth at the other end. Murmuring quiet words of reassurance, Cal flipped a noose over her neck. She jumped in surprise, then bawled and crashed into the corner of the pen.

They let her calm down, then quietly eased her toward the center, where Cal snubbed her to a stout post, shortening the rope until she couldn't move. She fought the rope briefly, then shuddered and gave up, her head low and sides heaving.

With Cal at her head, Seth gently checked her progress. He frowned as he stepped back and reached through the pen for a capped syringe lying on a hay bale. "She's got twins, and they both want to be first.

After I do a tail block we're going to need an extra set of hands here."

Cal nodded. "I'll scrub up."

Seth uncapped the syringe with his teeth, visually measured off an area of hide at the top of the cow's tail, and then swiftly slid the needle in. She didn't so much as twitch an ear in response. "This heifer doesn't have much room. Kate? You've got smaller hands."

She'd been watching, mesmerized by Seth's quiet competence, and at first the words didn't register. "What?"

"Ever delivered any babies?"

Nodding, Kate thought back to several—one in a car parked at the side of the road, one in a cramped apartment. Each had been an incredible miracle. Unforgettable.

"This is just a little different. Scrub up and come on in. These little guys aren't going anywhere without some help, and she's probably gone too long already."

While she washed up, he briefly explained the procedure as he slipped a separate noose over each front leg of one calf jammed in the birth canal, then handed the ends of the ropes to Kate. "See how limp the heifer's tail is? The anesthetic will keep her inner muscles relaxed so she doesn't fight against us. Between contractions I've got to repel one of them back. During contractions you've got to ease the other one forward, okay? Once they're positioned better she might manage on her own."

"And if she doesn't?"

Seth frowned. "Let's hope she can. She might not make it if we have to wait for the vet."

"Isn't she...uh...going to lie down, or something?"

"A lot of 'em calve standing," Cal interjected, steadying the cow against the post as she shuddered and strained.

Nothing in human labor and delivery had prepared Kate for the sheer physical strain of assisting a cow. Working with the animal's own rhythm of labor, Kate tugged gently on the calf's legs. Absolutely nothing moved. She might as well have braced her feet on a curb and tried to pull over a streetlight with her bare hands.

"This ain't a tea party," Cal growled. "Get your weight into it."

With the next contraction Kate pulled harder, then backed up and leaned into the effort. Ten minutes later there still hadn't been any progress.

"Doing good," Seth said in a low voice, adjusting his grip. "The other one is in good position now. We're almost there."

And then, as she hauled on the ropes again during another contraction, a single calf finally slid forward. In a rush of fluids it slithered out and landed at Kate's feet—sodden, dark and still. Then it jerked and blinked.

Cal bent over to clear its nose and mouth, then dragged it to the side. Moments later, the other twin arrived.

The wonder of it all swept through Kate on a tide of emotion as she stared down at the small calves.

Cal fished through the pockets of his denim jacket and withdrew a bottle of iodine, then reached down to treat each umbilical stump.

After unwinding his lariat from the post, he lifted the noose from the heifer's neck. She stiffly moved forward a step, then turned and lowered her head. Seth took Kate's arm and propelled her away from the calves. "Time to go," he said, keeping himself between Kate and the new mother. "Now!"

From outside the pen, he and Kate stood shoulder to shoulder and watched as the cow circled her calves, sniffing and gently licking them from head to tail. Her soft moos sounded like a lullaby.

"They're so sweet!" Kate said, transfixed. "Isn't it wonderful?"

Cal snorted as he headed down the aisle toward the door. "I'm going out to check the heifers again. Freckles will do the dawn run, unless you want to?"

"I'll take it." Seth glanced at Cal's retreating back, then shifted his gaze down to meet Kate's. "You can go on back, if you want. I'll stay and make sure these calves get started."

Kate heard the weariness in his voice. "Started?"

He shrugged. "Twins are smaller, not as strong. I have to make sure they both stand and suck. If one doesn't, the other will get most of the colostrum."

"I'll stay."

"You don't have to…" His voice trailed away as he looked down at her. His eyes darkened. His lashes lowered. Kate sensed his deepening awareness of her, his intention to kiss her despite every resolution they'd made back at the school. A rustle of bedding in the pen broke the moment.

One of the calves managed to stand partway, its legs spraddled wide and body swaying. After a moment of precarious balance it flopped onto the straw in a tangle of knobby knees and long legs, a startled look in its eye. Its mother gave it a firm lick that scooted it several inches across the floor, hummed maternal encouragement, then gave her other baby a nudge.

Five minutes later both calves were wobbling on spindly legs, then one staggered into the other and both fell in a heap. Soon they were lurching around again, tipsy little creatures bent on success.

Kate chuckled as they finally got to their feet once more. "Determined, aren't they?"

"Calves and foals have to be on their feet in a hurry or they're easy prey for the coyotes."

Kate washed up first, shivering as the icy water sluiced over her skin, then she pulled on her coat and tugged up the zipper with shaking fingers. When she was done, Seth stripped off his spattered T-shirt and bent over the pail of water.

Oh, Lordy, what a chest. With an indrawn breath, Kate tried to turn away. Her muscles didn't cooperate. Being a cop meant keeping fit, and she'd seen a lot of muscular bodies at the fitness center over the years. Not one of them had ever affected her like the one in front of her now—lean and hard, with thick-sculpted muscle that owed nothing to a pristine gym and everything to the demanding life of a rancher.

Her pulse kicked into overdrive, fueled by sheer,

raw desire. *Just a physical response. Nothing more than that.*

But it was. She now knew he was a man of substance. She'd seen him handle life-and-death situations with easy confidence. Risk his own welfare to save livestock. Work long, grueling hours. And she'd seen him with his daughter, infinitely gentle.

When he pulled on his sweatshirt she blinked, tore her gaze away from his chest and found him looking back at her, his eyes twinkling. He'd caught her ogling him like some silly teenager. Heat rose in her cheeks.

"Great pecs, there," she said gruffly, trying for distance.

That twinkle faded into something darker. "Thanks," he said in a low, intimate voice. "For helping. And for coming to Mandy's play tonight."

His voice reverberated through her with a lazy sensuality that made her feel warm, yet made her shiver. "I was glad to go. Mandy's quite a girl."

Seth cleared his throat. "I want to apologize for telling you to stay away from her when you first arrived. I misjudged you, and I'm sorry. Friends?" He offered his hand.

Friends? If only she could forget how she'd felt when he kissed her, and stop imagining what would ignite between them if they ever went further.

Hiding her regrets, she shook his hand and ignored the sensations that raced up her arm and settled around her heart.

TWO WEEKS LATER, Kate knew why Seth had warned her about calving. Round-the-clock surveillance, cold nights and sheer hard work had exhausted everyone. Most of the cows did fine, though several had needed assistance. The two-year-old heifers had a harder time. "Just like young teenagers," Cal had explained. "Maybe they can have a baby, but they aren't gonna be as ready for it as an older cow."

Two stillbirths occurred, leaving the mother cows heartbroken. They endlessly searched the herd, calling for their calves, and the sound tore at Kate's heart. With Seth's intervention, one of them finally accepted a calf abandoned by its mother and the other accepted an orphan. Then two calves were born too weak to stand and suck, which meant Mandy got to bottle-feed them in the warming shed.

Night and day, every two hours, someone rode through the herds looking for signs of trouble, playing midwife at a moment's notice, doctoring navels with iodine, hauling in chilled calves.

The calves were coming more frequently now. The temperatures began to drop. At the end of the second week, the stress was showing on the faces of everyone at the ranch as they layered on extra jackets and went out to check the herds. Kate's last decent pair of jeans had snagged on a barbed-wire fence, and she needed to take a trip into town for a few extra pairs.

"Anyone need anything while I'm in town?" Kate asked over breakfast.

Outside, dawn was breaking, cold and gray. The aroma of strong black coffee, bacon and waffles filled the air as Della moved stiffly around the kitchen.

Breakfast, thank goodness, was one meal she did well.

"A couple 500 cc bottles of Phi-Pen-G."

"Phi what?"

"It's a penicillin for sick calves."

"Do I need a prescription?"

Seth shook his head, then took a long swallow of coffee. The weary look in his eyes made him look another ten years older. He thought for another minute. "And iodine. Cal might need refills on his heart medications. He rode most of the night, but he should be up for breakfast in an hour or so."

Seth had ridden the herds on the midnight shift, then had caught just two hours of sleep before being called back out for a breech. He hadn't shaved for two days.

Della pulled a grocery list from beneath a refrigerator magnet and silently handed it to Kate, then shuffled back to the stove.

"Arthritis kicking up again?" Seth gave her a look of concern. "You should get in to see the doc."

With a shrug, Della served steaming waffles and bacon, then set a pitcher of warmed syrup on the table. "Weather's gonna change," she said, painfully easing herself into her chair.

"Let me do the kitchen before I go outside," Kate offered, looking at the breakfast clutter on the counters.

Della stabbed a strip of bacon with her fork. "I can manage."

Kate knew Della considered the kitchen her private domain and that it would do no good to insist. Kate turned her attention to Seth. "How many calves do we have so far?"

He put down his fork and leaned back in his chair. "Last count was around a hundred-seventy. Not including the four we lost. Another six weeks and we'll be done." He gave her a weary smile. "How does this compare to your city job?"

Kate realized with a start that she hadn't even thought about her life back in Minneapolis for more than a week. The grueling cycle of life, birth and death, and countless hours on horseback had consumed her.

That, and her increasingly wayward thoughts about the epitome of tall, dark and dangerous sitting across the table from her. Her cardiovascular health had to be incredible, because her heart pounded foolishly whenever he came into view.

Seth chuckled, then took a long swallow of coffee. "If it takes this long to compare your city life to this, you must be trying hard to be tactful."

"Not at all. It's...not what I expected, and my first preconceptions were wrong."

He looked at her then, meeting her gaze. "So tell me," he said slowly. "I'd like to hear."

"Well...I thought you'd be some aging cowpoke." Giving him a slow perusal from head to toe, she took a deep breath. "And you definitely aren't."

Amusement glimmered in his eyes. "So I'm not bald and bowlegged. Go on."

"And...I thought this place would be desolate—"
"It's peaceful."
"Barren—"

"Beautiful."

"And that it might be deadly boring."

He gave a shout of laughter at that. "Is it?"

She fervently shook her head. "Hardly."

"So tell me," he said, his voice soft and low. "What do you miss about being a cop?"

The moment of camaraderie shattered as her memories flooded back. In an instant, she was kneeling by Rico, soaked in his blood. Facing an irate husband on a domestic call. Cuffing a teenager high on crack.

"It was my life for ten years," she said. "I made a real difference every time I went out on the street. The feeling of being needed, of helping so many lives, is a powerful draw. The adrenaline rush of danger and excitement is almost addictive. A cop never knows what the next moment will bring."

Seth studied her for a moment, the glimmer in his eyes fading. "Not exactly like living on an isolated ranch."

"Not exactly." She smiled. "Yet I never expected the sense of excitement and satisfaction I feel here, and I never realized how beautiful this country is. I'm glad to be here."

"For a while, anyway, right?" He almost looked regretful.

"For as long as I should stay." That initial shimmering awareness had steadily grown into a palpable presence that throbbed between them like an extra beating heart. She lay awake at night thinking about him, wanting him.

Noticing the shadows under his eyes, she wondered if he did the same.

But whenever she was tempted to throw caution to the wind, she only had to recall her wedding fiasco fifteen months before. She'd been in love and had trusted her heart. Kent had walked out of her life without a backward glance.

It was a risk she just couldn't take again.

WITHIN AN HOUR, Kate was on her way to Folsum. A quick call to Joanna had given her a recommendation on a good jeweler, so she drove there first with the cruise control set on seventy and the local country-and-western station turned to high. Finding the jeweler took just a few minutes once she hit the city limits.

The little gray-haired jeweler squinted through his loupe for a full minute, then sighed deeply and looked up at her in consternation. "Where did you get this?"

Kate produced a folder containing the yellowed sheaf of documents her mother had given her with the brooch. "It's a family piece—many generations back on my mother's side. I'd like to have it appraised for my insurance policy."

He studied the documents. "What you have it in an old box for? And why you let it go unrepaired? This belongs in a museum, or in a fine case. You want to sell, maybe?"

"It's broken?" Kate leaned over his shoulder. "Where?"

Clucking his tongue, he rotated the brooch and indicated an area where the filigree formed a delicate tracery of vines and roses. "Here, by this largest rose. The emerald could be lost."

"I'd like it fixed. Can you do this type of work?"

"But of course," he murmured in a miffed tone. "Delicate work takes time and my schedule is quite full. I can get to it in a few days. Do you want to leave it or bring it back? We have a good safe and a new security system. You need not worry about it."

Kate debated. It might be a while before she could make another hundred-forty-mile round trip just to drop it off, and she would still have to return to pick it up. After the jeweler showed her the massive safe in the back, she agreed to leave the brooch.

"I'll need the appraisal document today, though," she said. "The insurance on it isn't adequate."

The jeweler positioned the brooch under a high-powered microscope and began painstakingly searching the glittering depths of the stones, making notes as he moved it in small degrees. With a flourish, he gave her the top sheet from his pad, kept the yellow copy beneath, then completed the repair paperwork and gave her that as well.

Kate stared at the papers in her hands. Swallowed. If she were to sell the brooch, it would more than cover the down payment on a decent house in the suburbs. And she'd kept it in an old pasteboard jewelry box. "Thank you," she breathed. "I—I'll be back next week to pick it up."

When she did, she would take it to a safety-deposit box right away. She found herself singing along to the tunes on the radio as she drove back to Salt Creek.

DRIVING INTO TOWN wasn't quite the experience it had been at first. Seth's effort at displaying acceptance toward her at the school play had dispelled some of the initial antagonism. Her old Mustang and Minnesota plates did not stir much interest. Still, as she parked in front of the farm supply store—the only source of clothes in Salt Creek—she felt the hairs rise at the back of her neck. She casually scanned the area as she stepped out of the car.

The small town was bustling with Saturday morning activity. Rows of pickups were parked nose-to-curb down its entire two-block length. Kids shouted at one another, ranch wives dressed in jeans and bulky jackets wrestled toddlers and grocery sacks out of the small food store. Ranchers leaned against tailgates, discussing the weather and cattle prices. No one seemed to be looking her way.

With a mental shrug, she walked into the store. The scents of feed supplements, livestock pharmaceuticals and motor oil were a combination she wouldn't ever forget. Nodding at the ponytailed teenager manning the lone cash register, she headed for the "clothing department," consisting of racks of jeans, flannel shirts and denim jackets. She grabbed several pairs of jeans. At the back of the store, she found a pint of iodine and, in a refrigerated case, the penicillin.

"These are on the Lone Tree account," Kate said, setting the bottles down at the cash register. "I'll pay cash for the jeans."

The girl peered at her through thick glasses. "You're Bob's granddaughter?"

Here we go again. Kate nodded. But instead of offering a subtle dig, the girl's eyes turned dreamy.

"So you get to live out at that ranch, with *Seth?* All alone?"

Kate stifled a smile. "Hardly alone. There're quite a few people out there."

"But," the girl returned in a stage whisper, "he's not, you know, *married,* or anything." She gave Kate an envious look. "I'd just *die* for a chance like that!"

"Well…" Kate's thoughts faded as she again felt that odd prickle of unease. Looking behind her in the store, she saw no one other than an elderly clerk shelving bags of dog food. The dusty front window of the store, liberally plastered with auction announcements, revealed no one outside.

And then she saw a figure in the shadows, across the street. A man, dressed in jeans and a heavy coat, a battered cowboy hat pulled low over his eyes. He was watching the store.

Handing the cashier three twenties for her new jeans, Kate tipped her head toward the window. "Any idea who that guy is—the one across the street?"

The girl leaned way over the counter and peered outside. "Who? Tom?" She shuddered in distaste. "They say he lived here years ago, then left. No one knows where he was, and a few of them wish he would go back."

Kate waited, silently encouraging the girl to elaborate. As with most teenage girls, it didn't take long.

"He's a bum." She lowered her voice to a conspiratorial whisper. "My mom says he got wounded in the head in Vietnam."

"What's his last name?"

The girl gave a bored shrug. "I don't know."

"He seems to be watching this store."

"He's always staring at someone," the girl scoffed, cracking her bubble gum. "Weird. Sometimes he talks to himself." She rang up the merchandise on the counter, then her hands stilled over the cash register. She gave Kate a look of sudden interest, as if ready to pounce on a delicious piece of gossip. "Has he been *following* you?"

Kate thought about the dark form lurking in the shadows the night of Mandy's play and the drunk who had come up to her afterward. Given the sense of foreboding she'd felt before coming in the store, she was pretty sure this was the same man.

But gossip would spread like wildfire if Miss Bubble Gum announced that Bob's paranoid granddaughter thought she was being stalked on the quiet streets of Salt Creek.

"No. Of course not. I just hadn't seen him around and wondered who he was." Pasting on a bland smile, Kate accepted her change and sack of purchases, then stepped out onto the sidewalk. With casual indifference, she was going to walk over and nod hello, maybe strike up a conversation with the guy. A little subtle interrogation could go a long way.

But when she looked up, he was gone.

In frustration, Kate wound through some double-parked pickups and walked across the street, scanning the area. A familiar feminine voice rang out from down the street.

Joanna, Nicki and Mandy were just a block down, heading toward her. Mandy had gone to their house after school yesterday and had spent the night. Joanna was hugging two bulging grocery sacks. Kate stepped forward and rescued the one slipping out of her grasp.

"Whew!" Joanna grinned. "Another minute and that one would have been on the street. Have time for coffee?"

No was the first word to spring to Kate's lips, but then she reconsidered. There were no time clocks at the Lone Tree. She hadn't had more than a few waking moments to herself in two weeks.

"Yeah, sure. I'd like that," she found herself saying. "Maybe at the drugstore, while they're filling Cal's prescriptions?"

Entering the drugstore felt like taking a step back in time. The pressed-tin ceilings, polished wood floors and old-fashioned soda fountain reminded Kate of something out of a 1940s movie. Parallel to the counter was a row of high-backed booths. The store carried everything from calf halters and udder balm, to jewelry and rental videos. Every time she walked in the door, she half expected to see people in period costume.

After settling the girls into the next booth with chocolate sodas, it didn't take Joanna long to get down to business. "So," she said, her eyes twinkling. "How's everything out at the ranch?"

"Busy."

Joanna laughed and leaned across the table. "Come on. How's everything going with Seth? You two ought to hit it off really well. Fess up."

"There's nothing to tell. We've managed to develop a good working relationship, I think."

Joanna rolled her eyes. "*Working* relationship? Are you ever missing the boat!"

Shifting uncomfortably in her seat, Kate passed the cream and sugar to Joanna. "So why didn't you ever go after him yourself?"

"Don't think I never wished." The look in Joanna's eyes turned reflective as she gave a soft sigh. "But some things just aren't meant to be. He and I are good friends, but we didn't have the right spark. It will take a powerful attraction to get him past all that his ex-wife pulled."

Firmly telling herself that she wasn't interested didn't stop the words from forming. "What did she do?"

"She walked out on him when their daughter was a baby and she never came back. I heard she was remarried soon after their divorce." Joanna gave a derisive snort. "Classy lady."

Kate looked down at her faded jacket, her short, chipped fingernails, then gave Joanna a rueful smile. "Well, I'm not interested in him, and I'm sure he feels the same about me."

Joanna leaned back in the booth and toyed with her napkin. "You know, I'd like to see his face when we got you dressed up."

"I really don't want—"

"Of course you do. You can't tell me it wouldn't feel good to see his mouth drop open when you walk down the stairs."

"What?"

Leaning forward, Joanna reached across the table and took Kate's hand. "The Rancher's Association has a dinner and dance every year, and you're going. I might even—'' Joanna tapped her lips with a forefinger ''—find you a date.''

''That sounds sort of pathetic, needing to find some poor soul to donate an evening.'' Kate grinned. ''How's everything going with Meadowbrook?''

Hesitating just long enough to acknowledge Kate's blatant effort to change the topic, Joanna grew more somber. ''Not well. The county has to approve our plans for expansion and they're balking. People think that bringing in more troubled youth would result in a major crime wave. I've gotten several angry letters from some folks in town.''

''And if it doesn't go through?''

''We've still got the old facility and twenty acres at the edge of town, but we can't offer the activities that we could in a ranch setting.''

A gray-haired man, backlit by the front windows of the store, approached the booth. Doc Anderson, Kate realized when he stopped and said hello.

''Weather's changing fast,'' he said. ''Radio says eight to ten inches, easy.''

''Snow!'' Apparently gifted with selective hearing, Nicki and Mandy shouted with glee from the next booth. ''No school!''

''We'll be plowed by Monday morning,'' Joanna said dryly, scooting out of the booth and standing up to pull on her coat. ''If the weather does hit.''

''Already started…just in the past few minutes or so. Take a look outside. You might need to head back to the ranch while you still can.'' Doc nodded toward

Kate. She saw none of his initial antipathy, heard no censure in his voice.

Joanna glanced at her watch. "I was planning on bringing Mandy home tonight after supper, but maybe she should go back with you now, just in case?"

"Sounds good. Mandy?"

Mandy's face fell. "But we were going to bake cookies and rent a movie and…"

"Another time, sweetie. But we can rent something here before we go. Why don't you go pick something out?"

With a dejected slump to her shoulders, Mandy turned to Nicki. "Help me find something good?"

The two girls left for the opposite end of the store. Joanna gave Kate a wink. "I can't wait to help *you* find something good."

Kate put her hands on her hips. This really had to stop, before Joanna embarrassed her to death in front of Seth and the entire town. "I'm not the frou-frou type."

"I never thought you were." Joanna gave her a once-over. "Size…eight? Ten?"

"No, I…"

"Twelve? Fourteen?" Joanna raised a brow. *"Really?"*

Exasperated, Kate reached for the keys in her jacket pocket. "Probably an eight, not that it matters."

"I'll bet you a lunch anywhere in Salt Creek that you won't recognize yourself when I'm through."

Kate burst into laughter. "There *is* no place to eat in Salt Creek other than Jim's Diner!"

"Folsum?"

"This is crazy."

Joanna gave Kate a knowing look. "You're afraid."

Kate started to reply, then bit her lip. She suddenly recalled Mandy confiding in her a few weeks ago. *Maybe we can be friends. You're not like all of those pretty ladies who want to marry my dad....*

Maybe it would be fun, just once, to see if she could measure up. And if she ended up a laughing-stock...well, she'd faced worse things in her life. "You've got a deal."

CHAPTER NINE

Mandy rubbed a porthole in the heavy frost coating the side windows of Kate's car and peered out at the snow. "This is going to be great for sledding!"

Kate gave her a quick smile, then turned her attention back to the road. The asphalt had been clear and dry on the way into town, but with every mile on the way home, the conditions had deteriorated.

Each cycle of the wiper blades swept a thick layer of snowflakes from the windshield. A few miles back, a tap on the brakes had sent the car into a brief skid before she turned into it and corrected the motion.

"Where do you like to take your sled?" Kate asked, keeping her voice casual.

"The hills above the north meadow, if I can get dad to take me in the snowmobile or four-wheeler. It's really super for sledding up there."

From the corner of her eye, Kate saw Mandy hunch over and hug herself.

"Can you turn up the heat?" Mandy asked plaintively. "It's cold in here!"

"Usually this heater runs hot, if anything. The thermostat may be going out." Kate reached over to turn up the heat.

The blower normally blasted the car's interior with

warmth. Now it barely provided a weak breeze. She shifted her gaze to the gauges on the dashboard, where the lights appeared to be…dim. Holy Hannah, the alternator light was flickering—an automotive distress call that sent a shaft of dread down her spine.

A gust of high wind blasted the side of the car, sending it into a sideways skid that carried them to the shoulder of the road before Kate managed to get the car under control again. Maybe it was just the heavy snow, but the power steering seemed…sluggish.

A quick glance at Mandy reassured her that the child wasn't aware of the danger that they were in.

"I'm sure glad I called the ranch. At least they know we're on our way," Kate said as she turned the wipers up another notch. "There are some blankets in a box up here on the passenger-side floor. Can you reach one?"

Mandy unbuckled her seat belt and hung over the front seat, snagged a blanket, then flopped back down. "Do we have more new calves?"

"I don't know. No one answered, so the machine took my message." She glanced back at Mandy. "Buckle up, sweetie."

Mandy dutifully buckled in, then unfolded the heavy wool army blanket and bunched it up around herself until only her face was visible. Ahead, the snow fell like a solid, swirling curtain of white. With the boundary of asphalt and shoulder obliterated, only glimpses of reflective signs and roadside markers provided any guidance.

Kate slowed from thirty down to twenty miles an

hour and peered ahead, forcing her death grip on the steering wheel to relax. *Easy does it. This is nothing compared to Minnesota,* she told herself firmly. *Level, straight roads, no traffic...just another dozen miles or so, a couple of turns, and we'll be stamping snow off our boots at the back door.*

The Mustang faltered. Bucked. Kate looked down for a split second, then looked again. The temperature gauge had risen into the danger zone.

The steering wheel grew dangerously stiff and unresponsive in her hands.

"Mandy, try the radio," Kate said, wrestling with the wheel as they plowed through a drift higher than the rest. The rear wheels spun, the back end of the car fishtailed. "Let's listen to the forecast."

Mandy reached forward from her cocoon and spun the radio knobs. "It doesn't work," she announced. "How come you drive such an old car?"

Kate shot a quick smile at her. "This old girl has been a good car. Not too pretty anymore, but usually dependable."

Unless a brand-new alternator belt goes. One with a three-year warranty.

In the darkness, her face lit by the dimming glow of the dashboard, Mandy looked doubtful. "We...we are going to get home okay, aren't we?"

"I'll make sure you stay safe. I promise."

The car lurched and skidded as they hit another drift. The wind rose, driving a blanket of snow horizontally across the road. Kate reached blindly under her seat for a small ice scraper, dropped it, then managed to snag it again. She scraped the thickening frost from inside the windshield.

From the corner of her eye, Kate caught the flash of a road sign looming out of the nearly impenetrable whiteness. They'd reached a T-intersection. The power brakes failed.

And seconds later, the old Mustang was airborne.

SETH GLANCED AT HIS WATCH, then gave Della a grim smile. "I'll be in and out all night, checking stock. We've got the herds moved up into the windbreaks and the boys put straw down already. But if this storm gets any worse…"

A feeling of unease rippled down his spine. He stood, paced to the front windows. The heavy curtain of snow obliterated everything beyond the glass. "This came up awfully fast," he said slowly. "And it was expected much farther south, not here. Surely Kate wouldn't have started home."

Della remained silent.

"Or she could have stopped to see Joanna and decided to give Mandy a ride home. Maybe tried to beat the weather?" He turned back to look at Della. "Were there any messages on the answering machine when you came in?"

"I—I didn't check. Ten minutes later, the power went out."

Seth shoved a hand through his hair. "She drives that damned old rear-wheel-drive car, but surely she would have put extra weight in the back." He frowned. "I have a bad feeling about this."

In the fire-lit room, the lines of Della's face looked

deep as gullies. She stared back at him, and even from a distance he could read the growing fear in her eyes.

"That twenty miles is a long trip in bad weather. Some of those turns…" She rose stiffly to her feet. "I heard on my portable radio that it could be minus-forty degrees by morning. If she's out there, she's gonna have trouble making it back."

"I'll tell the boys I've got to leave."

"I'll fix you some food and blankets."

"If the power and phone come back on, call me on my cell phone."

Within ten minutes, Seth headed out of the ranch in a four-wheel-drive pickup with a thermos of coffee and a basket of food at his side. Visibility extended only a few feet ahead of the bumper, though strong gusts of snow obliterated even that.

He crept along, as much by instinct as sight, down the highway, glancing now and then at the odometer. There would be a curve at around six miles, a sharp left turn at around twelve. And even as he struggled to keep the truck under control, he searched the darkness for any glimmer of taillights…or the shape of a Mustang.

He might as well have hoped to count grains of dust on the moon. There had to be eight, nine inches of snow on the ground by now. A drift loomed ahead. Steadying the wheel with both hands, he gave the truck a little more gas and plowed straight through it. Twin plumes of snow arced high above the cab at either side, like waves parting for a speedboat. The truck shimmied, fishtailed as it hit a bare icy patch. *Damn.*

Without a single visible landmark, he could have been in Alberta for all he knew. Sparing a quick glance at the odometer, he judged that a turn should be just ahead. He slowed the truck to a crawl, straining to see through the blanket of white just beyond the hood. He'd been out nearly an hour now. It seemed like a lifetime.

He nearly missed seeing the dark shape in the ditch. His heart thudding, he eased up on the accelerator and tapped the brakes. There was no way to back up safely, no visible crossroads for turning around.

Easing onto the shoulder, he parked as far off the road as he dared, though God knew how another driver could see the truck until it was too late, no matter where Seth put it.

Snugging down his hat, he grabbed the flashlight on the seat, launched out of the truck and slammed the door. His feet went out from under him. He caught the back of the truck, for one crazy moment feeling as though he were drowning in a world where nothing existed but bitter wind and the icy pellets of snow biting at his face.

Head down, leaning into the wind, he made his way to the back of the pickup, then felt his way beyond. In front of the truck's headlights everything had been white. Now the darkness swallowed him up. Looking back, he could no longer see the ruby taillights.

Cursing the wind, Seth shuffled through the deep snow. Slipped and nearly fell. How far back had the car been? Twenty or thirty feet? A hundred? He slid down into the ditch and swept the flashlight across its surface. There it was. *A Mustang.*

"Kate? Mandy?" he shouted, but the wind tore the words away. Knowing the noise would scare them, but that a shape looming outside the windows would terrify them more, he knocked on the hood of the car and called out again in warning as he made his way to the driver's door.

"Kate! Mandy!" He rapped on the top of the roof once again, then with his heart in his throat, he murmured a prayer and ducked down to flash a beam of light into the interior. Relief flooded through him at the sight of Mandy and Kate inside.

The startled look on Kate's face instantly relaxed. She hit the door locks and he slipped inside behind the wheel of the small car.

"Daddy!" Mandy launched forward over the back of the seat and grabbed him around the neck. "You found us!"

"Thank God for that," Seth murmured. He twisted around in the tight confines of the car and managed to give his daughter a one-armed embrace. Kate looked pale, but not particularly distressed. "Why the hell did you come out in weather like this? You two could have died out here."

Her eyes flashed. "We left Salt Creek in plenty of time. It was just starting to snow or I wouldn't have tried. We would have made it, but I think the alternator belt is shot."

Mandy gave Seth a big kiss on the cheek, then released his neck and dropped back. "It was too snowy to walk and Kate said it was safer to stay in the car. We've been camping!"

It wasn't until that moment that Seth detected the

scent of hot candle wax, felt the cold air seeping in through several inches of open window behind Kate's head and noticed the blankets piled on the back seat.

Kate struck a match and relit the candle nestled inside a coffee can. "Opening that door blew out our campfire," she said, looking up at him over the flame of the match before extinguishing it.

Seth stared at her. In the flickering candlelight her eyes were a soft, steady gray, her skin smooth as cream. His anger had been born of fear, he knew. And with equal certainty, he knew that Mandy had been safer with Kate than she would have been with anyone else.

Glancing at the stash of granola, chips, juice boxes and candy bars in a box between them, he cleared his throat. "Are you always this prepared?"

She laughed. "I'm from Minnesota, and I'm a cop. I'm *always* prepared."

Her eyes sparkled and suddenly they weren't just that steady, intelligent gray. They held mystery and humor and depth, and he felt her presence like the radiant warmth of a heat lamp. The Mustang grew smaller. More intimate.

Mandy bounced forward and hung over the seat once again. "Are we staying out here all night? We could, you know. Kate says this is good practice for camping out in the mountains."

Shaking off a flash of disorientation, he awkwardly reached up and ruffled her hair. "Just listen to that wind. Even with blankets it's going to be too cold out here. And once that candle burns down, you'll be sitting in the dark."

"Kate has a whole box of 'em!"

"I'll bet she does. But I've got a four-wheel-drive parked up on the road, and we'd better be on our way before someone rear-ends it."

"Bundle up, sweetie. We can bring those blankets." Kate pulled the car keys from the ignition and slipped them into her coat pocket, then grabbed her canvas purse.

"Ready?"

The bitter wind tore at their clothes and stole their body heat as they stepped out of the car. Seth slung an arm around both Kate and Mandy as they trudged through the deep snow toward the pickup. When Mandy slipped and fell, he swung her up into his arms and tucked her head against his neck. "Another year and you'll be too big to carry," he teased when they finally reached his truck. "Then you'll have to carry me."

Shivering, Mandy burrowed closer to him, clinging to him. He tightened his grasp around her. *If he hadn't found them...or there had been a wreck and Kate had been hurt, Mandy would have been defenseless.* The thought made him shudder from fear rather than the cold.

He settled Mandy on the back seat with her blankets around her and fastened her seat belt, then shut the door and caught Kate's wrist as she started to climb into the front passenger seat.

In the dim light of the truck's headlights reflecting off the falling snow, her face was shadowed with uncertainty as she looked up at him. "I'm sorry," she began. "I never would have—"

"No." Still holding her wrist, he looked down at her and saw the strain that she had so carefully hidden from Mandy. "Thank you. For keeping my daughter safe."

The words weren't enough, didn't begin to express his overwhelming feelings of relief and gratitude. He reached up and brushed away the snowflakes on Kate's cheek, then tipped her chin up until he could look down into her eyes. Without thinking, he lowered his head and kissed her.

Her lips were cold beneath his. She stiffened at the sudden intimacy. And then, tentatively, she responded to him. And everything around him faded until all that existed was Kate's hot, sweet mouth. From somewhere in the distance, he felt snow at the back of his neck and icy fingers of wind curl up through his jacket. None of it mattered until he felt her pull away and step back.

"Uh…you're welcome," she said, her voice shaky. She hesitated, then added, "Don't worry. I won't read more into it than there was, cowboy." Without meeting his eyes, she climbed into the truck.

Seth stood for a long moment, staring out into the night as his hammering pulse slowed. *What the hell have I done?*

They were business partners, nothing more. She'd be back to her Minneapolis career by midsummer. But ever since that first kiss, keeping his hands off of her had been damned hard.

He'd never wanted a woman so much.

DELLA MET THEM AT THE DOOR dressed in jeans, a sweatshirt and a down vest despite the late hour, her eyes glazed with fear. Knuckles white, her hands clenched the bail of a lit kerosene lantern.

"I've been worried sick," she said, reaching around Mandy in an awkward one-armed hug. "Are you okay?" She looked up at Seth. "Is she okay? Any frostbite?"

"She's fine, thanks to Kate." Seth glanced around the darkened kitchen. "Power and phone still out?"

Della nodded. "Come on in by the fireplace. I'll add some more logs and you'll all keep warm."

Seth bent to give Mandy a swift hug and kiss, then swung her up into his arms and gave her another squeeze. "Get some sleep. Same for you, Kate. I need to go check on the cattle, then I'll be back in."

Kate followed him to the door, zipping up her coat. "We're partners," she said simply. "I'm not staying behind."

He looked as if he were going to argue, then shrugged. "Grab an extra jacket and those heavier boots by the door. It could be a long night."

CHAPTER TEN

HALFWAY TO THE BARN, Seth stopped. "Are you sure you want to do this? Why don't you go back to the house."

Kate stubbornly shook her head. "I was useful last time, remember?"

With an exasperated look, he wheeled away and continued on, his head bent against the wind. A quick check of the calving shed revealed a bedraggled group of new calves shivering under the heat lamps and a new mother and her baby in the far pen. None of the hands were there.

"Could be they're at the bunkhouse," Kate said, rubbing warmth into her arms.

Seth studied the new calves for a moment, then tugged his hat down over his brow and headed for the door. "Maybe, but more likely they're out riding the herds. If we don't get a new, wet calf dry and warm in ten minutes or so, it won't even try to get up and it will freeze to death. "

Kate paused, listening to wind howling through the metal rafters of the shed. Just the sound made her feel bone-cold. "Can't all the pregnant cows be brought in?"

"There's no room for hundreds of cows inside and

they're not all likely to calve on a given night. We've just got to help the ones that do.''

As Seth had predicted, none of the hands were in the bunkhouse. Kate saddled Rowdy while Seth got Drifter ready, then they rode out of the barn with their collars turned up and hats tipped down. Rowdy balked at the barn door, shaking his head at the falling snow.

That moment of defiance no longer buffaloed Kate. With a whomp of her palm on his hindquarters, she made him step out into the night. He lowered his head and gamely waded through the drifts in the barnyard. She only had to rein him back once before he gave up and got down to work.

The saddle was cold and stiff beneath her jeans, the reins slippery. Kate looped them around the saddle horn, then reached back to tuck her sweatshirt into the waistband of her jeans. The sharp wind made it hard to breathe. She pulled a scarf over her mouth, keeping her eyes on Seth's back as he turned up into the one-hundred-acre pasture closest to the barn.

The pasture held a herd of two hundred heifers, roughly half with calves and the rest awaiting their arrivals. The snow finally slowed and quit, but the temperature dropped and the wind stayed strong. Faint moon glow lit the whitened landscape, revealing clusters of calves lying down, huddled together behind several three-sided sheds built to serve as windbreaks. Next to the calves were groups of watchful cows standing side to side, tails to the wind.

Seth rode up to the little groups and slapped his thigh, intimidating most of them into stiffly rising to their feet. "They need to get moving," he said. "They get tired and lie down together for warmth, but they're in danger of freezing if they stay down too long. They have to eat and they have to get their circulation going."

Once up, some of the calves found their mothers and started to nurse. Others just swayed on their feet like disoriented winos. Mooing softly, the cows sorted through the little group, sniffing backs and noses until they found their own calves.

"You ride through these and check out the other lean-tos farther up this fence line. Get 'em up and moving," Seth said. "Keep an eye out for any heifers that can't seem to find their calves. Sometimes a calf will drift along with the wind and get lost. I'll ride farther out to check the others. If you find any new ones or any too chilled to move, take 'em up to the warmers." He paused, reconsidered. "No, don't. I'll help you move them. New mamas can be pretty darn protective."

Before she could answer, he wheeled Drifter away and disappeared into the darkness. She shivered, hugged herself against the raw wind. And then got to work.

Kate lost track of time. Her hands and feet had gone numb long ago, her face felt as if it might shatter if she tried to speak. She'd dropped a rein so many times that she finally knotted the ends together. Rowdy's ears and mane were crusted with snow.

But the calves...she'd worked through the cows and calves all along the fence line, stirring them up, making them move, and felt a deep sense of accomplishment when they started to nurse. The night had turned still and crystal-clear, with stars that glittered like countless ice-chips against an indigo velvet sky.

From beyond the far shed she saw a form emerge from the darkness, like a dark ghost taking earthly form. Rowdy nickered and the shadow-horse responded eagerly. *Drifter,* Seth's horse.

Suddenly, despite the cold, Kate felt a flush radiate from the vicinity of her heart as she remembered Seth's kiss. Lordy, the man knew how to kiss. Just the memory made her toes curl and her soul heat.

Looking as bone-tired as she felt, he rode up beside her. "Time to go back to the house, Kate," he said, searching her face and frowning, "before you freeze to death. I'll bring in any calves that need to warm up."

"Got them."

He rose in his saddle and looked around. "Where?"

Kate felt a quiet sense of satisfaction. The city slicker had done all right, she commended herself silently. "A brand-new one is in the warming shed under the lights. I also trailed in two other mamas and their babies. The calves looked like they weren't doing too well."

"What?" Seth exploded. "Not by yourself!"

"It wasn't far. Who else was here to help?"

"Damn it all, Kate. These cows are dangerous." He reached out and grabbed Rowdy's rein, then sidestepped Drifter until his stirrup jostled hers. His face was just a dozen inches from hers. "Every instinct tells them to protect their calves. You could have been hurt.''

Kate reached down and pried his hand from her rein. "So be grateful for the help, then."

"Grateful?" He uttered a raw expletive that made his own horse dance sideways. "Grateful if we'd had to haul you to the hospital, or worse?"

"Don't worry about me." Kate reined Rowdy away and gave him a sharp nudge with her heels, sending him into a brisk trot toward the gate and the twinkling ranch lights in the valley below. Rowdy snorted and shook his head, clearly thrilled to be heading home.

Seth spun away and started checking the cattle one more time. As he disappeared into the darkness, Kate found herself smiling. He may have succumbed to emotion for a moment, but beneath his anger was concern for her. She thought back on his absolute commitment to the ranch and his daughter; his sorrow over the financial plight of his neighbors.

Whatever she may have thought of him at first, she now knew him for who he was: A man of strength and integrity. A man who could be trusted.

And despite all the lessons she'd learned about love and commitment—lessons she would never forget—she wanted him.

How was she ever going to deal with him now?

How was he going to deal with her now? Seth reached out to place a steadying hand on Drifter's arched neck and swore under his breath. The horse snorted and danced sideways, suddenly skittish since Rowdy had disappeared.

Making the gelding walk quietly back to the barns—and circling him tightly a few times when he didn't—Seth cursed the impulse that had made him kiss Kate Rawlins and forget every promise he'd made to himself in the last eight years. He'd been in love once, and where had that gotten him? Alone, lonely and trying his darnedest to be all things to a daughter cheated out of having a mother. Mandy deserved better. "Better" was *not* a tough city cop who planned to return to her career ASAP. No, if he ever risked commitment again it would be with someone steady, someone born and bred to ranching. Someone who would be a good mother to his daughter, and the rest of all that romantic love crap be damned.

Seth scanned the stalls and sighed with relief when he spied Kate's gelding down at the end. She'd gotten in safely, then. He saw that the men he'd passed on the hills—they'd been riding for several hours—had box-stalled their horses and left.

Seth unsaddled Drifter, rubbed him down, then threw a blanket over him, buckled the surcingles and sent him into a roomy stall with a manger full of hay.

Something moved at the periphery of Seth's vision. Startled, he spun toward it, his hands instinctively clenched.

Kate stepped out of the shadows. "I...uh...just put my tack away. Need any help with chores?"

She no longer sounded like a seasoned cop. The tentative note in her voice was unsure. That bulky down jacket disguised everything about her body, yet emphasized the delicate bone structure of her face. Her wind-chapped cheeks were rosy.

His heart had skipped a beat in automatic response to an unknown intruder. Now it picked up a faster rhythm. *You're a fool,* he told himself, even as he moved toward her. *Five minutes ago your head was on straight and now you want her.*

"You look cold," he murmured. "You need to get inside the house to warm up."

She shrugged lightly and he found himself transfixed by the dark sweep of lashes framing her eyes. The arch of her brows. The sensual curve of her soft mouth.

"If you don't need any help, I'll…" she murmured in a voice almost too low to hear.

Oh, he needed help. But it wasn't with the horses, peacefully eating in their stalls, or with the cattle. Not right now. Memories of their last kiss came back to him in a rush of heat and hunger and tenderness.

He brushed a hand lightly down her cheek. Lingered at her jaw. Then dropped his hand to her shoulder and found himself moving closer, until he was looking down into her eyes.

She tilted her head. "Did you want something?"

Oh, yes. Anticipation coursed through him, all the stronger because it could not be satisfied. Not here, in this cold and dusty barn. Not in the house, where his daughter and Della were probably asleep next to the fire.

Not ever, because he had responsibilities to the ranch, to Mandy and to himself.

''No...we'd better get back.'' Reluctantly, he lifted his hand from her shoulder.

A look of regret tinged with embarrassment flashed in Kate's eyes. She moved one step away before he gently caught her hand. ''Don't go,'' he said. ''Not yet.''

Staring down at her, he felt as if he were falling off a cliff into the unknown. His life was one of responsibility, of control, yet something about her made him think of unmade beds and long, hot nights, and of the kind of careless abandon he'd never been able to afford.

He gently lifted a hand to her cap and swept it off, then cradled her face with both hands and traced her mouth with his thumb. ''You're so beautiful,'' he murmured.

A smile played at a corner of her mouth. ''I can just imagine. In this coat plus two sweatshirts, after riding for hours, with cow poop on my boots...''

He frowned, trying to find the right words. It wasn't just her face or the clothes she wore. A deeper longing had settled in his heart from the day he'd met her. He gave a growl of impatience and lowered his mouth to hers.

He wanted to convey his thoughts in that one kiss. For her to understand both his desire and his regret. But when she swayed closer and opened to him, welcoming him, all rational thought disappeared in a heartbeat. Her mouth was hot and sweet. Arousal shot through him as her hands slid around his neck and held him close. *Oh, yes...*

"No," she whispered, drawing back. "I—I can't handle this. I'm sorry."

Seth released her, his blood thundering in his ears and his breathing harsh. "So am I."

In silence, they exchanged awkward smiles, and then headed for the barn door. He never should have kissed her, but it was getting harder and harder to stay away.

Gritting his teeth, Seth followed her back to the house.

SALT CREEK DIDN'T HAVE a name-brand gas station or a mechanic's shop with uniformed employees and sparkling-clean windows. It did have a hole-in-the-wall grease pit of a place with barrels haphazardly stored along the side of the building, windows that hadn't seen Windex in decades, and a three-hundred-pound owner named Sonny.

The phone at the ranch was working by daybreak on Monday and Kate called Sonny at eight. Within an hour he'd plowed through the snowdrifts with his ancient wrecker, collected her car and hauled it back to town. Kate couldn't have wished for better service.

Freckles dropped her off on his way to Folsum to pick up a new tractor clutch. Now she sat across from Sonny in his cramped office, waiting for her towing bill.

"Alternator belt, just like you thought, ma'am. Snapped clean through. I went ahead and fixed it."

"*What?*"

"No way you coulda driven it anyplace else." Sonny chewed on his tobacco a moment longer, then spat with startling precision at a coffee can next to his "desk," an old door laid over two-drawer file cabinets at either end.

He'd gone ahead, and now he would try to charge her double. With a sigh, she mentally counted backward and tried to focus on the suspicions that had been on her mind since last night. "I had that belt replaced six weeks ago."

Sunny chewed a while, lost in thought. "Shoulda lasted longer," he said finally. "Three, maybe four years."

"Do you think it was flawed?"

He continued painstakingly adding numbers, a pencil stub gripped in his massive fingers and a frown of concentration on his face. After a full minute he put down the pencil and looked up. "Belt still looked new," he said finally. "Never seen a new one snap like that." He shoved the bill at her. "Twenty bucks, plus the belt."

Startled, she looked up at him. "Plus the towing?"

"Nope."

"But—"

"Couldn't work on it if wasn't here, could I?" He smiled. "I did a lot of work for your grandpaw over the years."

His friendly gesture and easy acceptance of her warmed her heart. Kate grinned as she handed him the cash. "Thanks."

Stuffing the receipt in her pocket, she headed for the single bay where her car waited. She'd backed up to the curb and was ready to swing out into the street when she saw Eric Wright's gleaming silver Bronco approach.

The driver slowed down, looked out the window at her license plate, waved at her, then pulled up against the curb. In one fluid motion he stepped out and slammed the door. After glancing both ways, he jogged across the street and headed straight for her car.

The smooth, perfect tan on his face was proof that he and Alison had made the most of their trip to Cancún. Judging from the cut of his slacks and the fine leather of his coat, he was a man who could afford to go often.

She rolled down her window as he approached, wearing the expression of a used-car salesman moving in for the kill. "You must be Kate," he said, propping one hand on the roof of her Mustang and offering the other to her through the window. "I'm Eric Wright."

Kate managed a smile and shook his hand briefly, then suppressed a desire to wipe her hand against her jeans.

Squatting down, he hooked both forearms on the open window. "I have a proposition for you... something that would benefit us both." He jabbed a thumb toward Jim's Diner. "Cup of coffee?"

The words were casual, but something in his voice told her that Eric's proposition meant a great deal to him, and that he was broaching the subject with caution. "Sure. Why not?"

Five minutes of sitting across from him in an all-too narrow booth and she knew why not—when his knee brushed against hers for the third time. He leaned back in the booth and smiled at her. She felt her skin crawl.

"So," he continued. "I know how hard it is to deal with a partner, especially one who refuses to give up any control. Doesn't that sum up your situation? When you go back to Minnesota, you don't want to be bothered with some arid piece of dirt clear across the country. If you receive a top price, you can invest your money and get on with your life. Am I right?"

She'd come to Montana planning to collect her inheritance, sell out and go back home. Eric Wright was offering to help her do just that. But the choices that were clear before she arrived weren't so clear any longer. What would happen to Seth and Mandy, and all the ranch hands? Would the ranch go under if half of it were sold?

Seth loved every square inch of that land. To sell out would betray every dream he had of preserving a legacy for future generations.

Yet if she didn't sell, she couldn't make good on *her* vow to Rico's mother, which had been her sole reason for coming to Montana in the first place. "I'll think about it," she said finally. "I really don't know what my plans will be."

Eric's eyes narrowed. "You'll never make any money keeping the place," he countered. "Get out while you can, while the place is still solvent. I want to help you."

"Why?"

Eric's gaze flickered toward the door of the café,

then back to her. Jim's had been deserted when they'd come in, but now a couple of ranchers were strolling toward the door. He lowered his voice. "I'm a real estate investor. But in this case, I'd like to think I'd helped out Bob Rawlins's granddaughter."

Kate stood when Eric did, and met his gaze squarely. "Thanks. If I decide to sell, I'll be in touch."

The eerie intensity of his gaze and his satisfied smile told her all she needed to know. He thought he had convinced her, that she was just another gullible woman. But now she *knew* he didn't want the Lone Tree as a mere investment. He had far deeper reasons for wanting the ranch, and none of them were good.

She thought back to Alison's emotional departure after the school play, and the carefully concealed bruise on her cheek. Kate didn't yet know what the future would bring. But taking this man down a notch would make her stay in Montana infinitely more rewarding.

CHAPTER ELEVEN

BY SATURDAY, the snow had melted and balmy temperatures were back. "Spring comes early here," Kate called out to Seth and Mandy as she unbuttoned her heavy jacket. They were out in the corral, working with a sorrel foal.

"Spring?" Seth raised a brow. "It's only March first. All winter long we can have sixty-degrees one day and minus-thirty the next, and major blizzards have hit clear into April."

"Then I guess we Minnesotans are tougher," she teased. "When our winter comes, it *stays*."

Seth laughed as he turned back to the wild-eyed foal that stood at the end of a cotton lead rope, his forefeet braced. Talking quietly, Seth eased closer, keeping the rope taut, until he could stroke the colt's fluffy winter coat.

Its mother, a freckled white mare, stood tied to the fence, ignoring the proceedings. Judging from her placid demeanor, she'd seen a lot of her foals start kindergarten and none of it fazed her anymore.

Seth held the cheek of the foal's halter, keeping him steady as Mandy ran a brush down his side. The foal arched his neck and rolled his eyes, then swung his hindquarters away.

Seth pushed him sideways until he was parallel to the tall wooden fence, then stood at the foal's shoulder, effectively blocking his escape. "There you go, fella."

Even from a distance, Kate could almost feel the soft rumble of his voice against her skin.

She'd tried to forget the rush of feelings that had heated her head to toe when they'd kissed in the barn last week. She'd tried to treat him as she would a partner, a fellow cop with a wife and six kids. But that type of easy camaraderie was as false as her hope that they could go back to the way they'd been before that kiss.

If he walked into a room, she felt an electrical current enter with him. When he spoke to her, she felt his voice curl around her. And considering the way he avoided looking at her, she suspected he felt that same awareness and was trying just as hard to convince himself that it didn't exist.

The colt lurched forward, but Seth stepped in his way, his voice never changing its reassuring rhythm. "See, honey, we don't ever want to manhandle these little guys. We don't want them hurt. But we can't let them get away with anything, either."

Mandy grinned up at her father and again started brushing the colt's fluffy coat. "Can I lead him?"

He leaned down and picked up a rope, shook out a loop and draped it over the colt's rear end with the slipknot resting on the colt's spine. With a snort, the little fellow crow-hopped, trying to rid himself of the foreign object. Seth waited until he settled down, then tugged on the rope until the foal took a step forward.

"Good boy," he crooned. "Let me get him started first, Mandy. Then you can try."

After another step forward the colt reared high and fought wildly for its head, striking out with its fore-feet. His mother lifted her head and watched, then dropped back into a doze. In ten minutes, the foal was walking quietly with Seth, its swiveling ears the only sign of stress. "Okay, Mandy. You can come in, but I'll stay beside you."

Kate smiled to herself, watching him deal with both Mandy and the colt with the same quiet, easy approach...never raising his voice, never rushing.

He was good with the livestock and good with his daughter, and she found herself wondering wistfully about her grandfather. Had he possessed that same laid-back manner? If she had been here as a child, would he have nurtured her in the same loving way that Seth took care of his daughter?

Turning away, she went back up to the house. Della had gone to the mailbox. The house would be quiet and Kate would be uninterrupted. She took the steps two at a time and locked the door of her bedroom behind her. With quick movements she withdrew her laptop from the dresser drawer, hooked up the phone line, then settled on the bed with the computer nestled on her crossed legs.

Her searches on Seth and the ranch hands had revealed nothing suspicious, nor had the one on Della. Maybe Kate was worrying for nothing. Someone *had* been in her car that first week, but nothing had been taken, and nothing had been taken from her room. Perhaps that alternator belt *had* simply snapped. Unless something else happened, she would just keep her eyes open.

Her encounter with Eric popped into her mind as she logged onto the Internet. Kate thought for a minute, then keyed in the address of her favorite public records database and started a background check.

Eric Wright was clearly a man who had a lot to hide.

"MOM IS COMING TODAY!" Mandy chirped after lunch. "By three o'clock. She promised!"

Kate met Seth's gaze over her lifted coffee cup. "That's really nice, Mandy."

Seth cleared his throat. "If she can't make it, have Della call my cell phone and I'll come back so you can come with me to the J-Bar sale, okay? Your friends will be there."

Mandy shook her head. "Mom will come."

Over the sound of clattering pots and pans, Della harrumphed.

"Are the Petersons going to lose everything?" Kate asked.

"Yes. Foreclosure. Land, equipment, livestock, some of the household." Seth's voice suddenly sounded awfully tired. "Three generations on the land and they've gone under. It will break Hal to leave it."

"Are you going over to buy?"

"We couldn't finance more land if we wanted to. I'll bid on equipment we could use, but if I only manage to boost the prices, all the better. Every nickel is going to matter to them."

"I'd like to come along."

He stood, turned away. "Going to this sale will be like going to a wake."

AFTER THEY LEFT, Mandy curled up in a chair by the front living room window and opened a library book. The words and pictures soon ran together in a dizzying blur so she set the book on the floor. *Mom will come, mom will come,* she chanted to herself, her gaze fixed on the long lane that led out to the highway.

No one seemed to understand how bad it was at Eric's house, and how hard it was for Mom to get away. They all thought she didn't care about anything but her fancy clothes and the country club.

No one knew how much her mother loved her, but Mandy did. Someday Eric would go away and their family would be back together again. It would happen, because Mandy prayed for it every single night.

TWO HOURS LATER, Kate stood on the periphery of a group of ranchers who were moving in formation down a row of farm equipment, following the auctioneer and his assistant.

In the distance, Hal Peterson and his wife stood arm in arm on the porch of their house, looking shell-shocked as their possessions went under the gavel, yet unable to turn away. Their three young children played silently on the swing set in the yard, their eyes big and round and scared.

A well-dressed, silver-haired man at Kate's elbow nodded slightly at the auctioneer, spurring yet another flurry of bidding activity. "Decent tractor," he chortled under his breath. "I should be able to get it at a damn good price."

Kate felt a flash of anger at this man who relished the thought of capitalizing on the family's sorrow.

A burly man in a seed corn cap at her other side gave the bidder a withering look, then spat on the ground. "Sad day," he muttered, rocking back on his heels. He turned slightly and stuck out his hand. "Bill Turner, buyer for Midland Cattle Company. Aren't you new to these parts?"

After a brief introduction, they followed the crowd to the next tractor and then on down the line to a baler.

"I always liked doing business with Hal," Bill mused, cupping a hand around a match as he lit a cigarette. "His beef dressed out fifty-eight, fifty-nine percent every time."

Seth came up beside Kate and put a hand on her shoulder, gave her a curious look, then nodded a greeting at Bill. "He estimates within a half percent, and I don't think he's ever wrong. We go way back, don't we, Bill?"

Bill looked from Seth to Kate, then grinned. "Sure do."

"Figuring out what the Lone Tree stock is worth?" Seth said mildly.

"No, of course not." Sensing the tension in his stance, Kate angled a glance at him.

Seth shook his head slowly. "It's a bad time for anyone to liquidate, with land and cattle prices in the basement."

Bill gave him a knowing look. "It's never a good time."

The auctioneer started bids on a hay rake. Seth stepped forward for a better view, leaving Bill and Kate on the fringes of the crowd.

Bill smiled down at Kate. "Seth hates every damn minute of these sales, don't he?"

Nodding, she searched out Seth in the crowd. From his curt manner she'd thought he was irritated with her, but now his shoulders looked even more rigid, and his expression was grim.

And then she remembered what he'd said about his past—alienation from both sides of his parents' families, his father's suspected suicide and the foreclosure sale of his family's ranch. No wonder he hated sales.

Someone else had the high bid on the hay rake. Kate caught up with Seth and touched his sleeve. "No luck?"

He gave her a quarter smile, but there was no humor in his eyes. "No, but at least my bids helped drive up the price."

She fell into step with him and looped her arm through the crook of his elbow. "You're taking this almost as hard as they are. Are you worried about the Lone Tree?"

"No," he snapped. "Why don't you go get a cup of coffee or something?"

"And let you brood in peace? Not a chance."

"It isn't your business."

Kate laughed. "Yes it is, cowboy." She steered him away from the crowd. "And you've never discussed the problems in detail with me."

He looked down at her and scowled, then gave a resigned sigh and gestured toward a stack of hay bales by a tool shed. "Come on. You'll hear sooner or later, anyway."

Kate bought two foam cups of coffee at the refreshment wagon parked nearby and gave one to Seth, then they sat on the bales. She watched the steam curl from their cups and waited for him to begin.

After taking a swallow, he idly swirled the contents of the cup. "Another $15,000 note is coming due this month. The bank is balking about an extension."

"An equipment loan?"

"A loan for Bob's last medical bills. As I told you, there was no insurance, and when the medical bills started coming in he wanted to give up. I refused to let him and went to every length to find him the best care, hoping...but those efforts were my denial, not his."

Kate laid a hand on his arm. "It must have been hard."

"He was like a father to me." Seth contemplated his cup, then took another swallow.

"I'm glad he was," Kate murmured. And realized that she meant it. She'd had her mother until a few years ago, but Seth would have been a child alone if Bob hadn't taken him in.

Seth looked out across the desolate, rolling hills of the J-Bar. "My family legacy was one of failure, of being left behind by a father who couldn't face the struggle any longer. If the Lone Tree ever goes under, my daughter will face the same uncertain future I did."

"But she'll always have you."

"Yeah, well…" His gaze fastened on the periphery of the distant crowd, he gave a dismissive shrug.

Kate followed his line of sight. She didn't see anything at first, just the same cluster of ranchers bundled up against the chilly breeze, bidding on equipment, and a few dogs lurking around their heels. And then the crowd shifted, revealing a tall man with unforgettably pale blond hair.

Eric Wright.

He was a hundred feet away, but the sight of him made her feel as if spiders were crawling down her back. With a shudder she turned back to speak to Seth, but he was gone.

The sky turned leaden with the promise of rain by the time the sale ended at dusk. Seth had bid on several pieces of equipment. He invariably dropped out just before the final price. The crowd was dispersing as she followed Seth to his pickup.

Eric waved to her, caught up, then draped an overly familiar arm around her shoulders. "Can we talk for a minute?"

Kate stumbled. "What?"

"Careful, sugar." He tightened the grip around her shoulders, steering her behind some trucks parked along the side of the lane. Seth, several paces ahead, apparently hadn't noticed Eric approach.

"Take your arm off of me," Kate said evenly. "Or you'll lose it."

Eric laughed as he let go of her. "I do love your sense of humor. No wonder Seth keeps his eye on you."

"I've got to catch up to him. What do you want?"

"He won't leave without you. There isn't a man around who would forget to bring you home if he had the chance."

That crawling sensation down Kate's back returned. "If that's all you—"

"No," he said, his voice smooth. "Have you thought any more about my little proposal? I know you don't have the ranch in your name yet, but we could sign an agreement and then you wouldn't have to worry at all about the future."

"I'm not worrying."

"My offer will protect your interests, especially if Seth tries to take advantage of your lack of business experience. He surely doesn't want you to have a share of the ranch."

"You think he would do that?"

Eric gave her a bland smile. "Ranching is a whole different world from Minneapolis. You might not even realize what's going on and then, *wham.* You'd be out of luck."

Kate counted to ten, then turned to go. Seth had disappeared from sight, but she knew where the truck was parked. "See you around, Eric."

"No, wait—"

"I'm not interested."

He grabbed at her arm and held it in a punishing grip. "Hold on, sugar. Don't walk away from me."

Counting to ten again only gave her temper more time to rise. She grabbed his wrist, stepped closer, and with two swift moves had him facedown in the dirt with his hand bent up behind his shoulder blades and her knee against his spine.

"You need some counseling, Eric. Aggressive behavior isn't usually a successful business tactic," she said calmly, shifting more weight onto her knee.

He cursed, struggled. "You're breaking my arm!"

She leaned closer and spoke in his ear. "I'm not your sugar, and I'm not stupid. Your business propositions don't interest me at this time. And," she added, rising to her feet, "I don't believe Seth would try to cheat anyone. You, on the other hand, might."

Sputtering, Eric stumbled to his feet, his face purple with rage. "You're going to be damn sorry."

"I've got some information on you that would curl your hair. Don't threaten me again."

"Problems?" Seth appeared at Kate's elbow.

Kate looked up at him. The dark look on his face and tension in his stance showed that he'd seen more than enough, even if he'd been too far away to hear the words.

"He sort of lost his balance. You okay, Eric?"

"We'll talk later, sugar. I know you'll be interested." Giving them a bland smile, Eric dusted himself off, turned and stalked away.

During the drive home Seth answered in monosyllables when Kate tried to start a conversation. At the gate he glanced up at the broad wooden ranch sign hanging above the entry, then shook his head slowly.

"What's wrong?"

He steered around a pothole. "What are you planning to do when your six-month stay is done?"

I wish I knew. Her goals had been so clear before

she'd arrived. But now…she knew far too much about the ranch, the people, and what would happen if half the ranch were sold. "I honestly don't know," she said at last, twisting in her seat to look at Seth.

"But you're doing research on the idea."

"Research?"

"The cattle buyer and Eric."

"Chance meetings, both of them." She hesitated. "If I ever did want to sell, could you buy me out?"

"You could do that so easily? Just walk away from your family's land?"

She shook her head. "Not easily. Not anymore."

They'd reached the house. Seth left the truck without a word and strode toward the barns. Kate grabbed her purse and stepped out into the chilly air, feeling colder than she had all day.

As she drew closer to the house she discovered a familiar red Corvette nosed up to the edge of the lawn, hidden by the truck Della usually drove. Turning, she started to call Seth's name, but he'd already disappeared into one of the barns.

I should have guessed, she muttered, reading the personalized license plate as she headed for the house. *Alison.*

Kate recalled the bruise on Alison's face the night of the play and her own resolution to delve into Alison's life. Kate's encounter with Eric at the sale convinced her that now was as good a time as any. *You're doing it for Mandy as well as Alison,* she told herself.

Alison was heading out the door just as Kate reached for the handle. Clad in a silky turquoise jogging suit shot with gold thread, the woman sidestepped Kate and headed for her car without a break in stride. Kate moved faster.

"Could we talk for a minute?" Kate asked quietly, slipping between Alison and the door of her car.

Giving Kate a blank look, Alison lifted a wrist to check the time, but her gaze never veered to her watch. "Maybe another day."

"Please. For your sake. For Mandy's."

"I can't. I've got to go now, before—"

"Eric is still at the sale."

"But—"

"He's still at the sale," Kate repeated firmly. "Does he know you were coming out to the ranch?"

Alison hesitated, then nodded. Her wavy golden hair tumbled to her shoulders like an eighteen-karat waterfall. Her makeup was flawless, her clothing and jewelry tastefully chic. But the hunted look in her eyes was hard to miss. "I need to get home."

"Just ten minutes. Let's go back into the house."

Alison shook her head a little too forcefully, and Kate wondered whether she was thinking about dour old Della lurking about, overhearing uncomfortable truths.

"Then let's sit in your car for a bit, so the heater can warm it up before you have to leave. Okay?" Kate gave her an easy smile. "It's been years since I sat in a Corvette."

As soon as they slid into the low-slung seats, Alison started the engine and turned up the heater. "What do you want?" she asked finally, fiddling with her leather gloves.

"I'm worried about you, and I'm worried about

Mandy." At Alison's startled expression, Kate laid a hand on her arm. "Your cheek was bruised the night of Mandy's school play. I feel awkward even talking about this, because we barely know each other. But Mandy's a sweet little girl who loves you very much, and I don't want her to lose you."

"Please get out," Alison snapped. "I need to leave."

"Women often tell me they fell down the stairs." Kate gave her a wry smile. "Some say they tripped on a rug."

Alison gave an exasperated sigh. "I...I fell off my horse."

Kate waited silently, watching her expression. "I just want to encourage you to...get help, if you're in any trouble at home."

"How dare you suggest—"

Kate changed tactics. "Would you want Eric to treat Mandy the way he treats you?"

Alison froze, then her shoulders sagged. "It was...an accident. I made him angry. I...I forgot something and it made him look bad and..." Alison pressed her fingertips to her lips and closed her eyes. "I need to get home. Could you leave the car, please?"

"He has no right to touch you in anger." Kate lowered her voice and continued. "You could be anything, do anything you wanted. You could find a gentle, loving man who would treat you well." She paused a beat, then added softly, "What is Mandy learning from this? That it's okay for men to be like Eric?"

Alison didn't answer. A tear slipped down her cheek.

"Alison, I've seen this a thousand times. I'm a cop, remember?"

"He can be so charming, and sweet. But when I—"

"His actions aren't your fault." Kate took a deep breath, deciding how much to say. "But I'm sure he's delighted if you think so. Abusers can be manipulative, self-centered men, and I see that in Eric. While talking about a business deal he grabbed my arm and that's *not okay*. I sent him face first into the dirt."

A gasp erupted from Alison's throat. "He must have been so angry!" she whispered.

"If you want your marriage to work, you both need counseling. If he hurts you, you need to report it to the authorities. You can't let him rocket out of control, or you—and maybe Mandy—could end up hurt. Possibly dead. No man has a right to hit any woman. *Ever.*"

A wobbly smile played across Alison's mouth. She trailed her fingers around the steering wheel, then shot Kate a sidelong look. "You really dropped him to the ground?"

Kate shrugged. "I've taken tae kwon do for years, and started hapkido last year. It helps to have an advantage because most suspects outweigh me by at least fifty pounds."

Alison's smile grew wistful. "I wish I could have done that a time or two...."

"It takes a long time to develop those skills," Kate said firmly. "You need to start making some decisions. Do you want to save your marriage? Do you want to walk away? You need to choose what's best for you and your daughter.''

"What would I do?" Alison asked baldly. "My reputation for tasteful parties and my decent golf swing wouldn't pay the rent.''

"You could go back to school.''

"Right." Alison laughed bitterly.

"See a college counselor about financial-aid packages—grants, loans, scholarships. You could work part-time. There are lots of options.''

"But I'm thirty-one!''

"And you'll get older whether you go to school or not. Going back could give you a great career. Even if you decide to stay in your marriage, it could help give you confidence, put you in a stronger position. You wouldn't be dependent anymore.''

Her fingers drumming nervously on the steering wheel, Alison shifted in her seat, then jammed a CD into the stereo. "Look…I really need to leave. Thanks, okay?''

"If you ever need help, call me. Day or night.''

With an answering smile as fake as a three dollar bill, Alison fastened her seat belt. "Thanks.''

Kate watched as the Corvette roared down the lane into the deepening twilight. She'd done all she could for now. The rest was up to Alison.

CHAPTER TWELVE

ALISON HESITATED at the living room door. The fronds of an immense old Boston fern on a pedestal partly concealed her from Eric's view, but she still felt her muscles tense and her heart pound. *Leave,* an inner voice urged. *Before he sees you.*

His face flushed and his stride rapid, he paced across the room. When his shin connected with an eighteenth-century end table he uttered a vehement oath, spun around and shattered it with his booted foot. It had been her great-grandmother's. A piece that should have been in a museum.

Not bothering to survey the damage, Eric strode to the dining room table and reached for the bottle of bourbon at one end. With unsteady hands he held up a tumbler and splashed in a good two-fingers' worth, then doubled it for good measure. Lifting his glass to the light, he swirled the contents and then downed it all in two swallows.

"To you, Hayward," he growled. "And to spectacular failure."

Her courage gone, Alison turned to slip away but her toe caught the door frame. Eric spun around, his eyes glittering.

"Where the hell have you been?" he growled,

slamming his delicate glass onto the table. The tumbler shattered within his hand. The alcohol had to sting, but he didn't look down at the blood dripping from his fist. *"Where have you been?"* he repeated.

I can do this. I can do this. Alison stood a little straighter. "You know I went to visit Mandy this afternoon."

"Hoping to see good old Seth, I'll bet." Eric looked at her through slitted eyes. "But he was at the sale. I'm sure that just broke your heart."

"I *never* go to see him."

Eric's gaze shifted back to her trembling hands and his voice turned to silk. "Then why the hell do you look so guilty?"

She took a steadying breath and willed her heartbeat to slow. "I have a right to see my daughter. I miss her terribly. If you keep trying to interfere, I'll leave you."

"Right. And I'm the Prince of Montana." Eric glanced at the small cuts on his fingers, then closed his bloodied fingers around the neck of the bottle at his side. "You don't know how to do a damn thing on your own. Where the hell would you go?"

"I—I don't know. School, maybe."

"I know what's going on." He stood straighter and started across the floor toward her, and Alison fought the urge to spin around and flee.

"You think Seth will take you back. Well, I've got news for you." Eric gave her a satisfied smile. "He's gonna be out of business in no time, and he won't have two nickels to his name. And I'm gonna make it happen."

Alison eyed the bottle, then her gaze flew to meet Eric's. She moved back a step. "He loves Kate, not me."

Eric snorted in derision. "She hasn't been here that long."

"Maybe they fell in love at first sight."

Eric dropped the bottle to the floor, ignoring the shattering glass and the spray of bourbon against his slacks. When she turned to leave, he caught her arm in a viselike grip.

"Don't ever argue with me, sugar," he said softly. "And don't think you're ever gonna leave."

The moment he released her, she whirled around and raced for the stairs. At the top landing she paused and stared down at him. He hadn't moved.

"A locked door won't keep me out of *any* place I want to be, sugar," he called out softly. "But I don't want you right now. Believe it or not, you've just given me a damn good idea."

With a harsh laugh, he stepped over the broken glass and headed for his study.

THE NEXT WEEK FLEW PAST. The temperature hit fifty, and the frozen ground turned to nearly impassable mud. Then the cold returned, three inches of snow fell, and the corrals near the barns turned into a morass—typical mid-March weather.

Seth leaned against the tailgate of his pickup, watching Kate's Mustang zip up the long lane toward the house. She pulled up next to his truck and climbed out, then started toward him, her stride relaxed and a smile lighting up her face. The breeze blew her hair across her eyes. She scooped it back behind her ear with one hand. In the other, she carried a sheaf of papers.

"Hi, there, cowboy," she called out.

Over the past week he'd found a lot of excuses to stay clear of her. Hauling hay. Fixing fence. Riding through the distant herds. If Kate thought he was avoiding her, she didn't comment.

"Here's your mail," she said, handing him the stack in her arms. "I was going past the box, so I saved Della a trip."

"Thanks." He thumbed through the stack. Bills... bills...a few magazines, and...oh, damn. The Salt Creek Guaranty Bank.

"You don't look too happy," she ventured. "Anything wrong?"

He shrugged.

She leaned against the tailgate next to him, shoulder to shoulder. "I picked up the cylinder adapter you needed."

"Thanks. Did you put it on the ranch account?"

Kate nodded. Then she playfully leaned into him, bumping his arm. "What's up? I thought we were supposed to be partners, but you've been nearly invisible all week. I had to beg the boys to let me tag along so I wouldn't go stir-crazy around here."

He had to chuckle at that. Without intending to, he slid an arm around her waist and pulled her close. At the delicate scent of lemon in her hair, he fought the urge to draw her closer yet. "Freckles has a mile-high crush on you, from what I hear. Even Cal admits that you've been a lot of help."

She relaxed against him. Despite the thickness of their jackets, he could feel her warmth and her soft curves. Every sensation of the touch and taste and heat of their last kiss came back, swamping his senses. He stifled a groan and started to pull away.

Apparently oblivious, she snuggled closer and shivered, then reached forward and tapped the edge of the bank envelope in his hand. "Is this the note on Bob's medical expenses?"

"Uh…yeah."

"How soon is it due?" She looked up at him. "Will you need to sell more cattle?"

The words floated past him. He leaned closer, fascinated by the warm depths of those eyes, the softness of her mouth. Her breathing grew shallow. Her eyes widened.

"Hey, Boss!"

Cal stood by a corral, idly slapping a lariat against his leg. "Do you want me to go on out to the north pasture alone?" he hollered.

"Hold on." Seth looked down at Kate and willed his pulse to slow. "I don't know what's going on here, but it's getting a whole lot harder to keep my distance, Kate."

"We need to talk," she murmured.

He handed back the stack of mail, then turned away and headed for the barn. He needed something, but it sure wasn't that.

Talking was the last thing on his mind.

KATE WATCHED HIM STRIDE away, tall and broad and powerful, with a masculine confidence that called out to every hormone she possessed.

Whenever he came close to her, a blind need seemed to overtake every last ounce of common sense she possessed. His scent, the low, testosterone-laden sound of his voice swept through her and suddenly nothing else mattered. Not her life back in Minneapolis, not the goals she'd set before coming to the Lone Tree.

She shook her head and looked down at the sealed bank envelope in her hands. Painful thoughts about the years she'd lost, when she hadn't tried harder to establish contact with her grandfather entered her mind. His last days, when she should have been here with him.

An idea began to form. Maybe there was something she could do—a way to make some peace with the past. After a quick glance at her watch, she dashed up to the house, left the mail on the kitchen table and headed back to her car.

With luck, she could make it to Folsum and back to the Salt Creek bank by five o'clock.

"SHE *WHAT?*" SETH EXPLODED, pacing to the end of the telephone cord. "When?"

"Er…a half hour ago, Mr. Hayward. Came right in with the money and asked to see a loan officer."

Seth gritted his teeth. "It wasn't her damn loan."

After a brief hesitation, the bank officer continued. "It isn't something we would question, really. No one comes in and pays off other people's notes for them without having a vested interest in the business involved. The loan was due, and since Ms. Rawlins is out at the ranch we assumed...'' His voice trailed off delicately. ''Well, I'm sure you must understand.''

''I do now. Thanks.''

Seth hung up, then spun around and stalked to the back door, grabbed a coat and headed for the calving shed. He'd called to double-check the last possible payment date and had learned that Kate had gone to Salt Creek to pay off the loan. It made no sense. Judging from the clothes she wore and the ancient car she drove, she didn't appear to have much money. Certainly not anything close to the amount of the loan.

As soon as she walked into the barn, he confronted her. ''Where've you been?''

Startled, she pulled to a stop. ''I went to town.''

''And did what?''

''It isn't any of your—'' She stopped, caught herself and ventured a wary smile. ''I had business to take care of.''

''Which was...''

''Banking.''

''Because...''

''It needed to be done?''

''Why, Kate?''

She glared at him. ''In a few months we'll be legal partners. I chose to do something to help out.''

''It wasn't your responsibility.''

''Exactly how were you going to pay the loan off? Sell more breeding stock? Ship cattle that aren't ready?''

Seth stared back at her, a hollow sense of failure spreading through him. If the ranch was doing better...if the calves had been on different feed ratios last fall...

"I'm sorry," she said softly. "I never meant it that way. You're a good rancher and no one could work harder."

"I would have paid it on time. That debt was incurred long before you came out here. It had nothing to do with you."

"But it did, Seth." She lifted her chin in defiance. "I had something I didn't need, and used it to make peace with the past. I'm happy I did it. Let's leave it at that."

"I want to know how you got the money."

"Before my mom died she gave me an emerald brooch that had been in her family. She felt I should have it."

He stared blankly at her. "You sold a family heirloom?"

"Neither of us ever dared wear it. Mom always said it was an insurance policy against hard times."

"But you sold it to pay the note?"

"It seemed right." Moisture glimmered in her eyes. "Maybe if Bob and my mom had tried harder, we could have been a family. Maybe I could have changed things if I'd come out here sooner."

"So you gave up the brooch..."

"To pay off his last medical bills."

"When I get the money, you'll get back every nickel."

She shook her head. "No. I never got to know my grandfather. I wasn't even with him when he died, but now I feel as though I did something for him.

Allow me that much.'' She pivoted on her heel and headed for the house.

He watched until she disappeared through the door. It was past time to check the heavies in the lower meadow. Three calves were due for penicillin. But when he got back to the house, he and Kate were going to talk. He would find a way to pay her back.

THE PHONE WAS RINGING when Kate stepped into the house. She let it ring three times, hoping someone else would answer, then picked it up.

''I…I can't call the sheriff. The whole town would know….'' Alison's voice sounded fragile. Frightened.

''*What?*''

After a long silence, Alison continued. ''I tried talking to him the night of the J-Bar sale, but he got really angry. Now he's drunk, and I know he can get through this bedroom door. I'm scared, Kate.''

''Call the sheriff.''

''*No.*''

''Did he hit you? Has he threatened you in any way?'' The long silence said more than mere words. ''The sheriff can get there faster than I can. He can arrest Eric.''

''No! Everyone would find out. What would that do to Mandy? And Eric…I'm terrified of what he might do afterward. Please, just come.''

''This isn't smart, Alison.''

''Please!''

''Then I'll bring Seth.''

''No!''

Kate hesitated. "I'm on my way. But if he starts breaking down that door, promise you'll call 911."

Alison sniffled. "Yes."

After writing down the directions to Alison's place, Kate hesitated, then dashed up to her room to collect her Beretta and shoulder holster, then put on a bulky V-neck cardigan sweater and donned her heavy jacket again. With luck she wouldn't need to use her weapon, but Eric might need some convincing. Within minutes she slipped out of the house.

Seth was apparently still in the barn, and no one else was in sight. With a sigh of relief, Kate jogged to her car and took off. It was easier not having to explain her abrupt departure, though there might be plenty of questions when she got back.

Eric and Alison's sprawling home nestled in a grove of trees at the end of a long private lane just outside Folsum. Worth a half million, Kate judged, and easily the most pretentious home in town. Eric wouldn't have settled for less.

He met her at the double oak doors in front. "Changed your mind about our deal?" he asked, his words only slightly slurred. He gave her a satisfied smile. "Figured you would."

Kate let him usher her in. "Beautiful home," she murmured, glancing around the spacious entryway. "Is Alison home?"

"Asleep," he said nonchalantly, motioning toward the formal living room to the left. "Want a drink?"

"Maybe later." Kate purposely walked past the wide opening into the living room and scanned the rooms opening off the central foyer. Living room, dining, a large family room and kitchen beyond...the bedrooms were all upstairs, probably. "On second thought, I'd like whatever you're having...but on the rocks. With fresh lime, if you have it?"

Looking faintly disgruntled at her specific request, Eric headed for the wet bar she'd seen in the family room.

Kate spun on her heel and headed for the open staircase that curved up from the foyer. She took the stairs two at a time, then quickly searched the bedrooms. Four doors were open, revealing tasteful decor straight out of *House Beautiful*. A fifth led to a spacious bathroom with an immense Jacuzzi. The sixth door was locked.

"Alison?" Kate rapped lightly on the door. "Are you okay?"

After a moment of silence, soft footsteps approached the other side of the door. "Kate?"

"Open up. Eric will be here any minute."

Alison unlocked the door and opened it wide, her head lowered. "I want to leave," she whispered. "Can you help me?"

"That's why I came." Kate reached out and gently lifted her chin, then sucked in a breath at the dark red bruising across the woman's cheek. "We should report this."

Alarm flared in Alison's eyes. "No!"

"But—"

"His lawyer would have him released in no time. What then?"

"Kate, where the hell did you go?" Eric's voice bellowed up from the main floor.

Kate went back to the top of the stairs and hung over the rail. "I just went to find a bathroom. I'll be right down." She turned back to Alison. "Get your things together and be down in five minutes. I'll talk to him a few minutes about the ranch, and then maybe we can leave quietly without a scene. But whatever it takes, you will still be going tonight. Okay?"

"He's a different man when he's been drinking. Will you be okay?" Alison paled. "Did...did you bring a *gun?*"

Thankful for the bulky cardigan that concealed her shoulder holster, Kate shook her head. The less Alison knew, the better. If she frantically announced that Kate was armed, all hell could break loose.

Downstairs, Kate accepted the tumbler Eric offered and took a small sip, then set it down on a table in the foyer. "I really haven't decided what to do yet," she murmured. "But I'm curious. Why are you so interested in this particular piece of property? You don't own adjoining land, and in this part of the country a rancher would need far more than my share of the ranch to stay solvent."

Eric's eyes glittered. "Call it...personal."

Kate waited, silently encouraging him to continue.

At a sound behind them, he frowned and looked over his shoulder. Alison stood at the door, a coat slung over her arm and a suitcase at her feet. Car keys dangled from her hand, gleaming beneath the light of the heavy crystal chandelier hanging over the foyer. The bright light revealed the large reddened area on her cheek even more clearly.

"Where the hell do you think you're going?" Eric

glanced from Alison to Kate. "Is this why you came?" he demanded. "Did she tell you some half-cocked story?"

"I'm leaving, Eric. I should have gone long ago."

"The hell you are." Eric started across the foyer, but Kate stepped into his path. He halted and gave her a wary look.

"I know you've had a few," she said. "Don't do anything you'll regret. Lay a hand on either of us and you'll be arrested and charged before the night is over. I'll make *sure* those charges aren't dropped. The sheriff will arrive if I don't call him from town in the next fifteen minutes. He may even be suspicious enough to come, anyway."

Eric cursed, a malevolent gleam in his eyes. "You're tangling with the wrong guy, sugar."

"Oh, but I'm not," Kate said quietly, motioning Alison out the door. "I know quite a bit about you, more than most folks around here. The tax-evasion charges back in '95, that furnace-repair company in Billings…"

"I was a part-owner. I had nothing to do with what happened," he growled, his hands clenched at his side.

"The company bilked thousands out of elderly people, Eric. If you didn't know, you should have. Your lawyers deserved a bonus when they kept you clean on that one. What about the people who are currently investing in your property deals—do they know about your past? Does Alison know?"

He gave the door a furtive glance.

"What surprises me is that you've been able to

keep your past such a secret. Or is that a product of good connections and old money?'' Kate fingered the car keys in her pocket, then backed toward the door. ''Do yourself a favor and get some help, Eric. I don't know everything that's going on here, but I get the feeling that you need to work through a lot of problems.''

Outside, Kate found Alison sitting behind the wheel of her car, its motor purring and lights illuminating the curving drive leading out to the highway, its doors carefully locked.

Tears shone in her eyes as she rolled down the windows at Kate's approach. ''Thanks,'' she said. ''I wouldn't have dared leave without you here.'' She hesitated, then added in a low voice, ''Did you really tell the sheriff about Eric and me?''

''I told him that I had to talk some business with Eric, and that Eric had seemed threatening the last time he and I spoke. Yes, the sheriff will be coming out if I don't get into town and call him from a pay phone in the next few minutes. But no, he doesn't know how Eric has treated you.''

''Thank you,'' Alison breathed.

''I disagree with you on that score, though. The authorities should be aware. Are you coming out to the ranch?''

Alison stared at the steering wheel for a long moment, then shook her head. ''My parents sheltered me from everything. I married too young, then jumped right into a second marriage. It's time I learned to stand on my own feet.''

''Can you go to your parents' place?''

"They moved to California after Dad retired, and I need to be close enough to see Mandy. I have a cousin in Billings who's married to a lawyer. Maybe I'll go visit her for a few days and figure out what to do next."

Kate offered a hand, and Alison shook it. "Keep in close touch with your daughter. She misses you very much."

"I will." Alison reached into her purse and withdrew a small envelope. "Can you give this to Seth? There's a note inside for him, and one for Mandy. I'll call her in a few days, when I know a little more. Thanks for coming, Kate. I owe you."

Kate smiled, then stiffened as a wave of uneasiness slid down her spine. Years of law enforcement had taught her to trust her intuition. She watched as Alison drove off, then turned slowly, scanning the darkness. Finally she shifted her gaze to the house, knowing what she would see.

He was silhouetted at the living room window, a dark, rigid figure with his hands held stiffly at his sides. He'd disliked her before, and she didn't need to see his expression to know that his feelings had escalated to sheer hatred.

Alison wasn't the only one in danger now.

SETH WAS STANDING just inside the back door when Kate quietly slipped in after midnight. The sight of a dark figure looming over her, silhouetted against the dim light, sent her heart into momentary overdrive.

"Where have you been?" he demanded, glancing at the clock above the stove. "When I came in, I figured you'd gone to bed, but then I looked out and your car was gone.''

''I didn't know there was a curfew,'' she shot back, pulling off her boots and lining them up next to the door. ''Or is it that I failed to punch out?''

He blinked.

''Forgive me.'' She hung up her coat. ''It's been a long night.''

''I was worried about you.''

He reached out to rub the back of her neck. She leaned into his touch, savoring the gentle massage.

He followed her into the living room, guiding her to the sofa before she could head for a chair, then he sat down next to her and draped a hand over the upholstery behind her.

Her first impulse was to move away to safer territory, but feeling his warm strength next to her, with his faint masculine scents of leather and aftershave teasing her senses, felt like heaven. With a sigh she leaned her head against his shoulder and watched the embers pulse in the fireplace.

But the moment of sheer pleasure wouldn't last much longer, because he probably wouldn't like what she had to say. ''Alison just left her husband.''

''What?''

''I tried to talk to you earlier, but you didn't want to discuss it.''

''That's where you were?'' He lifted his arm away from Kate's shoulders and looked down at her. ''At Eric's?''

''Not because I wanted to do business with him,''

she said quickly. "Alison called and asked me to help her leave."

Seth launched to his feet and strode to the fireplace, then turned back. Silhouetted against the fire, he looked powerful, resolute. Impossibly masculine.

"So she's ditched another husband. Hell of an example for her daughter," he growled. "I suppose she has a third guy in mind?" Pain and anger reverberated in his voice, his stance. "Maybe someday she'll find someone good enough."

"She needed my help because she was afraid of him, Seth."

Seth stared at her. "He...*abused* her?"

"I think that marriage was probably a mistake from the first day," Kate said carefully. "She was afraid that he wouldn't let her go out the door."

"My God, she could have come to me for help!"

Kate shrugged and turned her hands over, palms up. "And admit to a second failure at marriage, especially to you?"

"She's my daughter's mother," Seth exploded. "Whatever my personal feelings, I would have done anything to help her if she was in trouble."

Kate felt icy fingers slip around her heart. Alison was now free, Seth available...and they both shared a deep love for their daughter. After a long pause, she gathered her courage. "Do you still love her?"

"No. We both knew our marriage was a mistake, but I never expected her to walk out on her baby. What kind of woman could do that?"

Kate reached out a hand, encouraging him to sit down again, but he turned back toward the fireplace.

"Did you ever ask her? Did you ever talk all of this through?"

"She hated the isolation of the ranch, and I couldn't imagine living anywhere else. Hell, she'd moved in with Eric before I even knew she'd left, and she married him the moment our divorce was final. Sort of a moot point, don't you think?"

"She's been paying for her mistake ever since," Kate said quietly. "Her life has been miserable, and it took a lot of courage for her to leave him."

Seth spun around. "*Mandy?* Did he ever touch my daughter?"

The rage and fear in his eyes nearly took Kate's breath away. "No, never. Alison never let Mandy out of her sight when she was visiting."

Drawing in a ragged breath, Seth closed his eyes. "If that bastard ever laid a hand on Mandy, I'll tear him apart."

Kate stood and moved across the room to stand behind him. Leaning her head against his back, she wrapped her arms around his waist. "Alison's planning to stay with a cousin and perhaps go back to school. Mandy will never have to be around Eric again." She waited a moment, then murmured, "Someday you and Alison need to talk about what happened between you."

"You helped her leave?" Seth folded his hands over Kate's.

"She refused to call the sheriff, because she was afraid Mandy would be hurt if word got out. You know how school kids are."

"Thank you, Kate."

She felt his words vibrate against her cheek. Inhaling his masculine scent, feeling the powerful curve of his back against her cheek, she ached for more than this embrace of friendship.

He turned within her arms and looked down at her, his eyes deep with vulnerability and hidden pain. Something else flickered in the depths. "I want you," he murmured. "I know it's wrong, but I do."

"And I—"

From somewhere behind them came the whisper of fabric. A muffled sob. They both lifted their heads and looked.

"You only wanted my dad," Mandy cried, her voice wavering. "I thought you were my friend, but now you've made my mom go away." Her voice broke on another sob, then rose. "I hate you!" She whirled around and ran up the stairs.

Kate stepped away from Seth and started after her, but he gently caught her arm. "No, don't. I'll take care of her."

"I'm sorry," she whispered. "I didn't realize Mandy was awake." Reaching into her back pocket, she withdrew Alison's envelope and handed it to him. "I hope this will help."

An hour later Kate still sat in front of the fireplace, thinking.

Seth would help Mandy understand. Life would go on, bridges could be mended. But Kate now saw what she had missed before: her feelings for Seth had gone far beyond mere friendship or physical desire. She'd left her heart wide open and hadn't considered the cost.

Whether or not he could ever love her, a relationship with him meant becoming a guiding force in Mandy's life as well. Stepparenting a child who wanted her real mom back. Alison may not be a perfect mother, but she was the only woman Mandy would accept in her father's life.

It was time for Kate to start thinking about returning to Minneapolis, where she could lose herself in her career once again.

CHAPTER THIRTEEN

KATE WAS STILL STARING at the last dim embers in the fireplace when quiet footsteps eased down the stairs. Seth crossed the room silently in stocking feet, with a crooked smile and a look of exhaustion in his eyes. Mandy shuffled along at his side, her eyes downcast.

"I read Alison's letters, and then let Mandy see the one addressed to her," he said in a low tone. "She won't go to sleep until she talks to you."

Releasing her dad's hand, Mandy lifted her tear-streaked face and took a faltering step forward, then launched herself into Kate's arms. "I'm sorry I was so mean," she murmured against Kate's cheek. "Dad always says we shouldn't go to bed mad at someone, because then they'll have bad dreams. Thank you for helping my mom."

"You're the sweetest little girl I know." Kate hugged her back fiercely, then gave her a kiss on her forehead. "Your mom and dad are very proud of you."

Mandy shuddered. "I'm just glad she won't be with that Eric anymore. He was such a creep."

Kate met Seth's gaze over Mandy's shoulder as she chose her next words. "Why didn't you like him?"

Her lower lips trembling, Mandy shook her head slowly. "I never, ever liked him. He was always yelling at my mom, and he made her cry. And he didn't like me, either."

"How do you know?" Kate lifted a gentle hand to brush Mandy's tousled hair out of her eyes. "Did he ever do anything or say anything bad to you?"

Mandy gave her a mystified look, then blushed furiously and averted her eyes. "No! We learn about *that* stuff in school every year. Eric wouldn't even talk to me when I was there."

"But you wouldn't ever be afraid to tell your dad if anyone ever did anything to hurt you, right?" Kate kept her voice low and quiet, and gave the child an encouraging smile. "Because he's a big, strong man, and wouldn't be afraid of anyone. And next to him would be the sheriff and his deputies, and all of your relatives and friends, wanting to keep you safe. Understand?"

Mandy nodded, while behind her the tension in Seth's face visibly eased. "Time to get back to bed, honey," he said, catching one of her hands in his own and then sweeping her into a bear hug.

Ten minutes later, Seth came downstairs. "I stayed until she fell asleep," he said quietly, settling onto the sofa next to Kate. He lifted a hand to touch her hair, then tucked a strand behind her ear. "We'd both like to thank you for what you've done for Alison."

His warm breath tickled her ear. Moving closer, he curved a muscled arm around her shoulders and drew her closer, until her back was firmly wedged against his chest. "I'm just not sure how."

Startled into a laugh, Kate twisted in his arms and looked up at him: the strong, lean jaw, the firm mouth, the deep chocolate eyes that had gone heavy-lidded and hazy with sensual promise. "You're not sure how…to do what?"

He nibbled on her ear, then trailed kisses down the side of her throat, sending delicious shivers tripping down her spine. "I could thank you like this."

He gently lifted her chin and looked deep into her eyes. "Or maybe like this…" He kissed her forehead, then the tip of her nose.

"But I think this would be best."

His mouth settled on hers, a potent combination of tenderness and passion, and she shivered with antic-ipation as his hands drifted lazily over her shoulders, down her ribs, and then back up again, his thumbs grazing the sides of her breasts.

Whatever reservations she'd had moments earlier were swept away, leaving her vulnerable and aching with need. When his hand brushed against her nipple, she arched into his touch, wanting more. And when his mouth moved over hers, possessive and hot, she answered with her heart.

But somewhere in the higher reaches of her con-sciousness a warning bell sounded. Her eyes flew open and met equal consternation in his gaze. "Della?" she whispered.

Flashing a lethal smile, he slid his arms under her thighs and behind her back, lifting her as easily as he might have lifted his daughter. Kate wrapped her arms around his neck and kissed his throat, tasting his skin and breathing in the elemental scents that were Seth's alone.

In a heartbeat they were in his room upstairs with the door locked. He released her slowly, letting her regain her equilibrium as she touched the floor.

"I've wanted you for longer than I can remember." His eyes twinkled. "Of course, at this point I'm not remembering much of anything."

"Thanks. I think," she said dryly, locking her hands behind his hips. Even through the heavy fabric of their jeans she could feel the heat of his arousal.

He sank his hands into her hair and kissed her again, deepening the kiss until her bones started to melt. "Tell me you want this," he whispered against her mouth.

If she could have answered, she would have. Breathless, her heart doing ninety in a forty-five, she could only sink back into him and kiss him back with everything that was in her soul.

Anything that felt this good had to be a crime, and a life sentence would be too wonderful to even imagine.

As if he could read her thoughts, he released her and began unbuttoning his shirt. Entranced, she watched as it opened all too slowly, revealing an expanse of hard muscled chest and a flat belly, the light bronze of his flesh and silky dark hair a beautiful expression of his mixed heritage.

The sight of him, tall and masculine, methodically undressing in front of her with his unwavering, wicked gaze fastened on hers, took her breath away. When he stood before her, magnificently naked and fully aroused, she nearly wept at the impact he had on her senses.

She raised a shaking hand to her own nondescript sweatshirt. Embarrassment washed through her at how she must look to him, but he gave her a heart-breakingly tender smile.

"Let me," he said softly. "Please."

His hands skimmed over her, then deftly whisked away her clothing until only the cool night air was between them.

She shivered. Whether from the cold or sensory overload she couldn't have said.

His eyes gleamed with predatory hunger as he swept her into an embrace. In a dizzying motion he lifted her and swung around. She was suddenly lying on the soft blankets of his bed with him looming over her, his forearms braced at either side of her head.

That wicked grin flashed once more, and then he dropped lower to leave a chain of kisses down her throat, her breasts. When he took her in his mouth, sensations rocketed through her. Wrapping her legs around his hips, she silently begged him for what she needed more than her next breath.

He reached for a bedside drawer, never taking his eyes away from hers.

"Look at me," he said softly, when he was ready. "Think about all the things you've ever wanted to experience, all the fantasies you've ever had. I'm here to make them happen, so that you'll never even imagine being with anyone else."

He entered her carefully, gently, as though he were afraid she might break. But when he began to move, that gentleness gave way to white-hot desire that consumed them both, and swept her into an avalanche of need and sensation and fulfillment that rocked her very soul.

THE SUNLIGHT STREAMING through the loose-woven curtains warmed her face. Kate stretched luxuriously, feeling satisfied and complete and…a little sore. With a start, she sat up and blinked at her surroundings. *Seth's* room. And she was alone.

Embarrassment slithered through her. Had she really been here last night? Wanton and reckless, stroking him, responding like a wild woman, begging him for more? She glanced furtively at the bedside clock and groaned. It was after eight. Mandy would be up watching Saturday cartoons or riding her horse by now. Seth would be long gone. With luck, her own bedroom door was shut, concealing the fact that she hadn't so much as touched her own bed last night.

She'd done a considerable amount of touching in Seth's bed, though. A whole lot. Just the thought made her skin heat and her toes curl.

Slipping out of bed, she searched the floor for her clothes. Her panties hung from the bedpost. Her bra dangled from the back of a chair. And her jeans…were here someplace.

Thank goodness the door to Seth's room was closed tight. Shutting her eyes, she breathed a prayer of thanks, imagining how this scene would look to Della.

Where she and Seth would go from here she couldn't begin to imagine. Last night had been an aberration, a moment of weakness to which they'd both succumbed. But the house wasn't that large and they weren't alone. And if they hadn't already been caught, it wouldn't take long.

Kate picked up her underwear, slipped on her jeans and sweatshirt and started for the door, then turned back to the bed. Lifting his pillow, she held it next to her cheek and wished for things that would never be.

AFTER A LONG, HOT SHOWER and a change of clothes, Kate headed for the kitchen in search of breakfast, and tried to forget last night. She might as well wish for a promotion to precinct inspector by next week. It wasn't going to happen.

Halfway down the stairs she heard an odd, crooning sound. At the bottom of the stairs, she discovered its source. Della sat in a small sewing rocker in the far corner, hunched over her fists as if in pain, but her head wasn't lowered. She was looking up at the wall, where a number of family photographs were displayed, totally unaware of Kate's approach.

"Belonged to me... It all belonged to me," she mumbled. "I gave you everything...." She reached up and reverently touched a photograph of Bob when he might have been in his thirties. "You meant for it to be, I know it...." Her voice trailed off. Tears plopped down on her fists. Her shoulders shook.

Kate drew closer. "Della, are you okay?"

The old woman reared back, her eyes unfocused. Then her gaze narrowed. "You slut," she snarled.

"You think I don't see what goes on here? You think I don't know?"

Kate's heart sank. "Can I get you something? Water or coffee?"

Della rose stiffly to her feet and stood in front of Bob's picture, as if protecting it. "It's all your fault, you know. Lorna thought she was too good for my boy and then she got herself in trouble." A wild light glittered in Della's eyes. "But I took care of it, I did. Then she was gone for good."

Kate stared at her. "Your boy?"

"My Tom. Then everything would have been set to rights."

Tom? A chill slithered down Kate's spine as she recalled the man lurking outside the feed store a few weeks ago. The drunk who had insulted her mother after the school play. *My God—could that man have been my father?*

Blood pounded in her ears. Her skin turned cold and damp. It took all she possessed to manage an encouraging smile. "Why should they have married? What would have been set to rights?"

Della's eyes glittered. "Just get out of my way. Stay away from me, and think hard about packing those bags of yours."

She shoved past Kate and hobbled across the room, leaving Kate standing alone in stunned silence. Who would know the truth? Seth? Doc Anderson? Cal? She lifted her gaze to the photo of her grandfather on the wall, wondering what secrets he'd hidden behind that confident smile. And then she remembered the box of old letters.

Maybe he could still share those secrets with her.

AT THE SOUND OF FOOTSTEPS, Kate looked up from the pile of papers in her lap.

Joanna peeked around the corner. "Are you decent?" With a broad grin, she lugged in two department store sacks and a dry cleaner's bag and dropped them on Kate's bed. "I'm here in my capacity as fairy godmother."

Kate scooted farther toward the pillows on her bed and stared at all of the loot. "What on earth did you do?"

"Mmm…just a little of this, a little of that. Nothing expensive. I hit my favorite secondhand stores when I was in Billings last week. They had a super-special seventy-five-percent-off rack, and practically paid me to take these things off their hands." Joanna kicked the door shut, then crossed her arms and gave Kate a stern look. "I did my part. Now let's see how well I did."

"What is this for?"

With a snort of impatience, Joanna moved to the bed and started burrowing through the sacks. "That annual Rancher's Dinner Dance, remember? You're going and you're going to be beautiful. Uh…not that you aren't, anyway. But packaging is everything, don't you think? Now, tell me what you think of this." She held up a burgundy cocktail dress with a neckline that had to end somewhere below the knees. "Or this?" She lifted a simple black silk sheath with a swirl of rhinestones that drifted over the bodice and then trailed on down to the high slit in back.

She tossed the dresses over the back of a chair, pawed through one of the other sacks, then triumphantly lifted two stiletto high heels, one in burgundy and one glittering with sequins. "Shoes," she offered helpfully. "So which is it, burgundy or black?"

Nearly dizzy, Kate started to refuse, but the impossibly hopeful smile on Joanna's face would have melted a granite heart. "I—I have no idea. And honestly," she added, regaining her sense of balance, "I don't know any of the people who would be there, and I don't have a date, and—"

"Oh, please." Joanna rolled her eyes. "Cal and the boys always go. Seth will be there. He ought to take you, because all the ranchers and their families around here attend. Speaking of men, I saw Eric's vehicle parked on the hill as I drove in. What the heck is he doing out here?"

"I don't have a clue," Kate shuddered. "The man makes my skin crawl."

After a long mutual silence, her gaze dropped to the treasures Joanna had brought. It just wasn't possible to sit there, cross-legged on her bed, and not reach out to touch the silky black dress draped just inches away. The rhinestones glittered. When had she ever bought such a dress? "You think it will fit?" Kate asked finally, her gaze still caught by its simple elegance. "And if it does, wouldn't I still look like I was playing dress-up? I've never worn anything like it."

Joanna gave her a smug smile. "You'll be a smash."

Trying to mask her unexpected eagerness, Kate

slipped out of her jeans and sweatshirt and lifted the dress over her head, then let it shimmer down into place.

Joanna closed the zipper and stood back, one finger tapping at her lips. "Guess not," she murmured.

"What?"

Joanna grinned. "Guess you don't need to try the other one on, after all. Unless you want to. This one looks as if it were made perfectly to measure. Go look in the mirror. Am I good or what?"

Kate started for the mirror, then turned back for the high heels and slipped them on. After weeks in cowboy boots the shoes felt strange, but she tottered carefully over to the full-length mirror on the closet door and looked.

The woman in the mirror wasn't Kate Rawlins, levelheaded Minneapolis police officer. She looked sinful, slender and entirely too wicked for her own good. "Oh, my..."

"Here, try the earrings."

The matching waterfalls of rhinestones made her look like a million dollars. And when Joanna reached up, grabbed Kate's hair and twisted it artfully on top of her head, the total picture was amazing.

"That isn't me," Kate breathed.

"It has *always* been you. You just haven't taken the time to use what you've got."

From somewhere downstairs a door slammed. Joanna listened for a minute, then shoved some bobby pins in Kate's hair to hold it in place. "Hold on," she ordered as she strode out of the bedroom.

Maybe it wouldn't be so bad to be dressed up like

this, just once. To feel like someone straight off the cover of *Cosmo*. It would be almost like going undercover, she realized with amusement. The guys back at the station would never recognize her.

From downstairs came a tumult of voices, then footsteps thundered up the stairs.

"We needed a second opinion," Joanna said, her eyes twinkling. "He's the only person I could find."

She stepped aside and Seth appeared in the doorway. "Joanna says you aren't feeling well?"

Joanna smiled. "I lied."

He pulled to a halt. Swallowed.

Looking up at him in the mirror's reflection, Kate managed a smile. "What do you think?" she asked, smoothing her hands over her hips.

The dress felt light as air. It clung to her like a coat of black satin paint, following every curve from her breasts to her mid-thighs. A corner of his mouth tipped upward. "I think that dress must be illegal."

"Looks pretty hot to me," Joanna said blithely. "I'm finding her a date for that Rancher's event coming up. What do you think, will the dress work?"

"She won't need a date."

"Of course she will," Joanna retorted.

Seth gave her an annoyed look. "Will you excuse us?"

"Whatever. Kate, I've got to get going. Nicki's dance class will be over in forty-five minutes. Let me know what you decide about the dresses, okay?" Joanna wiggled her fingers at both of them, then left.

Seth waited until her footsteps reached the bottom of the stairs before shutting the door. "You're looking for a date?'' he asked, his voice a low rumble in his chest.

"Uh...well, not exactly..."

He moved a step closer. Then another, until he was standing just an inch away from her, looking down into her eyes. Self-conscious, Kate took a wobbly step backward and reached for the back of a chair.

"Tell me your requirements. Tall? Short?" He trailed a hand from the base of her neck down her spine, then cupped her bottom and pulled her close. "Bald? Glasses?"

His warm breath sent tingles through her skin. She looped her arms around his neck and pulled him closer, until his mouth was moving over hers and last night came back to her in a kaleidoscope of images.

He pulled back and smiled at her. "Very, very nice, Kate."

The heat of a blush rose in her cheeks. She looked away, but he gently caught her chin with his fingertip and tipped it back, giving her a swift kiss. "Mandy's downstairs. I need to go."

She nodded, unable to speak.

As he turned away he glanced at the sacks on her bed, then at the stack of papers on the pillow. "What's up?"

Her ankles gave away and she wobbled on the blasted high heels. She scooped them off her feet and tossed them up on the bed. "Just looking at old letters. I've been reading a few of them each day."

"Letters?"

She eyed him uncertainly, unsure of how much to say, then threw caution to the wind. "When Mandy needed a costume we searched through a storeroom in the barn. I found a trunk that belonged to my mother. Did you ever see it?''

Seth sat on the edge of her bed and thought for a moment, then shook his head.

After a brief hesitation, Kate pushed Joanna's clothing sacks to the middle of the bed and sat down as well. At the sudden gleam in Seth's eyes she looked down. Stood abruptly and tugged her skirt down, then tried again. If the hem was any shorter, the dress would have revealed the color of her panties.

Seth grinned at her. "Great dress."

"What there is of it," she muttered.

His gaze dropped to her breasts. "*Really* great."

Looking down, she saw that the dress clung like a second skin, perfectly outlining her nipples. With a groan she reached behind him, grabbed her sweatshirt and pulled it down over her head. "It isn't something I'll wear again, believe me."

He sighed with disappointment. "You were telling me about the trunk?"

"Mostly filled with old clothes and mementos— my mother's prom dress, an old corsage. Plus a box filled with letters. Did you know that Bob wrote to my mom and me for years?"

"I knew he wrote now and then," Seth said slowly. "But I didn't know how often. Why?"

"My mother refused every last letter, as far as I can tell, and yet he still kept writing." Kate took a deep breath. "Some of the envelopes were stamped Return to Sender, but my mother wrote Refused on most of them."

Seth's mouth thinned. "He said they had quite an argument the night she ran off."

"She would never tell me what happened."

"Bob said that she went crazy and accused him of murdering her boyfriend."

Kate's mouth fell open. "Bob *murdered* someone?"

"Of course not. But he couldn't talk any sense into her. They argued and she left like a bat out of hell. He told me he was angry enough that he just let her go, and that it was the biggest mistake of his life."

Kate looked down at her hands. "Isn't it strange, how one night can change everything? From what little my mom said, I always blamed my grandfather. Now I know I was wrong."

Seth slid closer and pulled her into his lap. "Still, there were two sides."

"And far too much stubborn pride and anger. But after reading some of those letters, I guess I feel more sympathy for both of them than anything else. A misunderstanding led to a lifetime of anger. What a loss to both of them."

Seth's silence encouraged her to go on.

"I've always wondered about my father—about who he could be. Since coming out here, I've been more than a little worried about some of the possibilities!"

"Did you find any clues in those letters?" He nibbled gently at her ear, sending delicious shivers clear down to her toes.

She leaned into him, wanting more. "All I know is that my mom was seventeen when she got pregnant.

My grandfather was furious and sent her out east to have her baby. She would never say more than that.''

"Your father had to be a fine man to have a daughter like you, Kate. He would have been very proud of you." Seth dropped a kiss on her mouth, glanced down at her lap, and then looked up with the very devil in his eyes. "*Purple?* With *pink stars?*"

Her dress had hitched up beyond all claim to propriety, but suddenly she didn't care. Feeling more free than she'd ever been in her life, Kate bit back a laugh.

"Lock that door, cowboy, and we won't stop at the stars. This time, I'd like to try for heaven."

CHAPTER FOURTEEN

A WEEK LATER, KATE tightened the cinch on Rowdy's saddle, then gave him a quick pat on the neck. Riding almost daily had given her confidence on horseback that she'd never expected to gain in such a short time. Mostly due to Rowdy, who'd turned out to be more of a baby-sitter than a bronc.

Holding Mandy's horse by the reins, Cal's face contorted as he slid his chew to the other cheek and spat. "Gettin' along okay over there?"

Kate laughed. "I think you guys could put a two year old on this old boy and never have to think twice." She swung up into the saddle.

"You know where to go?"

"Southwest corner of the upper meadow, through the gates, then up on the ridge to the south. A hundred head of mother cows, all with calves, right?"

"Yep." Cal whistled old Belle to his side. "Just count and check through 'em. Any sign o' trouble and come back for help. Don't try to trail 'em in yourselves."

"We could, you know!" Mandy called out from the back of her gray gelding.

Shaped like an oversize bulldog, Frosty had a broad back and heavily muscled neck. The cowboys swore the old horse was absolutely bombproof; the only sort of mount Seth would entrust with his daughter.

Cal lifted his hat, shoved a hand through his hair, then jammed his hat back down over his head. "You go messing with those cattle, missy, and there'll be hell to pay with your dad. You all set up there?"

Mandy nodded and tapped the cantle bag that curved behind her saddle. "I've got the lunch—sandwiches, chips, cookies and juice. This will be fun!"

Cal waited until Mandy urged her horse into a lazy walk and crossed the barnyard. "You and Seth seem to be gettin' along pretty good," he said, studying the dusty toes of his boots. "Figured out what you're gonna do come July?"

I wish I knew. Over and over she'd been asking herself the same question, and with each passing day the answer became harder. Even though she and Seth had carefully avoided being alone together over the past week, the thought of going back to Minneapolis no longer filled her with a sense of anticipation.

To Cal, she gave a smile and a shrug. "I don't know. It would be awfully hard to leave here."

He tipped his hat back and looked up at her. "Maybe you should stick around."

"And drive you and Freckles crazy?"

"It might be a good thing for the boss, and for Mandy. Not that it's my business." He rubbed a hand at the back of his neck. "I figure we maybe jumped the gun a little. Figured you wrong."

At that she had to grin. "I did get the idea you weren't too happy to see me show up."

"People around these parts are loyal, clean through. We thought a lot of Bob."

"I'll regret till the day I die that I never had a chance to know him."

Cal gave her a piercing look. "Then you'd want to make sure this ranch never gets sold off, piece by piece."

"Like the ranches farther west, to the California crowd?"

"Divided in any way."

She looked at him helplessly. "It would be unfortunate."

Cal turned away and slapped his hand against his thigh, signaling Belle to follow. "When you think about the future, you'll know what's right," he muttered over his shoulder. "Sometimes there's other ways to skin a cat."

"Let's go!" Mandy called from the gate.

Nudging Rowdy into an easy jog, Kate shook out some slack in the reins and headed out. *Other ways.* Surely he couldn't know about her commitment back home, but maybe old Cal was right.

Maybe there was another way to keep her promise to Rico. Perhaps some group, some philanthropist, some company might be willing to help a worthwhile cause.

Lost in thought, Kate settled into her into her saddle and let her spine soften until she floated along with the two-beat cadence of the gelding's easy jog. Now that her muscles and joints no longer resisted Rowdy's gait, she'd discovered that he was smooth as silk.

They'd made it three miles up into rougher country when the saddle abruptly shifted beneath her as Rowdy negotiated a boulder-strewn path.

Before she could even think to grab his mane, she and the saddle slid off his back and onto the jagged rocks below.

SETH LEANED AGAINST the frame of the barn door, his arms folded, and watched Eric saunter toward him with a sheaf of papers in his hand and a self-satisfied smirk on his face.

Wright's aftershave arrived before he did—pungent and cloying, a definite step below the scents of the cattle and horses in nearby corrals. Fighting the urge to turn away and head back into the barn, Seth wondered how he'd managed all these years to rein in the overwhelming desire to knock the guy flat.

"Guess it's time we talked a little business," Eric said, his voice silky.

"We've never had any business to discuss. You must be confusing me with those ranchers you so kindly help when they're on the verge of foreclosure."

Eric bared his teeth in a smile. "You really don't know?" He opened a manila folder in his hand and thumbed through the papers, then withdrew one and laid it on top of the stack. "Taken any spills off a tough bronc lately?"

"Get the hell off this ranch." Seth turned to go back into the barn.

Eric waited a beat, then continued. "Think twice about that attitude."

"Think twice?" Seth spun around and was in Eric's face in a split second. "I've done nothing but 'think twice' since we were kids. If I hadn't, you'd have been face first in the dirt more times than you could count. What the hell is your problem?"

"You." Eric gave him a smug smile. "And now I've got you exactly where I want you."

Seth gave him a disgusted look. "What the hell are you talking about?"

"Kate hasn't said anything at all?" Seth heard the gloating tone in the other man's voice. "She's selling her share of the Lone Tree as soon as she meets the six-month residence requirement. I've made her an offer so generous that she can't refuse. You and I will be partners."

Seth turned slowly around and stared at him. "I don't believe it."

"Guess you two have been too—busy—to talk business, eh?" Clucking his tongue, Eric sifted through the contents of the folder again. "By the way, I did you a favor. I hired an investigator to look into her background, and the results were fascinating. I'll bet she didn't tell you about that shooting incident back in Minneapolis. The reason she came out here?"

He ran a forefinger down the top sheet in his hand. "An innocent teenage boy died. The report says she wasn't responsible, but I suppose it was all a cover-up. She was honest enough to insist it was her fault. Who would guess—a good-looking woman like that with a child's blood on her hands?"

Seth grabbed Eric's shoulder in a viselike grip and pivoted him toward his Bronco. "It's time you left," he said through his teeth. "Before I do something I'll regret later."

Eric scrambled to keep his papers together, then twisted away and looked Seth in the eye. "Kate only wanted her grandfather's legacy so she could fund a scholarship in the dead kid's name. Out of guilt, probably. From the first, she planned to sell out and go back to Minneapolis. Her precinct expects her back by the end of July. Did you think she would stick around? I expect a tough cop like her figured she'd have fun with a cowboy while she was out here."

Chuckling, Eric offered the stapled set of papers. When Seth didn't take them, he reached forward and jammed them in Seth's hands. "This is enough to make a man feel like ten kinds of a fool."

Seth clenched his hands at his sides, crumpling the papers. "Get out of here."

Eric sauntered to his vehicle and opened the door, then paused and looked back. "You can't afford to buy Kate's part of the ranch, but I can. And when I do, I'm going to make your life hell. I owe you, pal."

Anger burned through Seth like a wildfire. The temptation to go after Eric flamed higher when the man gave him yet another self-satisfied smile as he climbed into his Bronco.

Since childhood it had always been like this. A chubby, whiny outsider as a child, Eric had relied on his money and family name for social acceptance, and Seth had avoided him like the plague. In turn, Eric never missed an opportunity to goad and cause trouble for Seth in school, and had refined his tactics as an adult, apparently unable to move beyond his juvenile behavior. Ultimately, he'd contributed to the breakup of Seth and Alison's marriage. But this was his worst blow.

Until this moment the ranch had meant more to Seth then anything except his daughter. Eric's interference could jeopardize the ranch—and Bob's legacy—beyond hope, and losing it all would be a crushing loss.

But news of Kate's betrayal hit Seth like a shotgun blast to the heart.

They'd shared something strong. He'd been sure of it. Mind-numbing desire and unforgettable sex were just a small part of his deepening feelings for her. She was totally unique—strong and in control, yet with an inner tenderness that had touched his heart. He'd started to think in terms of *forever,* unable to imagine life at the ranch without her.

Had their relationship been a diversion while she waited to betray everything that mattered most to him? His heart turning to lead, Seth pivoted and slammed a clenched fist against the weathered siding of the barn.

He didn't feel the pain, even as warm blood dripped down his fingertips.

THE TRIP BACK TO THE RANCH was a whole lot less enjoyable than the departure. The hard soles and high heels of her Western boots couldn't have been worse for negotiating a rocky path. The wind had picked up, raw and penetrating. And Mandy's horse had refused to consider an extra passenger.

"Maybe he'll be better this time," Mandy offered,

patting Frosty on the neck. "He's never bucked before."

Kate eyed the placid old gelding, then shook her head. The gray may be childproof, but he'd clearly set his limits. The moment Kate had climbed up behind Mandy's saddle, the gelding's back bowed. He'd sidestepped, his tail lashing and neck arched high, and had mouthed his bit as though attacking it. The options were clear—get off or fly off. Kate had quickly slid back to the ground. She'd have enough scrapes and bruises from hitting the ground after the billet broke on her saddle.

"I still think you could ride Rowdy bareback. Or I could go bareback, and you could use my saddle," Mandy offered.

"Right. Then either I would fall off or you might." Kate grinned up at her. "Thanks, but I think we're safer this way."

Mandy frowned. "I've never seen a billet break like that."

"Guess I should be more careful about checking my equipment."

"But it was such heavy leather. Doubled, even!"

Maybe it hadn't broken on its own. The billet, which attached the cinch to the saddle on the offside, wasn't on the side she would face while saddling her horse.

After a time, the trail widened and Mandy fell back to ride next to Kate and Rowdy. "Are you…will you and my dad…are you going to stay here for good?"

"The ranch is a wonderful place to be, but…"

"Do you want to stay?"

''What I would like and what I have to do are two different things.''

Mandy looked down at her. ''Do you love my dad?''

Startled, Kate tripped over an uneven spot in the path.

Mandy didn't seem to notice Kate's discomfort. ''I used to pray that my mom and dad would get married again,'' she continued. ''Now I know they wouldn't ever be happy with each other, 'cause my mom told me so in her letter.'' Leaning back in her saddle, Mandy frowned. ''You sure must like being a cop.''

Despite her aching feet, Kate chuckled at the abrupt change of topic. ''My job was my life. Every day was exciting, challenging—and people depended on me to keep them safe. I enjoyed that very much.''

''We depend on you, too. You could stay here.''

At Mandy's earnest expression, Kate's heart turned over. ''I'd love that, but with grown-ups things aren't always that easy. I might look into a change, though. Over the last year or so I've thought about finding something directly involved with teenagers. Kids in trouble.''

''Do you ever talk to my dad? He listens pretty good. Maybe he can help.''

''I've been meaning to talk to him about a lot of things.'' *About what happened in Minneapolis. The funds I need to raise. And how I feel about him. Maybe we can talk tonight.* There were too many secrets, too many problems.

It was time to explain.

They'd reached the top of a knoll. Below, the path

meandered through a long, sweeping meadow, then up and over the next ridge. Kate winced as she stumbled over another rock. She looked up at Rowdy's back. Unless she dared ride him bareback, she would face a long walk home. "Do you think he'd let me get on without the saddle?"

Mandy giggled. "If he doesn't like it, he'll let you know."

She sounds just like her dad, Kate thought, remembering the first time she'd ridden Rowdy. "Thanks a whole lot."

Kate led the gelding up to a rock, gathered the reins in one hand and reached tentatively for a handful of mane. At the last moment, Rowdy neatly pivoted his rear away, leaving an impossible distance between them. Kate led him in a circle and moved him close once again. Again he moved away at the crucial moment, this time leaving Kate flailing her arms in a desperate attempt to keep her balance.

"They all do that," Mandy announced, sidestepping Frosty next to Rowdy and crowding him until he moved back.

Now that he was closer, Kate could grab his mane…throw a leg over his back…and have a nice ride home. Except he looked very, very tall. His back looked slippery. And the ground would be a long way down. "I don't know about this."

"Hurry up," Mandy ordered. "You can't let him think he can get away with anything."

Clenching her teeth, Kate gingerly slid aboard. Rowdy's familiar show of independence faded as soon as she was mounted. After a moment of vertigo, she released her death grip on his mane and managed a smile. "I did it!"

"Bareback is fun. It's a lot warmer, too." With that, Mandy nudged Frosty into a placid walk.

Rowdy fell in behind. Kate wobbled, then forced herself to relax. After a few minutes she found herself moving easily with his motion. His heavy coat felt like warm plush beneath her as his powerful muscles flexed and bunched with every stride. Grinning, she looked over at Mandy. "This is great! I feel sort of like a centaur."

Mandy giggled. "Let's canter!"

"No!" Kate retorted in alarm. "But maybe later…like next year?"

They were still laughing when they arrived at the barn. Kate pulled to a stop by a hitching rail and slid to the ground. She groaned as her knees buckled. Rowdy turned his head around and gave her a patient look.

"I think my legs turn into spaghetti every time I ride you." She laughed, giving the horse a rub behind the ears. "How are you doing, Mandy. Need any help?"

"I'm fine."

Mandy unsaddled her own horse and led him into a small corral next to the barn. Kate followed with Rowdy, and within a minute both horses were blissfully rolling on the ground.

Cal appeared and strode up to them. He no longer looked as friendly as he had before they left. "Cattle okay?" He directed his question at Mandy.

"We never got there! Kate's saddle broke and she fell off, and we ended up coming back."

"You didn't go on out?"

"I was bareback after that," Kate interjected dryly. "All things considered, I feel fortunate to be back here at all."

"We had to leave the saddle up along the trail, 'cause there wasn't a way to keep it on Rowdy's back," Mandy said.

Cal glowered at Kate. "I'll go on out and check the cattle and pick up that saddle," he growled. "Mandy, Freckles wants some help up in the calving barn. I think he's got some new calves for you to feed." He waited until she'd started for the barn, then turned back to Kate, his eyes glittering. "Seth's in his office. He wants to talk to you."

Surprised, Kate watched Cal stomp away. In the space of a few hours the man had changed a hundred-eighty degrees. What on earth could have set him off? Male menopause…gout…Della's cooking…? Shaking her head, Kate hung Rowdy's bridle in the barn and then started for the house.

SETH FELT HER PRESENCE the moment she stepped into the house. The slamming of the back door and the sound of boots dropping to the floor confirmed her arrival. When had he become so attuned, so aware of this woman?

With a curse he launched to his feet and strode away from his desk to the window. He was staring at the landscape when he heard her hesitate at the door, then cross the room in stocking feet to the upholstered club chair in front of his desk.

"Hi," she murmured. "What's up?"

He listened as she settled into the chair, and without turning around knew she'd folded her long, slender legs beneath her and would be resting her chin on the palm of her hand. He gritted his teeth. "Perhaps you can tell me."

"What?"

He rounded on her. "When were you going to tell me, Kate? Now? Maybe later? Or when we all woke up one day and found you gone?"

She stared up him, her face turning pale. "What?"

"Damn, you're good. Did you ever do undercover work and play some part to fool the bad guys?"

"Maybe you'd better explain so we'll both know what this is about."

He moved closer and leaned down to brace his hands on either arm of her chair, his growing hurt and anger driving him on. "Tell me why you came here, and what you planned to do when the six months were up."

"What I wanted before is very different from what I want now." She reached up and held a palm against the side of his cheek. An impossibly gentle touch that hurt more than if she'd hauled off and decked him.

"You know how much your grandfather loved this ranch. How much it means to Mandy and me. Yet you've planned to divide it from the word go."

"I—"

"Why did you bother to pay off that loan? Just to keep your investment safe until you could sell out?"

"No. I've come to care very much about the ranch. And, like I told you, helping with the loan gave me a feeling of connection to my grandfather."

Seth gave a short, humorless laugh. "I've been given reports from a private investigator," he snapped, tipping his head toward the crumpled papers on the desk. "I know about the kid who died, and how you told everyone that you were responsible."

"Y-you had me *investigated?*"

"It's all in that damned report...how you promised the kid's mother funding for some sort of memorial program. Admirable. But what about the future of the ranch? And what about us, Kate? What about being decent enough to tell the truth?"

"I was planning to tell you everything," she said dully.

Seth straightened, wincing as a branding iron of pain found his heart. "I understand your motivation for the money. The ranch never meant anything to you, anyway. But I don't understand how you could sleep with me, as if we mattered. God knows I cared more for you than I ever had a right to. But it was all just a game to you...a time filler, because you never intended to stay. Was sleeping with me part of your plan?"

She came to her feet. Her seductive hands lightly trailed from his cheekbones, to his shoulders and then to his waist. "Please," she said, her voice breaking. "It wasn't like that at all."

Grasping her wrists, he stepped out of her embrace and stalked to the door. "I know you'll be staying until your time is up. But stay the hell out of my way.

And stay away from my daughter. I learned some tough lessons after being married to Alison. Trust and honesty mean everything, and, lady, I don't think you know the meaning of either one.''

''Have you asked for an explanation? Would you even listen to what I had to say?'' She glared at him, then slowly shook her head. ''I guess it wouldn't matter, because you've already made up your mind.'' She turned away from him with a bitter laugh. ''We're two of a kind, you know that? We both value trust, but neither one can give it.''

Her words flowed over him, barely registering in his mind. It had to be damned disappointing to have her little ruse exposed, but she obviously didn't care about the pain she'd be leaving behind.

She might not care, but Seth knew he would never forget.

CHAPTER FIFTEEN

KATE STARED AT THE DOORWAY long after Seth
walked out. She had planned to tell him everything
later tonight. But he would believe that no more than
he would believe that she'd come to care for him
more than life itself.

He was the type of man who would defend and
protect his loved ones with his last breath. And one
who would never forget betrayal.

But why had he hired an investigator? She turned
back toward his desk and rifled awkwardly through
the papers he'd strewn there. The header on each page
read Twin Cities Investigations, Incorporated. *He'd
hired an agency in Minneapolis?*

Numb, she began paging through the documents.
financial checks, work history, even her past relationships were spelled out in detail. As a law enforcement
officer she had been on the other side of the fence,
but seeing herself on paper made her skin crawl. The
agency had certainly been thorough—they'd even ob-
tained the reports from the night of Rico's death.

Without reading further, she tapped the stack into
a neat pile and set them aside. Then she noticed another heavy vellum sheet of paper at the edge of the
desk.

It was the cover letter detailing the parameters of the investigation plus the fees and expenses charged. *At least it wasn't cheap,* she muttered to herself. And then the salutation caught her eye. *It hadn't been written to Seth—the report was addressed to Eric Wright.*

Relief poured through her, coupled with shock and anger. So Eric had chosen to retaliate, and he had done so with skill. Even now he had to be gloating over his success. But at least Seth hadn't ordered the investigation. He hadn't been suspicious of her motives even as he was making love to her.

Small consolation when their relationship was over.

THE FOLLOWING TWO WEEKS dragged by at an interminable pace. The hands barely spoke to her. Cal turned on his heel when he saw her coming. Seth left early and stayed out late, so she rarely saw him. Calving had slowed down. And Della seemed inordinately pleased by the dead silence at every meal. She'd actually smiled to herself at dinner last night and the effect had been eerie.

Kate spent more and more time on Rowdy, riding the boundaries of the Lone Tree, thinking about her options. Trying to focus on anything that would distract her from the shattered feeling in her heart whenever she thought about Seth.

At night, she researched grants and scholarships on the Internet, then wrote or e-mailed corporations, organizations and even private individuals who might be able to help establish a Rico Sanchez Scholarship for the Arts.

And all the while, she ached for Mandy, who hovered in the background, looking sad and confused over her father's edict to leave Kate alone. By Friday evening the little girl wasn't just hovering in the background. She was leaning over Kate's shoulder and watching the computer screen with rapt attention.

"I wish I could help," Mandy said, pouting. "Can I?"

Kate glanced toward her open bedroom door, then gave Mandy an amused look. "Aren't you supposed to be doing homework?"

"Done it." Mandy galloped her fingertips to and fro across the back of Kate's chair. "Dad says I can't be in here bothering you. But aren't we friends?"

"Of course we are."

"Then I can stay awhile?"

"Well…"

"Dad's outside now, anyway," Mandy grumbled. "But even if he's in the house I don't see him much, and when I do, he's really, really grumpy. I think maybe he's—" Mandy leaned forward to look into Kate's face "—really sad, or something. What do you think?"

"Umm…"

"I think he misses being your friend, too."

Kate felt a lump in her throat and didn't answer. She couldn't.

Mandy lifted her head and looked toward the open closet, where Joanna's two dresses hung among Kate's meager collection of shirts. "Which dress are you going to wear to the big party?"

Without looking up from her keyboard, Kate shook her head. "Neither, sweetie. I'm not going."

"But you have to!"

"I don't think I ought to. Your dad might be uncomfortable with me there, and I really wouldn't know anyone else."

"Joanna says she'll come and get you if you don't show up."

Kate laughed. "I'll bet she did."

"It's next Saturday," Mandy coaxed.

With a sigh, Kate turned away from the keyboard and took Mandy's hands in her own. "You are one of the sweetest little girls I've ever met. I appreciate what you're trying to do, but I'll be leaving soon, and if I went to that dinner I would probably make people uncomfortable."

"Maybe you'll meet some super cool guy there, like a real prince or something."

"At the rancher's dinner?" Kate gently tweaked Mandy's nose. "You've been reading fairy tales."

Mandy dropped her head, then looked up with a sheen of tears in her eyes. "I don't want you to leave. If you don't like my dad, maybe you'll see someone else, and then you can stay and still be my friend."

If life were only that easy. Kate turned off her computer, then enfolded Mandy into a hug and kissed the top of her head, thinking of just how much she would miss this ranch and the people who lived here…Seth, Mandy, Cal—even Della, for all her strange ways.

Kate had never been part of such a strong community of neighbors and friends, who helped one another at the drop of a hat, who stood up for one another and knew one another's families and past as well as their own.

The phone rang. Kate waited for someone down-stairs to pick up. On the fourth ring Mandy answered it, then handed it to Kate.

The unfamiliar male voice on the other end was deep, with the rasp of rough gravel. "You sure as hell don't take hints."

"What?"

"Maybe you ought to. Before it's too late."

"Who is this?"

The sound of a single rifle shot burst through the telephone line, loud enough that even Mandy jumped. And then the caller hung up.

Mandy drew closer, her eyes clouded with worry. "Who was that?"

"Just a friend playing a joke. He probably wonders if I'll guess who he is." Kate managed a smile. "Do you have any idea?"

The child shook her head.

"Then he's got us both fooled." She glanced at the clock on her bedside table. "It's probably time for your bath and pajamas. Sleep tight, okay?"

After a quick hug, Mandy left. Kate locked the door behind her then leaned against it. There were still too many unanswered questions about suspicious events. The night her car had been searched. The pos-sibility that someone had cut her alternator belt. The damage done to her saddle billet. And now a phone call, the first actual communication of a threat. Della's son? A ranch hand? Maybe even someone in town, someone she hadn't yet suspected.

Over the last hours she'd come to a difficult deci-sion, but knew in her heart that it was the only one she could make. She would continue her efforts until she found another way to establish that scholarship. But there was no way she could collect her inheritance. The ranch was Seth's heart and Mandy's future. They belonged here. No matter what the will said or the law allowed, she had no moral right to endanger the ranch.

She would leave Montana, and leave her grandfather's legacy behind. But first, she would figure out who was after her, and make sure no one else would be at risk if she left. It would be her silent, parting gift to the man and child who would always own a good share of her heart.

With a sudden flash of insight she knew just where to begin. Doc Anderson had been practicing in town since the 1960s and had known the Rawlins family well.

She would go see him tonight.

CHAPTER SIXTEEN

MANDY STARED AT THE CEILING wishing she could finally fall asleep. All she could think of was that weird phone call. Kate had pretended to be unconcerned, but her eyes looked surprised and worried. Was someone really mad at her—mad enough to cut up her saddle so she could get hurt?

Mandy rolled over and sighed. Dad would hardly talk to Kate anymore, and Kate was planning to leave, and everything was turning out all wrong.

At a rustling sound downstairs Mandy sat upright and listened. The back door creaked. She shot out of bed and flew to the window. Pressing her face to the frosty glass, she tried to make out the figure walking away from the house. *Kate?*

She was heading for her car.

Mandy's heart sank. Why would Kate go to town after the stores closed? Was she leaving for good? A tear trickled down Mandy's cheek. *But if I hide in her car, she'll have to turn around and come back. And maybe then…*

Mandy whirled away from the window, yanked on some pink sweats, then raced down the stairs.

IT HAD BEEN ONE HELL of a night. Not that they all weren't, this time of year. Seth stowed his gear in the tack room, then untied his horse and led it into a stall. Riding the herd, checking for calving problems and watching for sick or chilled calves had never seemed so lonely until now. All that time alone gave a man too much time to think.

And all he could think of was Kate Rawlins.

With a soft curse he latched the stall door and headed out of the barn. He pulled to an abrupt stop. The hands had headed to town tonight for poker. Surely everyone in the house was asleep by now.

But a white cloud of exhaust spewed into the twenty-below night air from the tailpipe of Kate's car. A slender figure climbed out and started scraping at the ice-coated windshield.

Memories of another night hit him like a knife thrust to his heart. Another woman who left under the cover of darkness…the wife who walked out without even saying goodbye.

He'd seen Alison take off, but pride and stubbornness had held him back when he might have gone after her. With startling clarity, the truth blazed through his thoughts like a meteor, blinding and overwhelming. If Kate left, he would never again find anyone else who could take her place.

He couldn't let her go.

Seth started forward, raising a hand to catch her attention if she turned around. But before he could call out her name, he saw something small creeping rapidly through the shadows along the side of the house.

And then he saw Della silhouetted in the doorway

of the house, her hair wild and bathrobe flapping in the wind. Her head swung back and forth, as if she were scanning the yard for something...or someone. She stepped ahead into the pool of light over the steps.

She held a rifle. With a guttural sound she lurched forward and stumbled down the steps, then headed to the right, toward Kate's car. Had she seen a coyote?

A few feet down she stopped. Lifted the rifle to her shoulder—and swung it toward the Mustang. *What the hell...*

"Kate! Look out!" His heart in his throat, Seth raced across the broad expanse of gravel. "Della!"

Kate whirled around, took one look at him, then spun back toward the house. Instantly she dropped into a crouch and lunged toward the back of her car.

Della pulled the trigger. The explosion seemed to echo in the frigid air, accompanied by the sound of a shattering windshield. Della lowered the rifle a fraction, then pinned her gaze on Seth and lifted the rifle once more.

Another fifty yards to go...no cover ahead. *Nothing.* Seth veered to the left and dove behind the black pickup. Della fired again, hitting its tailgate.

"Kate? Dad?" Mandy's panicked cry tore through his heart.

He rolled to his feet and darted to the back of the pickup. Scanned the yard. *Dear God, where is she?* From behind her car, he saw Kate crouch low and race into the shadows. A heartbeat later he heard Mandy's startled cry, then silence. Kate would keep her safe. Relief flooded through him.

Della stumbled forward, swinging her rifle wide. What in the hell was going on? Incoherently muttering, she took aim into the darkness and fired again.

He couldn't wait another second. If she'd started fully loaded, she would have another five rounds left, and if she calmed down she'd be capable of picking off a penny thrown in the air at a hundred yards. Seth spun around and darted to the left, using the other two pickups as cover. He slipped through the darkness, circled wide until he could take position behind a stack of firewood. He was behind her now. But there was a good twenty yards of bare ground to go.

She stopped, looked wildly around and seemed to focus on his position. At a noise behind Kate's car, she turned and fired into the darkness.

"Show yourself!" she screamed into the wind. "I'll find you no matter where you hide."

His heart in his throat, Seth took a deep breath and took off at a dead run straight for her.

She pivoted, swinging her rifle in front of her. Her eyes were glazed, her teeth bared. "You fool," she screamed. "You—"

He dove under her rifle barrel as she pulled the trigger. Grabbing her around the waist, he pulled her to the ground, twisting beneath her to cushion her fall.

With a savage cry of pain and anger she tried to scramble away. He wrenched the rifle out of her hands and then sat back, his heart still racing.

She stared at him like some wild animal, beyond all reason, then collapsed.

Kate came running. "You got her? Is she okay?"

"Where's Mandy?" Seth demanded.

"I took her to the calving barn. She's up in the hayloft hidden in the bales. She's fine."

Della's eyes flew open and focused on Kate. "You've ruined everything, you ungrateful bitch. Everything!"

Kate exchanged glances with Seth, then crouched a few feet away from the old woman. "What was ruined?"

Della's eyes glittered. "You were to marry my Tom." Her voice took on a strange, crooning tone. "You still could, you know. It isn't too late."

A look of horror crossed Kate's face. "My mother was to marry *Tom?* Why?"

"We belong here," Della said simply, her expression softening. "Bob loved me, you know. I spent my life here, making sure it was always kept just right."

Her face white, Kate touched the old woman's arm gently. "Was there any other reason Tom and Lorna should have married? Did Tom do anything to her?"

Closing her eyes, Della shuddered, wrapped her arms around her waist and began to rock herself, apparently unaware of her thin robe and the frozen earth beneath her.

"Let's go," Seth said. "We need to call the sheriff. I'll keep the rifle and get Mandy. Can you get Della back into the house?"

Kate nodded, then hooked an arm underneath Della's elbow and helped her up. At first, Della tried to twist away, but then she groaned and sagged against Kate's shoulder.

"Are you hurt?" Frowning, Kate stepped back and scanned her head to foot. "Your legs? Ankle?"

Della shook her head. Her mouth clamped shut, she hobbled forward. "I shoulda aimed better. I shoulda made my shots clean," she muttered to herself as they made their way back into the kitchen.

Inside, Kate helped Della sit down in a chair, then retrieved an afghan from the living room and wrapped it around the old woman's shoulders. In the bright light Della looked exhausted and weather-beaten, her eyes flat and mouth pressed into a grim line.

Kate thought back to the day she'd first arrived at the ranch.

Kneeling down in front of the chair, she took Della's cold hands within her own. "When I came here, you said you weren't around when my mother, Lorna, lived here," she said softly. "That wasn't true, was it? What happened back then?"

Della sat silently, her head bowed, eyes closed, until Kate thought she might be dozing. A single tear coursed through the deep wrinkles of her face. "He loved me, you know," Della whispered. "He never showed it, but I always knew. I knew what he felt inside his heart! I waited for Bob all my life."

"Bob loved you?"

Another tear slipped down Della's face. "He had Violet, but he loved me all the same."

"Violet—his wife?"

Della went on as if she hadn't heard. "Tom should have married their daughter, you know. But that Lorna was a wild one. As soon as my Tom showed interest, she up and went after some cowboy who wasn't fit to shine Tom's boots. She ruined everything! This ranch should have belonged to me and my boy!''

Kate shuddered, thinking of Tom as he was now: the surly drunk outside the school play, the scruffy guy lurking outside the feed store in town. No wonder Lorna had fled into the arms of someone else.

Uttering a silent prayer, she asked, ''Who got her pregnant, Della?''

Della seemed to shrink within herself. Her mouth moved soundlessly as she drew the afghan tighter around her shoulders.

''Who, Della?''

Her eyes bleak, the old woman raised her chin. ''That damned cowboy.''

Relief washed through Kate like a healing rain. From what she'd seen of Tom, she could well imagine him forcing himself on Lorna, impregnating her to gain a foothold on the Lone Tree.

''I made damn sure she paid for her sins,'' Della continued, her voice razor-sharp. ''I made sure Bob never got any of her letters and didn't mail the ones he wrote.'' Della's voice rose, and a wild gleam shone in her eyes. ''Worked, too. She quit writing, and even when his letters got past me, she returned them all unopened. He never went after her, and she never came back here. Ever.''

Anger clogged Kate's throat for all that had been lost because of one bitter, vindictive woman. Only now that woman was old, and confused, and probably suffering from dementia. And there would be no way to ever right the wrongs that had been committed years ago. But maybe there could be one last answer.

"Della," Kate murmured, taking the woman's gnarled hand. "You remember the night Lorna fought with Bob and left. What happened?"

The back door opened and Seth stepped inside, followed by Mandy. The child's face was chalk-white, her eyes revealing the terror she'd felt during the last hour. Kate gave her an encouraging smile, but motioned for them both to stay back.

"Della, you were going to tell me about that night."

The old woman stared blankly at her hands folded in her lap.

"Della? Please tell me. Did you fix everything that night, just like always?"

A frown furrowed Della's face. Then she lifted her head and smiled softly. "Oh, I told Lorna all about her boyfriend."

"Her boyfriend? What happened?"

"It's in the papers. Don't you read the papers?"

"Della, I don't have those papers. What did they say?"

"Why, when Bob sent her out east to have her baby, that boyfriend wouldn't take no for an answer. He got in his truck and took off after her, and he got killed in some accident on the way. Nobody here ever heard from him again, but I knew. A sheriff called from out east, 'cause this was the boy's last address."

"So he died."

"'Course, Lorna just thought he took off and dumped her 'cause she never heard nothing from him again."

Seth moved to Kate's side. "I'll call the sheriff,"

he said quietly. "Maybe now we should just let her rest."

"No—I'm so close. Just another minute."

Kate could feel her mother's heartbreak, imagine what it must have been like to bear a baby and never see the father again. "But the big argument was so much later—I was almost two when Lorna left the ranch for good."

Della shrugged. "She still could have had my boy, you know. But she was too good for the likes of him. So then I told her about how her daddy got rid of that boyfriend."

"You told her Bob had *murdered* him, and got away with it?"

"Whoo-ee, she was mad. Biggest helluva fight I ever saw! She took off and never came back." Della's eyes lit up. "They all deserved to suffer, you know. And I made sure they did."

CHAPTER SEVENTEEN

SUNSET BATHED the living room of the ranch house in pink hues as Kate and Seth collapsed into the chairs flanking the fireplace. Last night, after extensive questioning, Paul Cameron had taken Della with him back to Salt Creek, where she spent the night before being transferred to a hospital in Folsum.

Mandy had been in a state of shock, but finally fell asleep after Kate sat with her and recounted every amusing story she could recall from her days as a street officer.

After that, Seth had disappeared into his own room for the rest of the night. Numb with grief, Kate had packed her belongings and stowed them in her car, and then waited for morning.

She figured she would leave as soon as everyone was awake. But at dawn Seth had left without a word and didn't return until hours later. He walked into the house with his jaw set, sent Mandy out to see the latest calves and steered Kate into the living room.

Now he sat across from her, his elbows braced on the arms of his chair and his fingers steepled in front of him. He stared at Kate with heavy-lidded eyes. "So you were leaving us last night," he said flatly, his eyes dark with emotion. "Just like that? Not a word?"

She wished she could control the yearning in her voice and the heartbreak that had to be evident in her eyes. Never would she find another man like him. These last, unexpected moments were a precious gift. She stared at him, absorbing everything about him, wanting to remember these moments with absolute clarity forever.

"I was leaving to talk to Doc Anderson, because I thought he might know some answers about the past," she said simply. "But after that, yes, I planned to leave."

"Because of your career."

Because I love you too much to stay. "I don't belong here."

He flinched. "In leaving now you'll forfeit the ranch. Why, Kate? Why aren't you staying until July?"

"You've read the reports. You know why I decided to come out here. Well…I've done research, and I think there are other ways to fund the scholarship. I don't need any money from the ranch. And now I can get back to my job in Minneapolis."

"And that's what you want."

"Right."

"There's no other reason."

She fidgeted under his intense gaze.

"Even though you could technically stay the full six months and have the ranch as well as that alternative funding?"

She looked away, willing herself not to cry. *I never cry,* she told herself fiercely. *Never, never, never...*

"I didn't order that background investigation on you, Kate."

"I know."

"It...hurt to think you could make love to me and pretend to care, yet be planning to sell the ranch out from under us without a second thought."

Kate stared at her hands folded in her lap, her emotions surging through her on waves of pain...and love...and loss. "I knew the ranch meant more to you than anything. By the time we were...intimate...I knew I couldn't sell my share."

He moved across the space between them and rested his hands on her shoulders, then lifted her to stand next to him and stared down into her face. "I learned things last night that I should have learned long ago. When I saw you getting ready to leave..." His voice grew rough as he reached up and tucked a strand of her hair behind her ear. "I guess I saw what really matters. It isn't some legacy, or a piece of ranch land. It's the people on it. It's you, Kate."

Speechless, she stared up at him, her eyes burning and her heart pounding. She felt his hard, strong hands slide from her shoulders, down her arms and then curve around her waist. Warmth spread through her like molten honey, until she thought she might melt within his embrace.

"If it takes selling half of this ranch to honor a commitment you made back home, then that's what you need to do."

"But I don't—"

"Bob left half of the ranch to you and I'll be thankful forever that he did." Seth murmured. "Because at least for a while, it brought you here."

His deep voice vibrated through her as he tucked her head beneath his chin and held her tight. The strong, steady beat of his heart matched her own.

"I've already signed over my pension to start a scholarship fund," she said against his chest. She took a deep breath. "The ranch belongs to you and Mandy, not me. You've lived your lives here, worked endless hours…I won't take that away from you."

"My independent Kate," he said, his voice laced with amusement. "Take charge, full speed ahead. Do you ever make joint decisions?"

She drew back and looked up at him. "You make me sound impetuous."

He gave a shout of laughter. "Never that. But tell me, Officer, do you think you could share your life with someone—as equal partners?"

A sliver of painful memory shot through her, aimed with deadly accuracy at her heart. "I did think so once."

He gave her an amused look. "I remember reading about that in the damned report. Surely you couldn't think that a man like Kent was right for you. The day he walked out was the luckiest day of your life."

Suddenly she realized Seth was right.

"Kent only wanted me if he could change me," she muttered.

"Heaven help the guy who would try."

"I'm not stubborn," she retorted.

Seth stroked her ash-blond hair and tucked that

same recalcitrant tendril behind her ear once again. "Oh, definitely not."

His smile slipped as he cradled her jaw in his hand and ran his thumb over her lips. "Why didn't you tell me about the problems you were having? Cal told me about the saddle billet. Mandy said you thought some-one tampered with your car. How many other things happened?"

A hot flush rose in her cheeks and she tried to look away, but he tipped her chin and looked into her eyes, his own eyes clouded with worry.

"You suspected *me?*"

The feeling of heat rose higher in her cheeks. "At first, I wasn't sure...."

"Good Lord, Kate. Me?"

"You had the most to gain. But then, I just kept trying to figure it out on my own. I've never been a strong team player...that's one reason Rico Sanchez died. If I'd called for backup that night..."

"No, Kate. I saw those reports. Did you ever read them?"

"I know I was exonerated of all responsibility. They say I made a routine stop and couldn't have known about the ambush. But I'll always know that I handled it wrong. I charged in there without think-ing. If I—"

"It *was* an ambush," Seth said firmly. "Grieve for the boy who died, but don't make it your fault. The gang set up Rico as bait, and threatened to kill his little brother if he didn't wave to you with a smile on his face. No one would have known they were lying in wait."

"I should have sensed trouble. I should have called for backup," she repeated.

"Does an officer call for backup every time someone waves to him on the street? Second-guessing your decision will never change what happened. Those guys had a lot of firepower there—maybe your backup would have been killed, along with more of the kids on the street. Who knows?"

Kate gave him a rueful smile. "You're turning into my precinct counselor, here."

A sudden feeling of peace, of salvation, washed through her as she remembered last night. She'd been armed, but instead of taking charge, she had relinquished control of the situation to Seth and had rescued Mandy from Della's wild aim. This time, a child had lived.

Seth led Kate to the sofa, then sank down and pulled her onto his lap. "You need me, not a counselor."

If he only knew how much. Kate laid her head against his shoulder, breathing in his warm masculine scents. Her blood seemed to thicken and heat in her veins, throbbing through her, pooling deep inside.

"I need to tell you something, Kate. I—"

From outside came a sharp rap on the back door, then the door opened and heavy footsteps stomped into the entryway. Two thuds marked the removal of a pair of cowboy boots.

"It's Paul," called out a voice. "Anyone here?"

With a sigh, Kate slid off Seth's lap and they both stood to greet the sheriff as he walked in. He looked from one to the other, his mouth tipped up in a know-ing smile.

"Been quite a day, hasn't it?" He settled into one of the chairs by the fireplace and hooked one ankle over the opposite knee. Seth and Kate sat back down on the sofa, at either end. "Just thought you folks would want to hear what's happening with Della."

Kate bit her lip. "Is she okay?"

"They're doing some psychiatric testing. I expect she'll be in the hospital a few days, at least. From what I've seen before, I'd guess she might end up on medication, and need to be in a facility of some kind."

"What about her son?"

Seth and Paul exchanged glances. Paul cleared his throat. "You never did come talk to me about the problems you were having out here, Kate. I can un-derstand that you wouldn't know who to trust, but I would have been real happy to help you."

"What about Tom?" Kate persisted.

"All the way into town she rambled on about how her son should have had the Lone Tree, and how you should never have come out here. Once I had her taken care of, I picked up Tom and brought him in for questioning. Seth knows a lot more about the ranch's history than I do, so he came in early this morning and helped me sort everything out. We'll be filing charges against Tom tomorrow."

Seth nodded. "Della apparently brought him out to the ranch a few times, when she knew we'd all be gone. He cut your saddle billet and went through your things a few times to try to scare you off." A muscle flickered along Seth's jaw. "He also admitted to a threatening phone call, and to slicing your alternator belt just enough to make sure it would snap somewhere out of town."

"We discovered that he has quite a record back in the Midwest," Paul added. "Apparently a little incarceration did him some good. Della really put the screws to him, but he wouldn't do anything more serious than the damage to your car. He said he could see she was starting to go off the deep end, and he didn't want to end up back in jail."

Kate leaned back, her mind reeling. "I'd suspected him, but I also thought maybe Eric was behind some of my problems."

"Eric would have been another good possibility," Paul muttered.

"But why?"

Paul flicked a glance at Seth, then gave her a grim smile. "Since he was a kid, Eric had this competitive streak that never quit where Seth was concerned. Grades, sports, girls—he always seemed to come in second-best. After Seth married Alison, Eric must have been drunk for a week. I think he'd had some sort of crush on her since sixth grade."

"Well, he married her before the ink on our divorce papers was dry," Seth said mildly.

Paul snorted. "She filed for a restraining order last week. I've made it *real* clear to Eric about what will happen if he defies that order, and I may have to take off my badge to do it."

"That will stop him," Seth said. "He's always

been worried about preserving that pretty nose of his.''

They walked Paul to the door, then both shook hands with him. ''Thanks,'' Kate murmured, holding his hand a few moments longer. ''I appreciate everything you've done.''

Paul ran a fingertip around the brim of his hat, his brow furrowed. ''In talking to Della and Tom I found out some things about the past that you might want to hear sometime...if you'd like to stop by my office.''

''Can you tell me now?''

Paul flicked a glance at Seth. ''It's a little personal.''

''That's okay. Please?''

Paul looked down at his hat and cleared his throat. ''I also talked to some folks around town—Doc Anderson for one. I don't know if Lorna ever told you about your dad. He was a fine young man, from what everyone tells me. Doc could give you more details, if you want.''

''Thanks,'' Kate said softly, touching Paul's sleeve.

After Paul left, Seth turned to Kate and took her in his arms. ''Mandy will be back in the house in a few minutes. Before anything else happens, I need to ask you something.''

His hands trembled on her shoulders, his eyes filled with tenderness and love. ''If you leave, this ranch will mean nothing. When I go out to ride the herds, I'll always feel as if you should be with me. I'll want to turn around to talk to you—and you won't be there.''

With both hands cradling her face, he brushed a swift kiss against her throat, then settled his mouth over hers and kissed her hard and deep. When he lifted his head, his eyes had darkened with such need that it took her breath away.

"You can't go back to Minnesota. I need you here. I love you," he whispered against her mouth. "Marry me?"

Kate's knees nearly buckled. She threw her arms around his neck and pulled him down for another kiss, trying to convey everything that she felt in her heart and soul. "Forever and ever, cowboy."

EPILOGUE

One year later

"NOW TELL ME that the annual Rancher's Dinner and Dance wasn't worth waiting for." With a grin, Joanna waved a hand toward the crowd on the dance floor. "Best steaks anywhere, good company, a great band. And every one of those ranchers is wearing *clean* boots." She eyed Kate's rounded stomach. "I'd still like to see you in one of those great dresses I found for you last year, though. Maybe *next* year?"

"Maybe." Kate smiled back at her, then looked up at Seth, who stood behind her chair with his large, warm hands on her shoulders. They'd missed the event last year, because they'd been in the Tetons on their wedding trip.

"Or maybe not," Seth mused. "We'd like to have three or four more babies. With luck, Kate will be pregnant again."

Kate laughed. "That's what *he* thinks."

With a sigh of fulfillment, she looked at the friends around her. Life was so incredible. At the edge of the dance floor, Cal and Freckles were attempting a polka with Mandy and Nicki, who were nearly breathless with laughter.

Seth brushed a kiss against Kate's temple. "It's been a good year." His beloved voice was a delicious rumble against her skin. "But it's time you slowed down and started taking it easy. I worry about you when you aren't at home."

Joanna chuckled. "You know the boys and I are like a gaggle of mother hens, watching out for her," she said dryly. "Kate hiccups and I have at least five kids coming for me at the speed of light."

"It's true. I think the whole lot of them deserve to be godfathers when this baby arrives." Kate closed her eyes and arched her neck into Seth's wonderfully warm touch as his hands massaged the tired muscles in her shoulders and neck.

Contentment washed through her as she thought about all of her blessings.

A year ago she'd been alone, planning to go back to a sterile apartment and a career that could no longer be the substitute for all her life had been missing—family, a home, a community of good friends.

And now she had Seth. A wonderful stepdaughter. And a new life growing within her that brought tears of joy whenever she felt him—or her—flutter-kick beneath her hand. Everything she'd loved best about being a cop she had found right here, working with high-risk kids at Joanna's Meadowbrook youth facility.

And everything she'd loved about Seth had been increased a hundred-fold when he supported her decision to work and had donated a hundred acres of the Lone Tree to Joanna's facility.

Kate awkwardly shifted her weight, then rose and

moved into the familiar curve of Seth's arms. "I love you," she said simply, losing herself within his dark gaze. "If we were home, I'd show you exactly how much."

He laughed. "I can't wait that long."

Lowering his mouth to hers, he kissed her with such tenderness and love that she felt her heart fill her chest and tears burn beneath her lashes.

Her grandfather had left her part of the Lone Tree, but his gift had brought her so much more—a legacy of belonging, of family, and of love beyond measure. Glancing heavenward, she sent him her heartfelt thanks.

And then she wrapped her arms around Seth and kissed him back.

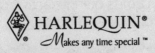

Come escape with Harlequin's new

Series Sampler

Four great full-length Harlequin novels bound together in one fabulous volume and at an unbelievable price.

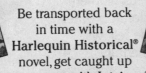

Be transported back in time with a Harlequin Historical® novel, get caught up in a mystery with Intrigue®, be tempted by a hot, sizzling romance with Harlequin Temptation®, or just enjoy a down-home all-American read with American Romance®.

You won't be able to put this collection down!

On sale February 2000 at your favorite retail outlet.

Back by popular demand are

DEBBIE MACOMBER's

Hard Luck, Alaska, is a
town that needs women!
And the O'Halloran brothers
are just the fellows
to fly them in.

Starting in March 2000 this beloved series returns
in special 2-in-1 collector's editions:

MAIL-ORDER MARRIAGES, featuring
Brides for Brothers and *The Marriage Risk*
On sale March 2000

FAMILY MEN, featuring
Daddy's Little Helper and *Because of the Baby*
On sale July 2000

THE LAST TWO BACHELORS, featuring
Falling for Him and *Ending in Marriage*
On sale August 2000

Collect and enjoy each MIDNIGHT SONS story!

Available at your favorite retail outlet.

HARLEQUIN®
Makes any time special ™

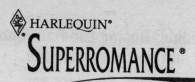

HARLEQUIN® SUPERROMANCE®

**They look alike. They sound alike.
They act alike—at least some of the time.**

Two Sisters by **Kay David**
(Superromance #888)
A sister looks frantically for her missing twin.
And only a stranger can help her.
Available January 2000

The Wrong Brother by **Bonnie K. Winn**
(Superromance #898)
A man poses as his twin to fool the woman he thinks
is a murderer—a woman who also happens to be
his brother's wife.
Available February 2000

Baby, Baby by **Roz Denny Fox**
(Superromance #902)
Two men fight for the custody of twin babies.
And their guardian must choose who will be their father.
Available March 2000

Available wherever Harlequin books are sold.

HARLEQUIN®
Makes any time special ™

Return to the charm of the Regency era with

GEORGETTE HEYER,

creator of the modern Regency genre.

Enjoy six romantic collector's editions with forewords by some of today's bestselling romance authors,

**Nora Roberts, Mary Jo Putney,
Jo Beverley, Mary Balogh,
Theresa Medeiros and Kasey Michaels.**

Frederica
On sale February 2000
The Nonesuch
On sale March 2000
The Convenient Marriage
On sale April 2000
Cousin Kate
On sale May 2000
The Talisman Ring
On sale June 2000
The Corinthian
On sale July 2000

Available at your favorite retail outlet.

HARLEQUIN®
Makes any time special ™

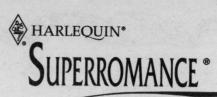